EBURY PRESS

THE VELVET HOTLINE

Arsh Verma is a 2017-batch Haryana cadre IPS officer. He is an alumnus of St John's High School, Chandigarh, and Hindu College, University of Delhi. Besides writing, he enjoys drawing comics and playing golf. The author can be contacted on Twitter, @arshverma, and Instagram, @arshverma15.

Celebrating 35 Years of
Penguin Random House India

THE VELVET HOTLINE

ARSH VERMA

EBURY
PRESS

An imprint of Penguin Random House

EBURY PRESS

USA | Canada | UK | Ireland | Australia
New Zealand | India | South Africa | China | Singapore

Ebury Press is part of the Penguin Random House group of companies
whose addresses can be found at global.penguinrandomhouse.com

Published by Penguin Random House India Pvt. Ltd
4th Floor, Capital Tower 1, MG Road,
Gurugram 122 002, Haryana, India

Penguin
Random House
India

First published in Ebury Press by Penguin Random House India 2023

ISBN 9780143463603

Typeset in Adobe Caslon Pro by Manipal Technologies Limited, Manipal

www.penguin.co.in

For Dad

Contents

ONE

MERRY EUPHROSYNE

Two days from now, Ayingbi Mayengbam would find a person with half their head blown off. Not that she knew it then, of course.

In that moment, all she saw was a class full of kindergarteners, on the cusp of their very first summer vacation.

'Holiday homework, Bing-bee ma'am? Holiday homework, Bing-bee ma'am?'

The chant, originally started by one or two, was gradually adopted by everyone else. Ayingbi wasn't sure they even knew what holiday homework was. And no, there wasn't any. 'Not this time,' she grinned. 'Next year, perhaps.'

One budding artist had made Ayingbi a greeting card. Seeing him, others too had ripped sheets from their notebooks, folded them in half and frantically scribbled Ayingbi messages of their own before the last bell rang. And when it did, they all began to cheer.

Their joy permeated the room like sunlight, and Ayingbi unconsciously tried to draw in more than she would by simply basking. At twenty-nine, she had lived just about enough to know that the high of leaving school for summer vacations was something one spent the rest of one's life chasing.

'Happy holidays, Bing-bee ma'am! Happy holidays, Bing-bee ma'am!'

'Go on! Happy, happy holidays!' Ayingbi sang back, hugging each of them as they flooded towards the door. 'I'll see you all next month—hopefully in one piece, yes?'

Some waiting parents wanted to make a parent–teacher meeting of it. Others stuck around to hector an admission of their progeny's embryonic talents out of Ayingbi.

'They're all bright kids,' Ayingbi stiffly maintained, in no mood to take sides.

The brightly-coloured corridors of the elementary school had almost emptied by the time she finished work and headed home.

Ayingbi, the first of her family to have left Manipur, lived alone in a small, second-floor flat above a bustling market. There wasn't much to see outside the bedside window—there were tall buildings across the street and a new flyover had taken over what little view remained.

In the evening, her friend Nimisha called.

'Hey, Bum! I spoke to your mom. What's this I'm hearing about a summer job?'

'I'm looking for one,' said Ayingbi because, with the summer to herself, she was.

'Well, why didn't you say so? I have just the thing. Good pay, too.'

'It's not really a money thing, Nimmi. I'd be open to volunteer work.'

'Same as always, our Saint Ayingbi. So, like vocational stuff?'

'Yeah.'

'Well, I'll keep my eyes peeled. Indian sign language classes, stray adoption, tree plantation, etcetera, etcetera. Whatever you need, I'll hook you up! Anyway, I gotta run. Family dinner, ugh. Just called to get the skinny on the job thing. Later, Bum!'

After the call, Ayingbi pondered her own dinner plans. Today, she'd order in. From tomorrow, she'd get back to cooking her own meals.

She arranged the ordered Chinese takeout boxes over a newspaper spread on the bed and turned on her laptop to watch some twee K-drama Nimmi had recommended.

She was folding up the newspaper afterwards when an ad caught her eye. It was for a foot cream. Ayingbi wondered if there would be anything about job openings. She flipped ahead to the classifieds and found a vocational-work column.

There was an opening for blood donation healthcare assistants, but you needed medical experience. There was something about building homeless shelters, but it was manual work, only open to able-bodied men. Some surveys. Not something Ayingbi was particularly interested in.

She picked up the week's pile of newspapers from under the bed and began to sort them out one by one. Finally, she found an opening that looked interesting.

'MERRY EUPHROSYNE'—HELP WANTED

From the description, it looked like a suicide-prevention helpline.

All it asked for was proficiency in spoken Hindi and English, a college degree, and some vague, subjective requirements like good listening skills, patience and a kind heart.

A suicide hotline, thought Ayingbi. It wasn't what she had in mind. But it sounded interesting—helping out people in distress.

She singled out the page and restored the rest of the newspaper pile beneath the bed.

Tomorrow. I'll make the call tomorrow.

The ad had actually slipped out of Ayingbi's mind the next morning, and as she sat at the window with her cornflakes, she heard tyres screeching, cars honking and heated voices from the street below. It was not uncommon. The street was one-lane, but it could be milked by three enterprising vehicles at a time. Right then, on the opposite balcony, she saw someone lowering a rope with a looped end. It looked like a noose. Moments later, the rope was raised again, now bearing a basket full of bananas.

The eerie noose analogy triggered a chain of thoughts, culminating in a reminder that Ayingbi had to call up Merry Euphrosyne.

She did look it up before making the call. It was an international NGO that had opened a few local chapters. The website had a polished and sober look, with official-looking accreditations. She checked news results and found reputable references.

It was certainly volunteer work. Perhaps more high-stakes than what she had anticipated, but it seemed exciting, and she liked the adjectives the ad had used: 'kind-hearted' and 'patient'.

Ayingbi decided to call.

The office number was busy the first time.

The second time the call was answered, but after enough rings for Ayingbi to sense reluctance at the other end. The voice was gruff and irritable, and it was easy to paint a physical form around it.

'Hello, this is B.S. Srivastav from Merry Euphrosyne. How may I help?' The polite words felt undissolved in the general tone, like sugar stirred into a bowl of coarse sand.

'Hi, I'm calling about the ad you put in the newspaper,' said Ayingbi. 'It said you were recruiting.'

'Which ad?'

'In the *Morning Herald*. Couple of days ago.'

'Oh. Okay, okay.'

'I'm interested, and I'd like to know more.'

'Come. Come.'

Ayingbi could almost imagine the hitherto unseen Srivastav reclined in a chair, picking his nose and examining what the fingertip drew.

'When should I come?'

'Tomorrow evening. Five p.m.'

'Do I need to bring my resume?'

Papers were shuffled at the other end. 'Sure. Sure. Get.'

'And anything else?'

Silence.

'Just come,' said Srivastav irritably, and he cut the call.

*

The dusty elevator opened directly into what appeared to be a common waiting room for two offices.

The one on the right had 'Merry Euphrosyne' written in snazzy red letters on a glass wall, behind which many call centre-type cubicles were visible. The one on the left looked like a somewhat shady massage parlour.

Ayingbi made an enquiry from the receptionist and was directed towards the stainless-steel waiting room chairs.

Two people were already seated—a woman, nibbling on the lid of a smoothie cup and across her, a man, trying to herd bubbles out of his phone's screen guard. Ayingbi took a seat with the woman. Her nostrils picked up a synthetic fruity flavour, and the man's gaze rose momentarily to see who had joined them.

Ayingbi wondered if the three of them were vying for the same job. Vying? Was vying involved for volunteer work?

But the man, having finished smoothing the creases out, got up, and trudged away to the lift.

At 5.15 the Merry Euphrosyne door opened, and a stocky man walked out, carrying a stack of forms.

'Euphrosyne?' he asked the woman sitting next to Ayingbi. She nodded.

The man handed her a form. 'Please fill this out.'

'Me too,' said Ayingbi.

'Pardon?'

'I'm here for Merry Euphrosyne, too.'

'Oh, right.' The man managed to keep his eyebrows down as he handed Ayingbi a form as well. Maybe he had assumed she was here for the massage parlour.

Afterwards, he led them inside, through the office's cubicle maze. The walls were low enough for Ayingbi to see a sea of headphone-covered heads nodding and bobbing. There were smaller offices for meetings and the walls had inspirational posters with messages like 'Be Patient, Be Compassionate, Be Kind' or 'Where There's a Will, There's a Way'.

Finally, they were led inside a small meeting room, with student chairs and a filled-out whiteboard. The man gestured to the seats.

'My name is Vikram,' he said. 'I'm an AAO here. First of all, welcome!'

Ayingbi wondered what 'AAO' stood for.

Vikram then gestured to the whiteboard. 'Your journey at Merry Euphrosyne will begin with an orientation, rigorously designed to give you all the skills a good operator requires.'

The whiteboard had a sketch of a sad-looking caller on one end, linked, with a looping phone cord, to a smiling operator on the other. A list of negative words (lonely, confused, depressed) spiked out of the caller while the operator radiated 'optimistic, helpful, polite, considerate'.

Ayingbi immediately began to make notes. The other woman didn't.

'Our philosophy is simple,' said Vikram. 'You receive a call on the hotline. You take the call. The caller will explain their problem. You listen to them quietly and patiently. Operator's Bible, Rule Number Eight: we do not interrupt them while they are talking! Once you receive verbal reassurance that they will not do anything dangerous, they will cut the call. Rule Number Eleven: we never hang up on them! Rule Number Seventeen: we do not make unfulfillable promises!'

'All that is fine. When do we start?' asked the other candidate.

'Right away, if you like.'

'Perfect. Do we get to choose our own cubicles?'

'Uh, we'll have to see when the time comes.'

'When the time comes?'

'Eight weeks from now, if all goes to plan.'

The woman looked bewildered. 'What do we do till then?'

'Dummy calls, training modules, conversation skills, ancillary services. It's serious business, isn't it? You need proper training first.'

Fair enough, thought Ayingbi. But . . .

'Ancillary services?' said the other woman. 'We're just going to be bringing everyone coffee, aren't we?'

'Decaf for me,' grinned Vikram. 'I'm only joking, of course. Ahahaha . . .' He quickly sobered up, seeing nobody else was laughing. 'Now, being a hotline operator is an art. We must be patient, we must be compassionate, we must . . . be kind. Ah! Somebody noticed the board!' He grinned at Ayingbi, who had mouthed 'be kind' alongside. 'Now's as good a time as any to look at the briefing booklet.'

He handed both Ayingbi and the other woman identical backpacks emblazoned with the jazzy Merry Euphrosyne logo. There was a thin booklet inside. The paper was powdery and of poor quality; the binding threads were already showing.

Ayingbi flicked through it. There were instructions on leading questions, judicious use of humour, how to study tone and voice, how to keep reluctant callers talking, and the importance of confidentiality.

'Depression is better understood now than ever,' declared Vikram. 'We are at the cutting edge of it.'

'At the cutting edge of depression?' said Ayingbi.

'Exactly.'

The other woman, who had been sullen ever since learning it would take a whole eight weeks before they operated the hotline, suddenly left her seat to take a call. She did not return. Undeterred, Vikram continued lecturing Ayingbi alone.

'The three guiding R's: Reassure—make them know that it will be all right. Reason—use logic and patient argument. Reciprocate—make it a lively, two-sided conversation. A three-pronged approach.'

Ayingbi rather disliked Vikram's handling of the subject of depression. Like the office itself, it felt corporate and sterile. She eventually decided to give him the benefit of doubt. Maybe it had been normalized for him—like a mortician who has conducted so many autopsies, he could be cheerful talking about them.

With that said, eight weeks did feel like a very long time.

'I have experience,' said Ayingbi.

'Oh, you do?'

'I've worked as a counsellor in a drug-rehabilitation facility.' Ayingbi didn't quite believe those credits would be transferable here, but she did think it was worth bringing up. 'I have work ex, is what I'm trying to say.'

'Okay . . . so what do you want?'

'I've only got a month and a half to work here,' said Ayingbi. 'I was wondering if this orientation period could be trimmed a bit. I'm sure I'd be up to it.'

Vikram flipped open a page in the booklet, no doubt looking for a rule against it.

'Eh, I think you'll have to talk to the AO. His office is two doors down.'

*

B.S. Srivastav, Administrative Officer—read the sign on the frosted glass door.

This must be the chap she had spoken with over the phone. Ayingbi knocked, and she heard a grunt of permission from the other side.

Srivastav's office was overly air-conditioned and smelt of a fifteen-minute-old fart. The wall behind him was covered in framed thank-you notes and testimonials, as well as a framed and garlanded picture of someone who looked like him, but forty years older.

Ayingbi matched Srivastav up to the mental picture she'd made of him after their phone call and found a close fit. He was cramped at his desk, engrossed in a noisy mobile game, the blast from the AC rippling the locks of his combover like an octopus's tentacles.

Ayingbi left the door open.

'Mr Srivastav?'

'Yes, yes.' Srivastav set his phone down. His hand reached into a greasy newspaper packet and withdrew a pakora.

'I'm here to volunteer for the hotline,' said Ayingbi. 'We spoke over the phone. You asked me to come today evening . . . '

Srivastav popped the pakora, and without wiping his greasy fingers, smeared them across the smartphone, starting a new game. Ayingbi's voice trailed away as the phone began to emit little video-game sounds.

'Okay. So?' said Srivastav, somewhat smugly, still looking at his mobile phone, jiggling his shoulders from side to side.

'Well, so, uh, Vikram tells me there's a two-month orientation before we actually man the lines.'

'So?'

Somehow Ayingbi had guessed it would not be so easy.

'Well, it just so happens that I have been involved in counselling before,' she said. 'I've worked with victims of drug abuse for six months and . . .'

'Doesn't matter. Everyone starts at zero.'

'I could be a useful asset to your organization,' said Ayingbi, preparing to reach into her handbag for her resume. 'I have experience. But I also have only a month and a half . . .'

'Hello, madam, this isn't interview.'

Ayingbi pressed on. 'Yes, I know this is different. All I'm asking is for you to give my experience proper consideration and see if I may be eligible for a position with more responsibility a bit sooner.'

'So, you understand that this is different,' said Srivastav, still not looking up from his game. 'Then, I don't see the problem. You have problem with that, you join Thai massage place next door. You can start on day one. Very little training needed.'

You can never get used to racial taunts. The ones who said you could, lied. Ayingbi felt her face burn. Srivastav still hadn't looked at her. He didn't know he'd hurt her feelings. Ayingbi was also beginning to feel funny around the middle. She knew that time of the month was coming.

'Also, important thing,' said Srivastav, raising a greasy finger.

'What?'

'Close door. All air go out.'

Ayingbi reluctantly shut the door. 'Will you at least take a look at my resume? You *did* ask me to bring it along.'

Srivastav groaned. He reluctantly set aside the phone and seized the folder she passed him. He began to flick through it. Ayingbi winced as he left disgusting finger stains on every page.

'Okay,' he said, bundling it shut and handing it back.

'So will you consider my request, please? I see a lot of people operating the lines are very young.'

'Nobody cuts the line,' tutted Srivastav. 'Everyone starts at zero. Even me. Even God.'

Ayingbi's temper began to rise. 'I wasn't talking about cutting any—'

But then Srivastav interjected: 'Disinfecting headphones.'

'What?'

Srivastav was looking at a calendar pinned to the board behind him. 'Interns have to disinfect the headphones twice a month. Today's the lucky day.'

'Fine, whatever.'

Srivastav seemed pleased as Ayingbi got to her feet.

'In the end, we are one big family,' he said.

Oh, fuck off.

'No wait, that's tomorrow,' said Srivastav, frowning at the calendar. He looked disappointed. 'All right, sit with Sonal. Make notes. See what she does.' Then his eyes widened, revealing bloodshot corners. 'Only observe! You do not take calls yourself!'

*

Sonal looked barely out of college. She was dressed in vibrant clothing, and had so many clips and barrettes in her hair that the headphones were easy to miss. She appeared to be listening to reggae music while playing Spider Solitaire.

Ayingbi sat next to her on a very tall red plastic stool, notebook open in hand, feeling rather foolish.

She tapped Sonal on the shoulder. 'So what happens now?'

'I told you,' said Sonal impatiently, tugging down the headphones. 'Nothing happens. We sit and wait for a call. Chill!'

Ayingbi tapped her on the shoulder again. Off came the headphones again.

'What?' barked Sonal.

'How often does someone call?'

'The hell do I know? They don't make appointments, do they? It's not a part of anyone's friggin' daily routine, is it? Whoops, it's time for me to cry in the shower, but I haven't got ten thousand steps in yet.'

'We're supposed to spend the time when there isn't a call responding to emails,' said Ayingbi, checking the manual. 'I looked at the list. There's a huge backlog.'

'Listen to me, what's your name?'

'Ayingbi.'

'Yeah, whatever. So, the manual, it's bullshit. It was written because they had to write something down. Human nature is erratic and unpredictable. You feel me?'

'I guess . . .'

'You can't pin that shit down to these guidelines. You gotta go with the flow, right?'

'Mmm . . .'

'Lemme give you an example. This place tells us to treat all calls seriously. But what if it's a prank call? Then, what do we do? Do we listen to them or do we tell them to suck a sack of mouldy old dick?'

'So, what do we do?'

'Like I said, babe,' said Sonal. 'Chill the fuck out and . . . fuck! Was that the four of spades? Did I click too fast? Fuck!'

Ayingbi sat back on the stool and sighed.

First Srivastav, now this Sonal.

She wondered if Merry Euphrosyne really was like a call centre, in that it routed calls from all over the world. Probably not—there was way too much downtime here. Had to be local only.

One set of male eyes, three cubicles down, kept peering towards Ayingbi every few seconds. Just when Ayingbi was beginning to get uncomfortable, the floating head left the cubicle and headed in her direction, until a barrel-chested young man was standing before her. Ayingbi braced herself for conversation, but the man ignored her entirely and, grinning to himself, reached out and plucked at Sonal's headphones, causing them to smack hard on her ears.

'Ow!' said Sonal, scowling as she looked around. 'Piss off, Ribs.'

Ribs did not piss off. He stood there, leering. Ayingbi stared at him, afraid of what might happen next. She had an uncomfortable apprehension.

Sonal turned back towards the computer and began clicking on nothing in a show of busyness. Ribs stood there, staring at an imaginary point between Sonal's shoulder blades. Then he began to inch closer, till he was leaning into the back of her chair. Sonal emitted a tch as he placed both hands upon her shoulders.

Ayingbi cleared her throat, so perhaps Ribs might be wakened to her presence. No such luck.

'No . . .' whispered Sonal, as Ribs's hand slid between the back of her chair and Sonal's shirt. Ribs was grinning shamelessly now, looking pleased at his daring.

'I'll complain to Srivastav, you bastard,' protested Sonal, arching her back and wriggling about.

The hump of her chest sagged an inch. Judging by the satisfied, validated look on his face, Ribs had unhooked her bra through the shirt. Sonal shrugged him aside.

'Five minutes,' whispered Ribs.

'No. Get lost.'

'Two minutes.'

'I said beat it!'

'Twooo.'

'Get lost, you creep—'

'Twooooooooooooo,' crooned Ribs.

'Jerk. I'll kill you, I swear!' exclaimed Sonal, though with muted resistance.

And Ribs began to bump rhythmically into the back of the chair.

The display was awful; it was as if they weren't in a fairly busy office. To Ayingbi, perched on the stool like a baby in a high chair that wouldn't understand what was going on, it was the least sensuous thing in the world, the polar opposite of erotic. Sonal's head tipped back and she began to croon a dim, affected, tuneless moan, like a lost goat bleating on a faraway hilltop.

Finally, Ribs's toils bore fruit and Sonal plucked the headphones off.

'I'm going to get a Pepsi,' she said, as if Ayingbi hadn't been around for the past five minutes. 'You want anything?'

'No,' said Ayingbi truthfully. 'What do I do if there's a call?'

'Take it,' shrugged Sonal indifferently. 'It's probably going to be some wet-dick phone sexer anyway.'

'No,' said Ayingbi. 'For real. What do I do?'

'Nobody's gonna call,' said Sonal firmly, pulling off the headphones and pushing herself off the chair. 'Just sit in my seat.'

And then she and Ribs were gone.

Ayingbi slowly took Sonal's place. The squashy leather chair was warm and comfortable from Sonal's shape and presence. She imagined the grimy corridor outside and wondered where on earth Sonal and Ribs were even going to find a spot. Her eyes fell to the sign 'Where There's a Will, There's a Way' and she wondered no more.

She looked at the computer screen. The words, 'CALL INCOMING' were pulsing in green letters on a black background.

Ayingbi blinked. She looked again.

CALL INCOMING.

Oh.

That wasn't good.

Coming to herself, Ayingbi pounced at the leather headphones, also still warm, and clapped them over her ears—she could hear a 'dididi-doo' type ringing through them.

'Shit,' she muttered.

Somebody was calling the Merry Euphrosyne hotline and the call had been routed to Sonal.

Ayingbi stood up straight, pulling the headphone wire taut. 'Sonal?' she called out, though she knew Sonal was not there. 'You're getting a call.' Then she called out to the cubicle maze surrounding her. 'Anyone free to take a call?'

The people in the cubicles to her left and right were both on calls of their own.

'Hello!' called out Ayingbi again. 'Can . . . um . . . anyone please take this? I'm still in orientation, so . . .'

The phone was still ringing. Ayingbi's heart began to thump.

Ayingbi half-shouted, 'Please, somebody, take this!'

No response from anyone. The phone had been ringing for a while. It might not stay ringing much longer.

Shit.

Ayingbi finally clicked on the green 'receive call' button on the computer screen.

'Merry Euphrosyne!' she said, in a voice that was all cheer, making a conscious effort to sound sincere and enthusiastic.

It wasn't a prank call. It wasn't even some wet-dick phone sexer.

TWO

NUTS ON A MILKSHAKE

'The movies . . . are a fantasy,' groaned a voice—female, middle-aged, slurry.

Movies? Ayingbi wondered if she had misheard. What kind of opener was this? She took a deep breath. Maybe best to go with it. 'Why, yes, ma'am, they are. That's why people enjoy them.'

'No . . . you don't understand . . .' growled the caller. 'They mislead . . . They do not tell it like it is . . .'

'Tell it like it is?'

'Accurately . . .'

Not off to a great start. 'Uh, madam, are you in need of help of any kind?' said Ayingbi helplessly, flipping pages in the manual, looking for a script she could stick to.

The slur in the woman's voice deepened. 'Help?'

Ayingbi finally found a series of questions that looked useful. 'Are you presently thinking distressing thoughts?'

'What . . . distressing thoughts?' The woman sounded more and more unfocused.

'Are you in any kind of danger?' said Ayingbi breathlessly.

'What . . . danger . . . why do the movies lie?!'

Again, with the movies.

'I don't know,' said Ayingbi. 'Uhh . . . which movies . . . uhh . . . are you talking about?'

Stupid. This was stupid.

But then the woman whispered, '. . . rat poison.'

Ayingbi's heart skipped a beat. 'Rat poison?'

'Why don't the screenwriters do their research?'

'Did you say rat poison, madam?'

'They write whatever comes to mind.'

'What were you saying about rat poison?'

The woman sighed. 'The movies . . . lie. A person takes rat poison—they die. And here, I just got a stomach ache.'

Fuck.

Ayingbi stood up, forgetting she was wearing headphones, causing them to pop off her ears. Sonal was still nowhere in sight.

'Hey,' said Ayingbi, peering into the neighbouring cubicle. 'I got a suicidal person here!'

Her cubicle neighbour didn't hear her. Ayingbi reached out and tapped his headphones to get his attention. 'Suicidal caller,' she said.

'Then talk to them,' he mouthed, gesturing to show he was on a call himself.

'I don't know how! What do I say?!'

'Tell them to go to a loved one, if there's one nearby. If they're seriously thinking of doing it, take down their address. Make sure you tell them you mean to give their address to the police. If they've already attempted it, tell them to call an ambulance or call one for them.'

'Please, can't you—' pleaded Ayingbi, but then she heard the tinny voice of the woman speaking on her own headphones. 'Yes, I'm here, madam,' she said, quickly reattaching them to her ears.

'I drank a whole bottle,' sighed the woman. 'And I feel nothing.'

Ayingbi squirmed. 'A whole bottle of rat poison?'

This was way beyond her pay grade. This was unprofessional on the part of everyone involved. She should not be allowed to take these calls, while the concerned authority was griming her knees outside.

'You know when you order a milkshake?' said the caller. 'And it comes with a topping of mixed nuts? You scoop them all out in the first bite, so you can get to the milkshake? That's what it tastes like—mixed milkshake nuts.'

'She's ingested rat poison,' said Ayingbi, twisting away the mouthpiece, standing up again and peering into the neighbouring cubicle. 'What do I do?!'

The man, still on his call, looked up at her with annoyance. 'Someone drinks poison. What do you do? You get them to a hospital.'

He seemed a pro. Ayingbi wished the call had gone to him instead.

'Please, it would be better if you—' pleaded Ayingbi, gesturing at her headphones, but the man raised a hand at her and began to hastily scribble something down. He obviously had his hands full.

'Madam, you have to get to a hospital,' said Ayingbi helplessly, twisting the mouthpiece back in front of her lips.

'Hospital . . .' slurred the woman. She was sounding way less cogent now.

'Is there someone else I can talk to?!' said Ayingbi, trying her best to sound in charge. 'Please, a friend or family member? Anyone in the house? Maybe a neighbour?'

'There's nobody here . . .'

'Could you please give me your address?'

The woman did not respond. Ayingbi then heard, with a leap of relief, the sound of retching.

'Yes . . . that's right, get it all out,' she heard herself mumbling, praying that this was sound medical advice. 'Aid the gag reflex.'

Unlike Sonal.

More retching.

'There you go!' cried Ayingbi. 'Aren't you feeling better?! Aren't you?!' She wanted to reach out through the phone and yank the woman by the shoulders to get her to say so. But the woman didn't say anything. In the background, Ayingbi could faintly hear a dog barking.

'Please . . . don't call anyone . . .' the caller finally croaked.

'I won't . . .'

' . . . I need help.'

'Yes, that's what I'm here for!' said Ayingbi, furiously wagging her head.

'I live in Charter Enclave.'

'You live in Charter Enclave, good,' said Ayingbi feverishly, writing it all down on Sonal's notepad. 'Where exactly?'

'The house that looks like shit.'

'Heheh,' gasped Ayingbi, breathing heavily. 'You'll have to be more specific, ma'am.'

'Fuck it, what's there to be specific about? Life's a scam, and there's nobody at the refund counter.'

'The refund counter?'

'Oh my God.'

'What?'

'I see it!'

'What??' said Ayingbi, slightly leaving her seat.

And then, there came a scream, a scream so terrible it seemed to bare the woman's soul. The kind that lassoes every muscle in your neck, the kind that can't be conjured up on demand, a scream emanating from a little primal reservoir confronted with unfathomable, indescribable terror.

There was a click and the line went dead. Her heart pounding in her chest, Ayingbi glanced at the monitor:

CALL ENDED AT 7:36 P.M. DURATION: FIVE MINUTES, TWELVE SECONDS.

*

Ayingbi looked at the notepad to see what she'd written. It was all barely legible because her hand had been trembling so badly—'MILKSHAKE NUTS' and 'GAG REFLEX' and 'SHIT HOUSE'.

Sonal, meanwhile, had returned, bearing no sign of any dishevelment whatsoever. 'Any calls?'

'Um, yeah, there was one, actually,' said Ayingbi. 'Someone swallowed rat poison.'

'That's fucked up,' said Sonal mildly. 'What did you say to them?'

'Um, I asked if there were loved ones nearby and to get medical aid . . . and . . . then she threw up, I guess.'

Loved ones. Ayingbi had heard the term twice in the past few minutes, and already, it sounded corny.

'Good,' said Sonal. 'You did everything right.'

'I did?'

'Yeah, you hit all the marks. That's basically the entire handbook.'

'It is?'

'Sure. You did fine.'

'There's no chance she's going to try again, right?'

'Not our cud to chew.'

'What do you mean?'

Sonal removed a hanky from her purse. She patted it to her lips. 'I mean your job is done. She drank poison. You spoke to her. She threw up. Gold star. You're a hero.'

Ayingbi bit her lip, unconvinced. 'Except . . . I don't think she was fine, at the end.'

'Too bad. Can't be helped.'

'Er . . . if I'm being honest, I'm a bit worried.'

'You won't last two days here if you fret about that shit,' said Sonal harshly.

'She did give me her address, sort of.'

Sonal frowned. 'You can't take responsibility for everyone, sis. You go running off for a follow-up, three more calls will go unresponded.'

'Like you did, just now?' said Ayingbi coldly.

'I mean it! This is literally Rule Number One! We. Don't. Chase. Calls.'

'Can't we tell the police?'

'Wow,' snorted Sonal. 'Hello, officer? *Maybe* this person took poison and *maybe* she lives on this street. Could you go check up on them, please? Good luck with that. Now, do you mind? You're in my seat.'

Ayingbi knew this would be a lost cause. She stood up suddenly, ripping her headphones off. 'I'll be back,' she said, storming down the office, already unzipping her handbag for the keys to her pink Scooty and flipping the Merry Euphrosyne backpack over a shoulder.

'No, you won't,' said Sonal, resuming her seat and putting the headphones back on.

*

Ayingbi had judged Sonal for poor work ethic earlier, and now, she was judging her for stone-heartedness. But she knew, deep down, that Sonal was right. It was dangerous and foolhardy, what she was doing.

And besides . . . the caller was probably fine. The poison was already out of her system, before it could be digested, absorbed, whatever. She'd be fine . . . of course, she'd be fine . . .

And yet, even knowing all this, here was Ayingbi, riding to her house at full speed, against her better judgment.

This is stupid, and I'm going to regret this.

On the way, she halted at a chemist, where she clumsily purchased medicines a poisoning victim might need.

Charter Enclave was a middle-class colony, with several streets radiating out of a children's park. Most of the residences appeared to be flats, and Ayingbi wondered if she'd misheard a detail.

The caller had clearly said: '*House* that looks like shit.' She enquired from a loiterer and was guided further down, to a row of two-storey houses.

What now?

Slowly, Ayingbi began to roll the Scooty down the road, trying to read every nameplate. It was only when she had nearly reached the end of the lane that one name stood out.

Mrs Something Something, LLM.

Mrs.

This was the first nameplate not identified by a male name or family surname.

This was a woman's house.

It could mean she lived alone.

It could also mean there were no family members nearby.

Ayingbi quietly stared at the silent, dark-grey house. The gate was an arc of beige wood with a marble ramp in front, like a speed-breaker. Unlike in the neighbouring houses, there did not seem to be a light on inside.

Ayingbi parked the Scooty. She went through the little baggy from the chemist shop, finding a bunch of emetics and activated charcoal.

Ayingbi's only source of hesitation now was that the house did not look like shit.

But she supposed everything would seem pretty shitty after drinking rat poison.

She dismounted, swept towards the gate and rang the bell. A few seconds later, a dim Westminster chime sounded from within.

But nobody responded.

A rickshaw tinkled past; there were two girls huddled in the back, shawls over their heads, their faces illuminated by their mobile phones. A dusty wind, drying and unpleasant, made the leaves of the trees overhead shimmer.

Ayingbi thought of those 'trespassers will be shot' signs they had on fences in America and wondered if she would be liable for prosecution if she went in uninvited.

After some thought, she rang the bell of the house next door. Not long after, the door swung open and a middle-aged man appeared. The ice tinkled in his whisky glass as he trod towards her. His pyjamas were too long and half his shirt buttons were open.

'Yes?' he growled, his manner unfriendly.

'Um, hello!' said Ayingbi, squinting at his chest hair. 'I was riding by, and then I heard a scream from that house.'

The neighbour looked at the indicated house. 'Hmph. I wouldn't worry about it. She's always screaming in there.'

'Who else lives with her?' Ayingbi asked politely.

'No idea.'

'Uh . . . does she have a dog?'

The man frowned. No doubt he thought she would toss it into a cooking pot.

'I don't know. Be on your way. Stop hanging about.' He was undoubtedly mistrustful of her. Ayingbi didn't want to jump to racism—after all, it was late, and she was enquiring about an uncongenial neighbour.

'Sure, I'll go. Can you just . . . um . . . check if everything's okay . . . maybe give her a call?'

'I don't have her number,' said the man shortly, and carefully nursing his nightcap, he headed back inside, slamming the door shut.

'Hello!' Ayingbi cupped her hands and yelled at the silent house. A stray, snoozing under a nearby neem tree, raised its head. 'Hello!'

Leaves shuffled as the dog rose, shook itself and approached Ayingbi.

Ayingbi petted it, wondering if she could send it in as an advance party. She had made up her mind. Having already committed to foolishness, now was not the time to stop. Ayingbi unlatched the gate, marched around a white car, whose windows were beige with dust, and stood at the front door. She peered through the side window—she could see a prayer room, through an exposed rectangle the curtain did not quite cover.

Ayingbi covered the doorknob with her handkerchief and gently twisted the heavy door open. There was a faint scent of incense and old books. She looked around for the source—a wall of legal volumes.

The name on the house nameplate, squeezed between the letters 'Mrs' and 'LLM' was already forgotten. But where was Mrs Elelem herself?

Ayingbi moved out of the prayer room, ducking beneath a low doorframe. A dark, dimly lit corridor lay before her.

SLAM!

Ayingbi jumped and turned around wildly to find the heavy front door had slammed shut behind her. It seemed to be one of those doors that closed slowly at first and then quickly as it completed its course. The slam had kicked up Ayingbi's heart rate.

She began to move through the corridor. In the darkness, a low shadow, about knee-high, moved in front of Ayingbi, crossing what looked like the open kitchen door.

'Hey,' Ayingbi blurted out, immediately raising her hands. 'I'm sorry, I heard a scream, just wanted to check it out.'

A little whine emerged from the darkness, and a Labrador Retriever, somewhere between puppy and adult, emerged, tail tucked firmly between its legs.

'Oh . . .' said Ayingbi. The Labrador squeezed itself into the gap beneath the first stair of a nearby staircase, where it continued to whine, its eyes glowing green in the dark. Ayingbi supposed she should be grateful it was only a

Labrador—it could easily have been some other breed, not as agreeable.

Maybe it was time to dip, after all, thought Ayingbi. This place was nothing but bad vibes. She stepped inside the kitchen, where the smell of fresh vomit hit her nostrils. Ayingbi exhaled sharply and, covering her nose with the crook of her elbow, began to feel around for switches with a hanky-protected finger. She managed to click on a tube light, bringing a disgusting scene into full view.

There was a glutinous pool of grey vomit on the kitchen counter. Next to it was an emaciated-looking cat, the exact same shade of grey, dipping its paw into the sick, licking it and nodding. Licking it and nodding.

'No, get away from it,' hissed Ayingbi, remembering what was in the vomit. When the cat refused to be shooed away, Ayingbi bodily picked the cat off the counter and on to the floor, whereupon it immediately shot out of the kitchen.

Ayingbi knew the puke confirmed that this was the place. Maybe it was time to call in the cavalry. She withdrew to the corridor, now fractionally brightened by the kitchen light, and saw a curtain, gently shaking. Maybe this was where the cat had run into. Ayingbi followed. Beneath the stairs, the dog was still whining.

Behind the curtain was another darkened room. Again, Ayingbi swept her handkerchief-clad hand across the wall by the door, searching for switches.

She found them.

Clicking on lights in this house just seemed to present Ayingbi with more and more bad news, and an awful sight blinked into life.

Mrs Elelem was sitting in a dining-room chair, her head tilted back and slightly to a side, her mouth wide open. A little too wide open—in fact, a good portion of her head was missing from the back. There was a very clean hole—Ayingbi could see a diagonal sliver of the microwave oven through it. The blood spatter was a misty crimson rainbow across the wall, glimmering with bits of bone and brain.

Ayingbi's throat constricted. She was too late.

She stood there, rooted to the floor, while her gaze rose up the wall, trying to see how high the blood spatters went, and then lower, where bits of brain matter were glued to the wall and, finally, down to the floor, where pieces of skull, that had gotten unstuck, had fallen. The cat was tiptoeing across the remains, smelling the little bits of brain, choosing choice bits to clean up.

Ayingbi could feel the vomit rising up through her like magma in an erupting volcano.

She did not want to leave behind more pudding for the puss, so she threw up into the polythene bag of medicines she had brought. Mrs Elelem wouldn't be needing them now.

Mrs Elelem wouldn't be needing anything, ever again.

Why had a gunshot not been heard or reported? Ayingbi forced herself to look back and under the table, where she saw a little black pistol with a very long nozzle. She'd seen those in movies—they called them silencers.

But then again, as Mrs Elelem had said—'the movies, they lie'.

It suddenly hit Ayingbi that, not an hour ago, she had been speaking with a person who was now dead.

Ayingbi's brain was filling up with what felt like television static. She saw herself like in a dream, in one of those mental how-did-I-come-to-be-here scenarios.

There's nothing more to do here.

She's gone.

Ayingbi wrinkled her nose. The smell was already bad—rust and iron, Mrs Elelem's perfume (she had not died ungroomed) and now, Ayingbi's own sick. She wiped her mouth and spat a glob of acrid saliva into the bag of medicines, now half-full of her own gunk. Her stomach had begun to churn and curdle.

Oh no. It was coming.

'Fuck,' Ayingbi murmured, closing her eyes. It was sharp and severe when it was early.

She squeezed her eyes, trying to discipline the pain. It was the cat's hissing that made her straighten herself. The cat had puffed itself up, and its pupils were entirely rounded, mumbling little mow-mow-mows at Mrs Elelem. Outside, the dog's whining had stopped.

There was a whoosh of movement behind Ayingbi— she spun around to look; there was nothing there. *Enough! I'm outta here.*

Ayingbi turned the light off and retreated outside, already feeling for her mobile phone. She would call an ambulance, that's what she would do.

But the thing was already in the corridor; Ayingbi very nearly walked into it.

It could easily have passed for a piece of misshapen wall. Ayingbi could not describe what it looked like, because it did not look like anything at all. The thing was so unearthly in form and construction. It was there, waiting in the corridor, where it had not been moments ago. An invisible, unidentifiable force, which made its presence apparent without being seen, heard or smelt. It was there. It could not have been more there if it tried.

'Oh . . . ' grunted Ayingbi. She knew she was being regarded. Did the thing have eyes? She couldn't say. She just knew her presence had been acknowledged and appraised. The thing moved, and Ayingbi shrank sideways to make way. The thing hesitated for the fraction of a second when it was right alongside Ayingbi and then it pulled on ahead, into the dining room.

A great groan emerged from the room in the voice of Mrs Elelem, like she was trying to imitate the voice of a vacuum cleaner. It was the groan of a person trying to feebly resist something being taken from them. But the person in question was dead and in no position to resist anything.

The pain in Ayingbi's belly seemed to be the only thing keeping her moored to reality, a rope to guide her out of the terrifying other-worldliness of her own predicament. She felt a spasm in her middle, which she instantly took as a cue to—

RUN!

Ayingbi bolted out the house, feeling the relief of fresh air hit her face. There was a new car, a blue one, on the road. There appeared to be someone in there.

Perhaps a man.

But Ayingbi did not stop for hellos. She ran down the driveway, fumbling for her keys. The stray bolted when it saw her arrive. She clambered on to her Scooty and kicked the kickstand off, pedalling off the road with her feet while she keyed the ignition in.

Please start!

The movies also lied about vehicle engines not starting when quick getaways were required, for the Scooty growled into life at once.

Ayingbi ploughed through the busy city streets, the pain in her stomach getting worse and worse.

Just give me another hour.

No such luck.

It happened on a red light, which was too busy for her to run. She slumped over the handlebars, groaning in pain.

Ayingbi drove the rest of the way back slowly.

When she reached home, whimpering, she slid off the Scooty, took her handkerchief and swept it across the seat. In the dim light of the staircase, she checked the hanky for the verdict.

Yes, too late, indeed.

Ayingbi squelched the rest of the way up, already unfastening her jeans, which she dropped to her ankles as soon as she was inside, before waddling into the bathroom to get cleaned up.

Afterwards, Ayingbi lay in bed and began to cry softly, hugging a hot water bottle to her stomach. She cried herself to sleep, because sleep would not come any other way.

At some point, she heard her phone ringing.

She let it ring; she did not answer.

THREE

THE TEETERLING

There were two missed calls from last night. One was from Srivastav, followed by a curt message telling Ayingbi she was fired.

Can't fire a volunteer, dumbass.

The second was from an unknown number.

With too many mysteries to deal with right now, Ayingbi decided to call the unknown number back.

'Good afternoon,' said a pleasant male voice, receiving the call. 'Is this Ayingbi Mayengbam?'

'Yes.'

'Ah, thanks for calling back. My name is Dr Rastogi. I am a clinical psychologist, specializing in cognitive behavioural therapy, with a dabbling interest in psychotherapy. Now, the circumstances of this call may seem strange, but if you have a minute, I have a proposition for you.'

Ayingbi was puzzled. No doubt she needed therapy after last night, but—

'How'd you get this number?'

'I'll get to it. Forgive me for guessing, but did you happen to leave the Merry Euphrosyne office last night to attend to a caller? The place, I believe, was Charter Enclave.'

'How do you know?'

'Well, it seems our mutual friend made two calls last night. I received the first, and you, the second. I was there as well. I believe our paths crossed briefly, just as you were leaving.'

'Were you the guy in the blue car?'

'Indeed. Judging by your manner of departure, I regret to hazard that we both were too late.'

'Do you work at Merry Euphrosyne, too?'

'Oh no. I run an independent crisis helpline. However, I did notice a Merry Euphrosyne backpack on your Scooty. When I contacted them, they were happy to give your number.'

That bastard Srivastav.

'Well, what do you want?' growled Ayingbi.

'My proposition is simply this, Ms Mayengbam—we would love to have you on our team.'

'Your team?' said Ayingbi, in a slightly raised voice. 'You mean this other *independent* helpline you speak of?'

'Well, yes. We thought you might be interested.'

'Sir, I have no idea what I might have done to give anyone that notion!' said Ayingbi shrilly. 'I've had enough of suicidal people to last me a lifetime! Goodbye!'

And she cut the call.

Put off as she was by Rastogi's call, one detail about it stood out—the man had nailed the pronunciation of her name. It was so rare that it always registered.

Even so.

There was no way she was going to work at a hotline ever again.

She'd seen enough.

Ayingbi lay in bed, trying to remember exactly what she'd seen while leaving Mrs Elelem's dining room. She had felt its presence with a blazing certainty, but she couldn't quite pin down the details to present as objective evidence, even to herself. It was bizarre.

She had half a mind to report what she had seen to the police, but then she realized she might be a suspect in yesterday's suicide case, once it was discovered. That no-good neighbour would certainly have a description of her to give the authorities. Besides, Mrs Elelem was already dead—Ayingbi did not need to get embroiled in a messy aftermath.

If I am to continue living a normal life, I must have some sort of closure regarding what I saw.

But it was hard.

The situation was even scarier when she imagined not what she had seen, but what she'd missed. Mrs Elelem, after throwing up, after counselling from two separate hotlines, had doubled down on her original decision.

Chilling!

Hotlines tell call operators not to go, for a reason.

I shouldn't've gone.

Why, then, had Mrs Elelem done it? Had she—Ayingbi—not been assuring enough in their brief conversation?

'You do not need to feel guilty,' Ayingbi told herself sternly in the mirror. 'Compose yourself!'

While Mrs Elelem decomposes.

Ayingbi smiled her first smile in two days.

Was she really going to while away the summer just because one thing didn't work out?

Maybe she needed to learn a new skill. There were lots of places offering Zumba classes. Maybe she could do volunteer work elsewhere. Perhaps at a dog shelter or an old-age home?

Reluctantly, she decided to call Nimmi.

'Bum!' said Nimmi cheerfully. 'Free for dinner tonight?'

'Hey, not tonight, no,' said Ayingbi. 'So, the volunteer thing, er . . . didn't work out.' She awkwardly massaged the back of her head. 'You said you had . . . something in mind. Does the offer still stand?'

*

'So, for the pre-wedding photoshoot,' said Dhaanvi, the wedding planner, snapping her fingers at the photographer, 'you want to imagine their grandkids poring over the photos. When the house burns down, these are the photo albums they'll be rushing inside to save.'

Up ahead, the rest of Dhaanvi's assistants were chivvying the betrothed couple up and down the steps of the haveli's lawns, while relatives chaperoned from the sidelines. Both bride and groom appeared gormless and without chemistry, with smiles that came on when the photographer twitched his finger and vanished the moment the photo was clicked. It looked more a business alliance than a union of soulmates.

The haveli, scenically located on a hilltop, was the ancestral property of some automobile magnate based elsewhere, and the lawns were often leased out for banquets or film shootings.

'Get some by that tree!' barked Dhaanvi, and the assistant photographer jabbed the couple in that direction with his portable LED ring.

'Oh, my lehenga is too tight!' huffed the bride, who appeared to have been fitted for it when she was eleven.

'Can we do a picture in which we're shaking hands?' suggested the groom.

'What are you? Team captains?' said Dhaanvi sourly. 'Why not something a bit more romantic?'

'High-five?' giggled the bride, and the groom put a hand to his mouth, looking scandalized.

'No,' said Dhaanvi flatly.

'You keep saying no to everything,' pouted the bride's mother. 'You wouldn't even let him have musical chairs at his bachelor party!'

'For the same reason we cannot have her bridal entry on a sledge pulled by swans,' said Dhaanvi patiently. 'It's a stupid idea.' She glanced at Ayingbi. 'You're taking notes, right?'

'Uh, yeah.'

Dhaanvi's phone began to ring, and Madhuri—her assistant whose job Ayingbi was vying for—scurried over with it. 'No!' barked Dhaanvi, after a beat. 'Tequila sunrises and mimosas, not margaritas! Everything's yellow for the haldi ceremony!' She cut the call and looked up at the couple. 'Maybe take your hand off her butt. These pictures will be going up on the reception, after all.'

'Can we do that picture,' said the groom, 'where I'm kissing her belly?'

'Kissing her belly?' frowned Dhaanvi.

'Yeah,' said the groom, jabbing his finger into the jutting ring of flesh between the bride's lehenga and *choli*. 'A little smoocheroo—right there.'

Dhaanvi clenched her teeth. 'Those are for pregnancy photo shoots. There needs to be a baby bump.'

'Maybe he could wear a stethoscope and sort of listen to my stomach,' piped in the bride.

Dhaanvi's eyelid twitched. 'Again . . . pregnancy.' Madhuri again scurried over with Dhaanvi's ringing phone. 'We have permission till seven-thirty!' she shouted into it. 'We need the sunset shots!'

The bride burst into tears. 'Mummy, mummy! My lehenga will not fit!'

Dhaanvi ordering a 'chai tea' was the last straw. Ayingbi walked away as Madhuri scuttered past, sticking a stirrer into a lidded disposable cup. Ayingbi checked the number on her phone from last calls. She hadn't yet saved it, but she remembered the name.

The phone had barely rung when Dr Rastogi picked up. 'Ms Mayengbam!'

'Um, hello,' said Ayingbi stiffly. 'I was wondering . . . if you could tell me more . . . about this place of yours.'

'Yes, absolutely! It's a suicide hotline, similar to Merry Euphrosyne.'

'Okay. Now, I'm open to your offer, but I'd like to know why you guys want me.'

'It's not that hard. What you did was very brave, Ms Mayengbam. Breaking protocol like that, to save someone else's life.'

'Yeah, I get that. But it was dangerous and irresponsible, too.'

'There are a lot of people in the world in pain, Ms Mayengbam. They need good people like you helping them. Going that extra mile, so to speak. We see your talent and drive as invaluable. I don't see your actions as irresponsible at all, but simply motivated by a strong desire to do good. At our hotline, we not only permit what you did, but actively encourage it.'

'Okay . . .' said Ayingbi. She felt like she was being buttered up. But she also knew she'd eat rat poison herself before spending a summer getting turmeric lattes for Dhaanvi.

'What say you, Ayingbi?'

'I don't know, Dr Rastogi,' said Ayingbi softly. 'I'm really not sure.'

'But . . . you called, just now!'

'I know,' said Ayingbi, tapping her mobile restlessly with her fingertip.

'You want to save lives, don't you?'

'Yes,' sighed Ayingbi. 'Of course I do.'

'And even though you had a nasty first time, I can assure you the real work of counselling people is very rewarding. I've been doing it for twenty-five years.'

'I'm sure it is. I guess I . . . just wanted reassurance.'

'Look, Ayingbi, are we legit? Are we crazy? You're going to have to roll the dice on us. Tell you what, why don't you swing by the office some time tomorrow evening and decide for yourself?'

'Okay,' said Ayingbi, with a deep breath. 'I'll give it a shot.'

*

Rastogi's office, located on the first floor of a somewhat run-down office complex, between a pirated-movies store and hair transplant clinic, was easily missed.

A garland of daffodils hung from the cheap-looking aluminium door, almost entirely concealing the signboard— 'Good Morning Helpline'.

Ayingbi ducked beneath the daffodil garland as she pushed the door open, almost running into the earpiece-wearing, grey-moustached man standing there . . . with a gun.

Ayingbi's heart skipped a beat.

'Oh no!' said the man, and Ayingbi immediately recognized the voice as Rastogi's. 'It's a water pistol! See!' He squeezed the trigger a couple of times, and thin water jets squirted out.

He indicated several potted daffodils, which appeared to take up every unoccupied corner of the office lobby.

'You must be Ayingbi!' said Dr Rastogi, giving the water pistol a little gunslinger spin as he pocketed it, and extending a hand for her to shake. 'I'm Dr Rastogi! Thank you so much for coming!'

Ayingbi shook his hand, staring at the potted daffodils.

'The police didn't come knocking, did they?' said Rastogi.

'Not yet,' said Ayingbi nervously. 'Will they?'

'I should think not. I think it will be better to not dwell upon the matter further. It is best that our presence at the scene be kept private.'

'You mean we don't report the suicide?'

'Just so,' said Rastogi evenly. 'What had to happen, happened. There is no point in implicating ourselves in an eventual enquiry.'

That was exactly what Ayingbi had been thinking, too.

'A neighbour saw me, though,' she said gloomily. 'So, I guess I'd be implicated anyway.'

'Our common client had tried to take her own life twice in the past year. I wouldn't worry too much about it, to be honest,' said Rastogi. 'The neighbours knew. Even the police knew.'

For a place that marketed itself as going out of their way to save everyone, Ayingbi couldn't help but feel that Rastogi was being rather cavalier.

Correctly reading Ayingbi's expression, he added, 'It's very sad, obviously, that she couldn't get the help she needed. But at a suicide hotline, even as we put in our best efforts, the show must go on.'

Ayingbi nodded.

'Why don't we talk in my office?' said Rastogi.

His office was almost as large as the lobby itself, and a rather ornate affair. There were more potted daffodils, and a bed folded into the wall. A second wall had a sword collection, each sword sheathed in velvet of a different colour.

'Yes, I like to collect them,' said Rastogi. 'My wife isn't a fan.' He indicated the seats in front of his desk, which was itself a bit of a spectacle.

It had a computer, two grey telephones, a drinking bird, a Newton's cradle and a statuette of a very ugly, blue-grey creature. There was another strange typewriter-like device sitting on the edge, wired up to switches, emitting a low-pitched, humming noise. The sound was eerie—something you heard in a very old alien movie.

Rastogi sprayed the potted daffodils with his water pistol, before sitting.

Ayingbi's eyes, still wandering all over the office, returned most frequently to the ugly gremlin on Rastogi's desk.

It had a very large, round head, all blue, with a small body, short horns and a wide, wicked smile. It held a pitchfork with a pointing hand instead of prongs.

Why would anyone want that there?

'So, to business,' said Rastogi, twiddling his earpiece. 'As you know, I want you as a call operator. I have two others—young, eager kids like you working the lines.'

Kids like you.

Ayingbi could never think of herself as a kid—it came with being a teacher. 'Where are they right now?'

'Chaitanya works the day shift, from six to six. His night-shift reliever, Hardeep, must've come in.'

'Will there be a training period?'

Rastogi nodded, but appeared to be busy with the humming device. He reached out and dragged it till it was directly in front of Ayingbi, partially blocking their view of each other.

'Consider this a test,' he said. 'Then, we'll know if you need training.'

He pressed a couple of switches, and the machine's humming turned into something of a wavering groan. It began to vibrate—the vibration made loose papers on the desk chatter and the drinking bird's water shiver. Rastogi then plucked a tangle of tapeable white wires out of a drawer, and jacked them into his side of the device.

'Do you mind if I wire you to these?' he said. 'Sorry, I don't have any consent forms, so I can only ask.'

Ayingbi nodded.

Two of the wired electrode stickers went on her wrists, two on her temples, and the last two on either side of her windpipe.

'Is this a lie detector test?' said Ayingbi, fidgety and somewhat nervous.

'No,' said Rastogi, making for a lampshade. 'I'm just going to dim the light now.'

'Okay,' said Ayingbi, and she closed her eyes with the dimming of the room.

'You can keep your eyes open,' she heard Rastogi say. 'Just relax . . . breathe. I'll give the instructions.'

The groaning of the device turned into more of a hungry rumble. It was making Ayingbi feel sleepy. Rastogi lit three candles on a candlestick on top of the device, and they immediately began to burn at quick but unequal rates. In their flickering light, Ayingbi could see him frowning at a reading she could not see.

'There's no pain, right?' said Rastogi.

'No,' said Ayingbi, slightly worried that pain was within the realm of possibility.

Rastogi was now checking his watch. After around a minute, he said, 'if you're ready, I'm just going to be asking some questions.'

'Okay.' It came out as a bit of a slur, surprising Ayingbi.

Rastogi pressed another button. A dull, radar-type pinging began to accompany the groaning. Rastogi gestured, first, to the little blue–grey demon. 'You noticed that earlier. What do you think it is?'

'Dunno. A little goblin.'

'What do you think it does?'

'Probably tickles people with that hand on a stick thing,' grunted Ayingbi. 'Looks the mischievous sort.'

'If you had to give it a name, what name would you give it?'

'Erm . . . Gobbly.'

'On a scale of one to ten, how distressing to you is the idea of dogs on wheels?'

Ayingbi thought about skateboarding dogs for a hot second. 'Oh, like, dogs with wheelchairs? Uh, five, maybe six.' It was dogs *without* wheels that needed them that was more distressing.

'Right,' said Rastogi. 'Moving on. You are offered immortality, with no diseases and perfect health. Do you accept it?'

'No,' said Ayingbi immediately. She hoped she wouldn't be asked to justify, and she wasn't. She was, however, asked: 'What per cent of the population would you say would take it? This isn't an experiment that has already been conducted, so there is no right answer.'

'Uh, I guess 10 per cent.'

Ayingbi wondered if she'd lowballed it, but Rastogi had already moved on to the next question.

'North Pole or South Pole?'

Ayingbi wondered what that had to do with anything. 'South.'

'Why?'

'Penguins, I guess.' There was a sentence Ayingbi thought she'd never say today. 'And no polar bears.' She blinked, for a moment thinking she'd nodded off. 'The picture of them with their kills is scary, with the blood all over the snow.'

'Hmm,' said Rastogi. 'When you worked as a guidance counsellor, did anyone ever cry in your presence?'

'Yes,' sighed Ayingbi. 'Often.'

'Okay,' said Rastogi gently. 'Almost there. What comes to mind when you think of the colour purple?'

'Purple stuff,' said Ayingbi stupidly. Her head was just not in the game right now.

'Would you regard purple as an edible colour? Humour me.'

'Uhh . . . I guess? Maybe a luxury item. Like caviar.'

'Can you list some things that are purple?'

Ayingbi's mind immediately jumped to 'brinjal', but she didn't want to say it, for Freudian reasons.

'Purple shirts,' she said. 'Purple pants. Purple flowers.' Ayingbi thought with all her might. 'The purple part of the rainbow.'

She felt like the drowsiness was both dumbing her down *and* making her talk longer than she would've liked to, but then, Rastogi turned the machine off. He got up and restored the light. The room seemed to grow cooler. The candles had all melted into puddles of grey goo.

'Thank you, Ayingbi. You can take those off, now.'

'So . . . when do I get results?' said Ayingbi, pulling the electrodes off.

'Oh, no results. Well, you passed, but we already knew that. I will, however, tell you what this is.'

He patted the little demon statuette on the head. 'This is a Teeterling. Little demon in Welsh folklore. They say it uses its staff to push people over cliffs. Well, not everyone. Only those who are . . . already standing on the precipice.'

'What kind of people are those?' said Ayingbi apprehensively.

'You tell me.' Rastogi gave a piercing smile. 'What our friend the Teeterling does, or is said to do, is to give people

that last, fateful nudge that pushes them over the edge.
Are you familiar with the behaviour of suicidal people just
before they commit the act, Ayingbi?'

'They don't do it straight away.'

'Exactly! They dither. They stall. They contemplate.
They work up the courage—yes, courage! It takes a level
of bravery to do it, regardless of what some heathens
might think! In all of it there is a pivotal moment—
lasting merely a microsecond, where you decide to take
the plunge. Either that moment doesn't come for you . . .
or it does.' He sighed. 'Well, having this little bugger
around reminds me of what we're dealing with. Of what
we're trying to avoid.'

Ayingbi nodded.

Rastogi cleared his throat. 'Anyway, I was thinking of
putting you in the day shift.'

Ayingbi immediately took umbrage. 'When do more
people call?'

'At night.'

'Then I would like to work in the night shift.'

Rastogi hesitated. 'I hadn't planned on it. For safety
reasons.'

'Because I'm a woman?'

'Naturally.'

'I can handle myself,' said Ayingbi shortly. 'Besides,
you sought me out, based on work I'd done in a night shift,
remember?'

'True,' mused Rastogi. 'I hope you realize this isn't
because of sexism.'

'No, no,' said Ayingbi. 'I get where you're coming from. And I'm telling you quite plainly that I'd like to work in the night shift, if that's where more calls come in.'

'Well, night shift it is, then. We're pretty flexible with hours, so if you want some modification, get in touch with Hardy and Chatty.'

'Okay.'

'Let's take a look at your office, then, shall we?'

They headed back outside to the office lobby, where Rastogi pointed to a glass-panelled fridge. 'I keep it stocked. Help yourself to whatever you like. And those are Hardeep and Chaitanya's cubicles.' Both cubicles were guarded by translucent, hard plastic curtains. Ayingbi could hear a muffled voice from one of them.

'I think Hardy's on a call, or I would've introduced you . . .' mumbled Rastogi. 'Anyway, here we are.' He led her inside a third cubicle. 'Not much privacy, I'm afraid.'

The cubicle had a plastic curtain like the others, a desk occupying two-thirds of the space, a squashy office chair, and a window with a cooler.

'Don't worry, the chair is very ergonomic,' said Rastogi, wheeling it around. 'Give it a go.'

Ayingbi sat—it felt like an electronic massage chair.

'Laptops are fine. Just, no headphones,' said Rastogi. 'You need to be able to catch the phones ringing.'

And, finally, the phones.

There were three of them on the table, in a perfect, equilateral triangle. They were old-timey rotary phones— the sort that made your fingertips hurt when you dialled a

Arsh Verma

number. The one on the right was deep purple. The one on the left was royal blue. The battered one at the back, with a velvet-covered coiled cord, was jet black. The wires from each of the phones vanished into a hole in the desk.

'Let me explain,' said Rastogi. He gestured towards the purple phone. 'That's the hotline phone.' Then he gestured to the blue one. 'And that's the office phone. Extensions are written right there.'

'What about that one?' Ayingbi indicated the black phone.

Rastogi reached out and pulled the receiver. He put it to his own ear, then handed it to Ayingbi, who did the same.

'See? It's dead. You needn't worry about it.'

'Then why is it here?'

'Too much of a hassle to get rid of it,' muttered Rastogi. 'I'd have to remove the table, call an electrician and everything. Maybe on a free weekend. Now, for the switch.' He pointed to a small, silver toggle switch on the wall. 'Whenever you're entering or exiting the office, you flip this switch. It lets me know where you are.'

It had two settings: 'HERE' and 'OUTSIDE OFFICE.'

'Okay,' said Ayingbi, remembering that this place encouraged leaving the office to attend to callers.

'Well, that's the tour,' said Rastogi. 'Any questions?'

'Uhh . . . I think I need to get my bearings a little bit.'

'Of course,' said Rastogi softly. 'I'll leave you to get settled.'

Rastogi left, and Ayingbi set down her handbag and looked around.

She exhaled.

Here she was.

Another suicide hotline.

Her heart gave a sudden flutter. This was serious business.

The blue phone suddenly rang, making Ayingbi jump. She panicked for a second, before remembering that it was only the internal office phone. She took the call.

'Thought I'd make a test call,' said Rastogi. 'Everything comfortable, Ayingbi?'

'Yes . . . everything's fine.'

'Is my voice coming through okay?'

'Yes.'

'Good. Give me a holler if you need anything.'

'Uh . . . Dr Rastogi?'

'Yes?'

'Am I really ready for this?'

'Hmm. Hold on, I'm coming back down.'

A minute later, Rastogi was outside Ayingbi's cubicle again. 'Maybe I didn't do a very good job of explaining it earlier,' he said. 'What I meant was, you have full flexibility—you decide how to engage the patient.'

'Yes, I get that,' said Ayingbi. 'But is there like a handbook or something I can look at?'

'I would encourage you to let go of that approach, Ayingbi. We don't really believe in scripts and protocols. We try to examine each case from the prism of . . . freewheeling empathy.'

'Freewheeling empathy?' Ayingbi was totally bewildered.

'Just another way of saying we leave it to our operators to devise their own styles.'

Ayingbi was not reassured. 'Surely some loose guidelines . . . I mean, what if someone has absolutely no idea what to say?'

Rastogi smiled. 'You could say there are dos-and-don'ts but nothing you, as a guidance counsellor, wouldn't already be aware of.'

'There's another thing. I still can't get behind this concept of attending to calls in person. It strikes me as very strange.'

'Or philosophy is a little different, Ayingbi. We feel that someone on the verge of taking their own life cannot always be suitably counselled over the phone.'

'But . . . what if the caller is a nutcase? Or drunk, or dangerous?'

'Ohh, no, no! You don't have to go after every call! You use your discretion! It can be all, it can be none! All we are saying is: we *will* facilitate it. We'll even pay for fuel, parking fees and tolls—the whole lot.'

'Hmm.'

'You're still not sold.'

Ayingbi appreciated that Dr Rastogi was being patient with her. She was no expert, but even with the explanation, the legality of what he seemed to be doing here seemed wishy-washy. Throwing her into the deep end without training. Attending to callers in person. No guidelines. Merry Euphrosyne, for all its perceived flaws, positively radiated a dull, by-the-book credibility.

'It's just all so . . . peculiar,' said Ayingbi, too polite to say 'shady'.

Rastogi sighed. 'Look, Ayingbi, when you joined Merry Euphrosyne, it was with a purpose, wasn't it?'

'Yeah . . .'

'You could've gone for any job.'

'I know what you're getting at, Dr Rastogi. I guess I did want to help people.'

'Let me give you an analogy, then. On holiday, why do families get together to exchange gifts, when they could simply send them? Why do businessmen travel across continents to seal trade deals? We often say "oh, this could've been an email", but could it really? What is it about personal contact that changes the entire dynamic of the equation?'

'The human touch.'

'Precisely. Now, coming to what we are doing. Could there be a more suitable candidate for saving lives than the actual human touch?'

'Maybe you're right, Dr Rastogi,' said Ayingbi. 'But there's still an inherent risk. Increased accountability, too.'

'Well, I've laid it all out for you, Ayingbi. Maybe give it a go for one night? See how you like it?'

Ayingbi thought about it. 'Okay. I'll give it a go.'

'Great! Well, I've already given you the drill, so . . . holler if you need anything.' Rastogi awkwardly patted the plastic curtain, then stumbled away again.

Ayingbi sat again.

Maybe it won't be that bad, she thought. Maybe in matters like these, basic humanity and compassion trumped technique.

She stared at the phones.

I should name them.

Ayingbi liked naming inanimate objects, and she did so with her first instinct, without stopping to ponder which ancient neural connections the names had sprung from.

The blue office phone?

'Phoenix.'

What about the purple one—the star attraction?

'Barney!'

And what about the dead one? It was entirely black, except for the white central dial. It should have a name, too.

'Tuxedo.'

Blue, purple and black . . . Phoenix, Barney and Tuxedo. Surely they would all become the best of friends.

Ayingbi wondered whether Hardeep was done with his call yet. She rose to check and maybe say hello, when a phone started to ring.

She knew it wasn't Phoenix, because the ring was different. This one was shriller, with a shorter pulse between rings. Ayingbi squinted from one phone to another.

It was Barney—the purple hotline phone.

She was getting her first call.

FOUR

CUSTARD–MUSTARD

Showtime already.

It felt weird to implement Rastogi's advice mere minutes after having received it. Ayingbi really did not want to sound robotic, or like an automatic answering machine.

She took the call, with her free hand reaching for her pen and notepad. Barney's receiver was thick and heavy. Slowly, she exhaled and raised it to her ear.

Here goes nothing.

'Hello! Thank you for calling—' Ayingbi fumbled with the name of her new place of employment, '—us.'

'Hi . . .'

Female voice, soft and timid.

'How are you doing tonight?' trilled Ayingbi, keeping her voice sharp and clear, so the girl would have no doubt Ayingbi was also a woman.

'Uh, not that great, actually. I really screwed up.'

'Do you want to tell me about it?'

'It's . . . very difficult to talk about.'

'No worries, take your time.'

The caller breathed heavily into the phone. Ayingbi thought she was mustering up courage, but was left disappointed when she said, 'Actually, let it be.'

'No, no!' cried Ayingbi. 'Look, I'm here. Let's talk!'

'I changed my mind. I have nothing to say.'

'I'll just call you back if you do that.'

'Are you allowed to do that?'

'No, but our phone has a button. We can call back the person who called us last, without actually getting their number,' said Ayingbi, inventing wildly.

'That doesn't seem right.'

'I won't pry too much. But can you at least tell me if you're in any immediate danger?'

'Uhm . . .'

'Are you at a risk of self-harm?'

There was a long pause. 'Yes,' said the caller finally.

'Are you thinking of hurting yourself?'

'More than.'

'Are you in the presence of a loved one?' asked Ayingbi, her mind hurrying to the safety of the tips she had learnt at Merry Euphrosyne.

'No.'

Ayingbi decided to relax and ease into the conversation. 'Look. I'm just a stranger on the phone. You can talk to me.'

'I'm not sure . . .' said the caller, but as she spoke, Ayingbi could hear a familiar train station announcement in the background.

'Are you at a railway station?!' said Ayingbi, restlessly playing with the coil of Barney's cord.

The girl sighed. 'Yes.'

'Are you running away from home?'

'Not exactly.'

'Are you thinking of hurting yourself with a train there?'

Hurting yourself with a train. It sounded silly, but anything to avoid dropping the K-word.

'I'm considering it,' said the girl. 'Seriously.'

A girl at a crowded place, thought Ayingbi. Maybe a face-to-face might not the be worst thing. She might get a hang of this new system.

'I could come over,' she suggested.

'Come over?' The caller sounded horrified.

'Yes, to meet you.'

'No! I don't want to meet you! Are you crazy?'

It did sound weird, now that the caller had said it. Ayingbi wondered whether she'd rushed that particular proposition. 'I won't report this to anyone. And I won't call you back.'

'Promise?'

'Promise,' said Ayingbi earnestly. 'Just please don't hang up.' She remembered how she'd pleaded with Mrs Elelem, and she had vowed to be, or at least come across as, more straightforward and professional going forth.

'I've done something,' the caller finally squeaked. 'Something horrible.'

'Whatever it is, you can tell me.'

There was the longest pause yet.

'Okay,' said the caller finally. 'I'd like to meet. I'm at Rahilgiri railway station. Not on the station, like off it, on the tracks. To the left when you enter. But please, don't tell anyone. And please, come alone.'

Ayingbi wrenched her hand free of the cord and reached for a pen. 'Cool. What's your name?'

But the girl had already cut the call. No matter. The name wasn't that important.

They had a rendezvous point.

Ayingbi reached for her Scooty keys, and flicked the silver switch on the wall from 'HERE' to 'OUTSIDE OFFICE'.

'Good luck,' she heard Hardy call out, as she swept out of the office.

*

Ayingbi was excited on the Scooty ride. It felt like a smart decision to do a face-to-face right out the gate. She wouldn't wonder too much about the process later.

Rahilgiri was a local railway station. Some long-distance train might stop here just long enough for you to run out and buy a packet of chips.

A train had pulled into the quiet, dimly lit platform when Ayingbi arrived, but nobody was getting on or off. At least a third of the space was occupied by sleeping squatters. Thankfully, it did not look like there had yet been an incident. Keenly aware that eyes were following her, Ayingbi walked down the platform till she reached its end, her roving gaze scanning for solo female faces. She gingerly lowered herself to the dark ground and clicked on her mobile torch.

The train began to move in the opposite direction, slowly at first, then picking up speed, giving Ayingbi the impression she was walking much faster than she actually was, until it was gone.

She followed the oily gleam of the tracks for about two minutes. There were shanties on her left. Far up ahead, she could see, like a colourful constellation, a vertical stack of three red lights, and another yellow one on the side.

And yes, there she was—a petite female figure—mooching on the tracks.

Ayingbi picked up the pace. The smell of ammonia was searing through her nose, and the uneven ballast rocks made it difficult to walk. Crows cawed from the power line overhead as Ayingbi approached the still, silent figure.

The puddle of mobile torchlight had heralded Ayingbi's arrival, and the figure straightened up as she drew close.

Ayingbi raised the mobile phone, and she saw a young, suit-wearing woman squinting down at her toes. There was a thick yellow stain of some kind on the suit—it looked like squirted mustard, or spilled caramel custard. One really couldn't tell.

'I lost my earring,' said Custard–Mustard, looking up at Ayingbi.

Again, the voice was a giveaway. This *was* Ayingbi's caller. Ayingbi did not make her sigh of relief audible, but quietly lowered her mobile torchlight, permitting Custard–Mustard the privacy of darkness.

'Where?' said Ayingbi, and Custard–Mustard's ears perked up. Just as Ayingbi had recognized her from voice, she too, had placed Ayingbi.

'Oh . . .' said Custard–Mustard. 'Oh.'

So, they both knew who the other was, even if it was yet to be acknowledged.

Ayingbi's lips were already dry. Now that she was here, she had no idea what to do or say. 'What are you doing here?'

Custard–Mustard's expression again stiffened. 'It's like I said . . .' she said, with an effort to change her voice. 'I lost my earring. There, somewhere.' She pointed at an indistinct patch of grass.

The wind played over the rails. A polythene bag rolled across the tracks like tumbleweed.

Ayingbi could play this game. She pretended to cast her torchlight over the grass patch.

There was a coo of a distant train. The *chhuk–chhuk* sound rapidly grew louder; the train did not appear to be stopping at Rahilgiri. Custard–Mustard's eyes found the front of the train, a great, yellow-eyed red wall. As it rattled towards them, Ayingbi quickly gripped Custard–Mustard's wrist tight, and Custard–Mustard's gaze flickered as the train engine hurtled past them at a 100 km an hour.

'Right,' said Ayingbi, releasing Custard–Mustard's hand after the train had crossed. 'So, you want to tell me what this is about?'

Custard–Mustard's eyes finally met Ayingbi's, and she bowed her head, ever so slightly.

Ayingbi did not break the silence at her own end. She thought of what Rastogi had said about the Teeterling. Custard–Mustard probably had one over her head right now.

And, finally, Custard–Mustard squeaked, 'Nudes.'

'Pardon?'

'Nudes. I sent my boyfriend . . . nudes.'

'Oh,' said Ayingbi, after a pause. 'Did he forward them to his friends?'

Custard–Mustard hugged herself and shook her head vigorously. She attempted to turtle her head into the neck hole of her suit.

'Did he upload them . . .' Ayingbi began, but then she stopped as she remembered one of the rules from Merry Euphrosyne. No leading questions.

'No,' said Custard–Mustard. 'He didn't post them anywhere.'

'Then?'

'He never got them. I posted . . .' Custard-Mustard now sounded like she was forcing the voice through a rock stuck in her throat, '. . . them to the wrong place.'

Ayingbi's heart sank. 'Where?'

Custard–Mustard attempted to mash her own face like a potato with her bare hands. 'Like a shitty group chat I don't even use,' she moaned. 'Someone had commented. I made a slight mistake. The group was inactive. All acquaintances. It was from a project thing years ago. They all got them.'

Fuck.

'And they're just so horrible . . .' Custard–Mustard burst into tears. 'I'm spread out in one photo and everything. Uhuhuhuhu . . .'

Ayingbi rushed and enveloped her in her arms. The blood was pounding in her head—she had no idea what to do, none at all. She thought of Rastogi, and his encouragement to think on her feet. So far, it wasn't going well. Custard–Mustard shuddered stiffly in Ayingbi's arms, not yielding to the hug.

'Didn't you delete the photo afterwards?'

Custard–Mustard bawled some more. 'Yes . . . but . . . it's out there now . . . it's in the wild.'

Ayingbi was feeling worse by the second. This truly was an awful situation—it was no good pretending otherwise. Even if Custard–Mustard had deleted the photo, people, acting on some depraved instinct, would've taken screenshots immediately.

Think, Ayingbi, think! Say something!

'People will forget,' suggested Ayingbi lamely. 'People have a short-term memory with these things. They are so wrapped up in their own—'

Custard–Mustard gave a dry, hollow laugh. 'Pratishtha Bhatia's sister ate her booger one time in first grade,' she said shortly. 'And even though she's an influencer now, it's all I can think of whenever I see her reels. Oh, they can forget other things, but this will not be forgotten.'

'Yeah . . . well . . .' said Ayingbi. She did not want to be silent too long, for fear of appearing out of ideas. She needed to keep conversation threads, ideas, suggestions, solutions—good, bad, whatever—going. To be silent meant to concede defeat.

'I sent it on the right chat! I know I did!' cried Custard–Mustard hysterically. 'I'm not stupid! I was cautious!'

Ayingbi knew that teenagers didn't have the sense not to expose themselves in front of a camera, but Custard–Mustard looked older than that. Ayingbi immediately reproached herself for judging Custard–Mustard. She must never do it again.

'How are your parents?' said Ayingbi. 'Like, how will they react?'

'Loving . . .' hiccupped Custard–Mustard. 'So . . . loving . . . They've always been . . . they've known about him . . . from the start . . . and now look how I've hurt them . . . Papa will never take it out on me . . . he'll take it out on himself! He'll kill himself! Oh, I've ruined their reputation! I can't go back! I want to die!'

'Sshh . . .' whispered Ayingbi, pulling her into a hug again. 'It's okay . . . it's okay . . .'

'I'm sorry, Mumma!' wailed Custard–Mustard. 'I'm really sorry!'

Ayingbi felt a lump rising in her own throat.

Get a grip, Bing-bee ma'am.

'Mum . . . mum . . . mummyyy . . . Mummmyyyyyy . . .' sobbed Custard–Mustard.

'What about your boyfriend?' said Ayingbi, waiting until the throat lump had gone.

'He knows, he's called like a million times . . .' Custard–Mustard began to blabber through her tears. 'I haven't taken his calls . . . how will I be able to look him in the eye now . . . I love him so much . . . I want to marry him . . . but why will he want me now?'

'Of course he'll want you!' shouted Ayingbi. 'You did nothing wrong.'

'Well, he'd forgive me,' shrugged Custard–Mustard.

'There's nothing to forgive! It was an accident!'

'Yeah, I meant he'd . . . he'd . . . know it was an accident . . . he's mature . . . too mature for me . . . what a guy, really.'

'Then I don't see the problem!' said Ayingbi, sensing an opening. 'You have a loving family and boyfriend! These are the only people who really matter! Who gives a shit what society thinks?'

'You know . . . it's easy to say these things . . . ' said Custard–Mustard. 'But it's not as simple as that . . . and you know it.'

True, mused Ayingbi. She tried a different tack. 'Come on, we can work this out! Have you maybe suggested the pictures are fake?'

'I . . . I . . . have . . . uhuhuhuhu . . . nobody will buy it . . . they'll think I'm only covering up . . . uhuhuhu . . . '

Something about the words 'covering up' hit her hard; Custard–Mustard began to bawl harder than ever. Ayingbi, as she hugged her, could feel a wet, warm stain from her tears blossoming on her own shirt near the collarbone.

'Look!' said Ayingbi, after they had pulled apart. She showed Custard–Mustard what she had looked up on her phone.

Custard–Mustard squinted. 'Ew, ew, ew! What's that?'

'Nude beach in France.'

'Ew, ew, ew. It's all gross old people. I could never imagine such a thing here.'

'My point is, maybe if we were in Europe, this would not be such a big deal.'

'There's a difference between France and India. Over there, everyone in the friend group has seen each other's wee-wee and cooter.'

'Back in the British Raj, it was quite common for women to not wear blouses,' argued Ayingbi.

'That was, what like, thousands of years ago,' said Custard–Mustard gruffly.

'Well, we have the tribals in Nicobar,' said Ayingbi. 'They're naked, too, right? And that's the present day.'

'Yeah, but they're savages. Cut off from the world. Almost animals.'

Ayingbi cringed. She had something in mind now. It was horrible. But just by making the custom of naturism seem not so culturally, temporally and geographically remote, she felt, for a slight moment, that Custard–Mustard might not want to throw herself in front of a train again.

'Heck,' said Ayingbi. 'Even back home in Manipur, it's not unusual for women to wander around topless all the time. And we're all well-educated, I can tell you that.'

Custard–Mustard looked at her. 'Really? I've never heard about that.'

'Sure! You've seen our clothing, right?'

Horrible. Simply horrible. Ayingbi was ashamed of herself.

'Uhmm,' said Custard-Mustard. 'It's . . . uh . . .'

'Revealing!' said Ayingbi. 'Exactly!'

'So, your point is . . .?'

'It's not as big of a deal as you think!'

Custard–Mustard peered hard at Ayingbi. She seemed doubtful. 'Seriously?'

'Totally,' said Ayingbi. 'In fact, you'd probably have gotten a bunch of nudes in return, if this had happened back at home.'

Custard–Mustard snorted. 'No way! That's ridiculous! You're just making stuff up.'

'Not at all. If I had photos, I'd show you.'

'Ugh, no thank you.'

'Come on,' said Ayingbi bracingly. 'It's just the clothes we were born in! Boys and girls, all roam around naked for the first few years of their lives, and nobody bats an eye. And then, suddenly, you need clothes, or it's obscene.'

'I get what you're trying to say . . . but it's not how things are . . . it just isn't . . .'

'I know it sounds like I'm trying to make things better, and I am, but I do think there's a matter of perspective as well. And it's not worth throwing away your life for. That's all I'm trying to do.'

'I want to believe you,' said Custard–Mustard. 'But how? You're convincing me now, but then you'll be gone, and I'll be alone.'

'Look, I'm not saying it's going to be perfect. Just assume the worst. Assume everyone's seen it. Imagine all kinds of shady guys ogling at it.'

'That's probably already happened,' said Custard–Mustard gloomily. 'Screw it. So, everyone's seen my tits!'

She began to laugh manically, then she began to sob again. 'Uhhuu . . . uhhhuu . . . I want to die . . . I don't want to deal with this . . . please, just kill me . . .'

Ayingbi sighed, once again patting Custard–Mustard's head, which was again buried into her neck.

'I'm like those tarts who whore themselves online!' howled Custard–Mustard. 'The ones who bottle their farts and sell photos of their feet . . .'

Ayingbi picked Custard–Mustard off, and gave her a sharp flick on the forehead. 'Enough, dammit! This is not like that, at all! You haven't bottled any farts!'

Custard–Mustard stopped crying. She began to sway on the spot, looking around blankly. 'This feels surreal,' she said, as the wind blew her ponytail back. The pinpricks of light from a faraway signal were reflected as dots in her eyes. The signal changed from red to green, and so did the eye pinpricks. 'I can't believe this is happening. I never thought I'd be here today morning. I'm not a sad person.' She gave Ayingbi a reluctant grin. 'Crazy how stuff just happens, huh?'

'Are we out of the woods here?' said Ayingbi warily. 'You're not going to kill yourself, are you?'

'No,' said Custard–Mustard. 'I don't think I have it in me anymore. I've just . . . spent myself.'

You and me both.

Ayingbi exhaled. 'Thank you.'

'Will you tell me your name?' Custard–Mustard asked Ayingbi.

Ayingbi wondered if it was the right thing to do. It was also important to protect her own identity. Ayingbi gave her a fake name, and then asked Custard–Mustard hers. Custard–Mustard also gave Ayingbi a name.

Was it a two-way lie?

Perhaps.

'You ready to phone home?' whispered Ayingbi.

Custard–Mustard held a button on her mobile phone until a bright rectangle of blue light appeared. 'Seventy-eight missed calls. Well, time to face the music.' She walked away.

Ayingbi, feeling the confession and breakdown would be unpleasant to witness, quietly walked away out of earshot. She could see Custard–Mustard talking on the phone; she could tell she was bawling.

She stared up at the power lines. The crows were gone.

Finally, Custard–Mustard began to wire walk on the tracks towards Ayingbi, arms held out, her manner slightly carefree.

'Would you get off the tracks, please?' said Ayingbi uncomfortably.

'I called them . . . and I called him,' said Custard–Mustard, staring gauntly.

'And?'

Custard–Mustard collapsed sobbing into Ayingbi's arms. 'They said it's going to be all right! Uhhhuuhhuhu! UHHHUHUHUHU!!!'

Ayingbi was fighting tears herself. *I'm human, dammit. I can damn well feel things.* She was most relieved about the boyfriend, regarding whom she had made a rather unfair presumption that he might have bailed. 'That's good,' she mumbled. 'He sounds like a great guy . . .'

'How could I have been so stupid! To have put him in a spot like this?! He's such a nice guy! How would he feel that everyone's seen me . . . like . . . that! How would he want to be with me? To touch me? Twenty years later, when we're married, people will still be looking at it.'

It was just wearying and unpleasant after a point.

'Can we please get back to the platform?' said Ayingbi. There was no point hanging around in a dark, smelly place.

'Can we hang around here a bit longer?' pleaded Custard–Mustard, looking dismally towards the distant railway platform.

Ayingbi could understand. Going back meant facing consequences. 'Of course. We can wait as long as you want.'

'Thank you,' said Custard–Mustard tearfully.

'My name isn't the one I told you earlier, by the way,' said Ayingbi. 'It's Ayingbi. Ayingbi Mayengbam.'

Custard–Mustard shook her head. 'I'd already forgotten. Well, I gave you the correct one, anyway.'

And fifteen minutes later, Custard–Mustard, with gritted teeth, clung onto Ayingbi and gave a swift nod, allowing herself to be steered back into civilization.

In the dim light of the station, Ayingbi could see soft, pretty features—bright eyes and baby fat in the cheeks, and a modest demeanour that suggested a sweet, wholesome, middle-class upbringing.

From a food stall, Ayingbi ordered golgappas.

Custard–Mustard's response to the first offering of golgappas was childlike. She hurriedly wiped her hands and accepted the leaf bowl, so the vendor would not have to wait too long.

She asked for the golgappas sweet. She finished one plate and asked for another. And another. She must've wolfed down fifty of them before wiping her hands on a dirty napkin impaled on a stick. Ayingbi suspected she might not have eaten that day.

'I feel better,' she said, and Ayingbi figured the golgappas had done their duty. She purchased a small water bottle so they could wash their hands.

'You know, I was thinking of this Korean show,' said Custard–Mustard. 'In the sex scenes, they show everything. And the Koreans are said to be conservative.'

'There you go,' said Ayingbi bracingly. Truly, a paradox for the ages.

Custard–Mustard's phone began to ring as she wrung dry her hands.

'They've reached,' said Custard–Mustard, glancing down at it. 'They're outside.'

'Won't they wonder what you were doing on a railway platform?'

'No, I told them I planned to leave the city or something.'

'Okay . . . good thinking.'

'Some friends messaged too,' said Custard–Mustard, opening her messages.

'And?' said Ayingbi tentatively.

'Supportive,' said Custard–Mustard, sounding dazed. 'Anyway, I better go. Thank you . . .' She pulled Ayingbi into a final long, lingering hug. And then she had pushed into the crowd, and vanished from sight. Ayingbi peered at the exit, half-wanting to witness the reunion, but she could not spot Custard–Mustard in the sea of moving heads. Perhaps, it was best to let some things be.

If there was anyone who deserved privacy right now, it was Custard–Mustard.

*

On the ride back to the office, Ayingbi tried to pacify herself with an imagined happyish ending.

Maybe her relatives would all embrace Custard–Mustard in a loving hug. It's all right, the aunties would chuckle. These things happen. No judgement anywhere. Maybe, tomorrow, Custard–Mustard and her co-workers would all have a good laugh about it. Maybe in a day or so, it would all be forgotten.

Too good to be true. Poor wretch.

By the time she was back at the office, Ayingbi knew she might get another call, so it was important to emotionally disentangle herself from Custard–Mustard's life as quickly as possible.

But it was hard.

Ayingbi moodily turned the switch in her office from 'OUTSIDE OFFICE' to 'HERE'.

'Mission successful?' came a call from Hardy's cubicle.

'Yeah, I think so,' said Ayingbi.

'So, you're gonna stay?'

Ayingbi shrugged, before realizing Hardy couldn't actually see her shrugging.

They had now made far too much small talk for Ayingbi to not say hello. She rolled her chair over to Hardy's cubicle. He was a stubbled, good-looking man about her age. When Ayingbi entered, he held out his fist for her to bump; Ayingbi noticed a gold wedding ring as she bumped it.

Hardy's cubicle was identical to Ayingbi's—only his phones were turquoise, yellow and orange.

'So . . . details!' said Hardy eagerly. 'What was it like? Who was the caller?'

'Some girl,' murmured Ayingbi. She debated whether it would be ethical to discuss the matter. It did feel like there was a client-confidentiality issue at hand. But since there were no names, and the issue was so vague, it did not feel wrong. 'Sent nudes to the wrong person—well, people.'

Hardy's face screwed up. 'Aieee. That's rough. What did you say to her?'

'I dunno. Lots of things.'

Ayingbi could barely remember now. The whole episode blurred together as a soggy whole. She could only remember flashes of Custard–Mustard's face, expressionlessly swallowing golgappas faster than the guy could prepare them.

'There's this other thing that happened, though.' Ayingbi was already upset about it. 'Kinda messed up. So, a lot of stuff I said didn't seem to be working, then I went ahead and said something really stupid.'

'What?'

'I told her, that in the northeast . . . you know . . . where I'm from . . . it's common to roam around naked.'

Hardy pulled a face. 'Huh?'

Ayingbi covered her face with her hands, deeply embarrassed. 'I don't know why I did it. It was so stupid.'

'But why?'

'Before that, I'd said that public nudity is not uncommon in Europe. But she wasn't convinced . . . Then I just thought that maybe giving an example of how public nudity wasn't frowned upon within the same country . . . would resonate more . . . so I said it's a thing in Manipur.'

'*Is* it a thing in Manipur?'

'Of course not.' Ayingbi blushed deep red. 'I played up stereotypes about my native place to save someone's life.'

Hardy laughed. 'That's not even a stereotype! I don't even know what that is!'

'Ignorance, then.' Ayingbi lowered her hands. 'Fuck, man.'

'Look,' said Hardy. 'Maybe it wasn't perfect in your head. But it got the job done. There's a lot going on, and we say stuff on the spur of the moment. It's fine. It's part of it. You'll know what to say or not say with time. But you saved her life. And really, with suicide, all bets are off.'

'I guess . . .' said Ayingbi. Then she shook her head. 'No. It's not okay. I deal with racism on a damn near-daily basis, and I know others like me do, too. It's just white noise at this point. I don't want to be responsible for one more negative stereotype about my people.'

'Honestly, I just think she'll remember you as the nice girl who saved her life.'

'I hope you're right. Really, I do. Because if not, this summer is going to be a total bummer.'

'It won't, trust me,' said Hardy. 'There's something you should know, though. Today's sounds like it was an impulsive case. Those are easier to handle. Wait til' you get to the ones with full-blown depression. Hoo boy. You never know if you've done enough, so it's better not to think about it.'

Ayingbi nodded. It had been on the back of her mind ever since she had left Custard–Mustard.

'Anyway, what about a cold one to celebrate?' said Hardy. 'I remember my throat was like sandpaper after my first call.'

That sounded like a good idea.

Ayingbi tried to stand, but found her legs trembling so badly she simply couldn't do it. She collapsed in her chair, staring at her thighs as if they were foreign objects. The physical and emotional drain had quietly slunk up on her as she'd been chatting away.

Hardy nodded knowingly. 'Stay here.'

He left the cubicle, returning with two cold beers. He popped one open, vapour hissed.

'Here.'

Ayingbi accepted the can with trembling hands, but as soon as it touched her lips, she smashed it down in eight seconds flat. Invigorated, she snatched the second, tore it open, and smashed it down too.

'Oh, I'll get another one . . .' mumbled Hardy, as Ayingbi wiped her lips with the back of her hand. He seemed both alarmed and impressed by Ayingbi's drinking ability.

Ayingbi grinned at him. The beer had given her doubts a gentle telling off. Suddenly, Ayingbi was feeling much better. Happier. She felt strong, energized and empowered, living at a level she hadn't felt in years.

And then she burst out laughing, with happiness and relief.

'I'm just happy she didn't jump in front of a train, that's all. And that she's back with her family. Of course I'll stay. I'll save every last one of them—you just wait and see!'

FIVE

THE SPLASH TROLL

There were no other calls that night. Ayingbi clocked out at six, getting home and going to bed just as the sun was rising.

When she woke, bright afternoon sunlight had set the curtains aglow, and life was babbling on the street below. There was drool on her cheek and crust on her lashes. She peeled one eye open and checked her phone. A quarter to two.

Ayingbi sat upright in bed, blinking, checking for headaches, muscle spasms or any signs of her body's venturing towards an irregular sleep schedule.

Her throat felt slightly sore—probably from last night's golgappas.

She checked for news of any suicides near Rahilgiri station—she'd been worried that the moment she'd left, Custard–Mustard might've charged back and swan-dived in front of the next train.

Luckily, there was nothing.

She also had a text message.

HEY.
COMPOUND PERIL.
EAT WELL, REST WELL.

—CHATTY

This must be that Chaitanya fellow—the one on the day shift. Ayingbi wondered what Compound Peril meant.

'Hey,' said Hardy, when she clocked in to work that evening. 'So, Chatty gave you a heads-up about Compound Peril, then?'

'Yeah, he said to eat well and rest well.'

Hardy nodded. 'Might be a busy night. Chatty got five calls in the day shift—pretty rare.' He began to count on his fingers. 'Stock market took a hit because of shivery Gulf oil prices today morning. Job layoffs in IT. Pollution at a seasonal high. Small uptick in onion rates, medical college entrance results in a few hours. All of them annoying on their own, but put them together—'

'Compound Peril?'

'Yeah. It means we can expect plenty of walk-ins. In general, early summer is the riskiest time of the year.'

'Really,' said Ayingbi, surprised. 'I would have thought it would be winter or something.'

Hardy opened his mouth to reply, when one of his phones—the orange one—began to ring.

'Later,' said Hardy hastily, and he reached for his notepad. Ayingbi supposed the orange phone was his Barney.

She returned to her own cubicle. For only her second time coming in, it felt oddly familiar.

Not long after, Hardy left the office for a follow-up, giving her a quick 'see ya' on his way out. Ayingbi wished him luck and then she sat there, already envisioning another tense encounter like last night.

She'd taken Chatty's advice and prepared a healthy multigrain sandwich. She did not want to go around eating junk again.

Ayingbi remained twitchy and on tenterhooks for the next several hours. Five call-free hours of her shift later, she began to feel hungry, so she unwrapped the sandwich and took a huge first bite.

Exactly then, almost as if it was being cheeky, Barney began to ring.

Ayingbi, choking on the sandwich, began to vigorously thump herself on the chest.

'Huglo,' she growled, yeti-like, as a golf ball of mushed-up sandwich painfully snailed down her food pipe.

'Hey,' said the voice. Adult male. 'Uh . . . you good?' he added, as Ayingbi continued to cough and sputter over the phone.

'Yes, yes, thanks,' muttered Ayingbi. She cleared her throat with a sip of water. Time to take back the reins. 'I'm fine, sir,' she said loudly. 'How are you?'

'Oh, quite lousy, actually. I'm in stocks. Just took a big, fat loss.'

'Ah, right. Would you like to talk about it?'

'You know, when the stock market falls, we say, 'this too will pass?' Well, it hasn't passed at all! It's sat down on a sofa and put its big, stinky feet up on a pouffe.'

'Look, sir,' said Ayingbi gently. 'How do you want me to help you?'

'I want to be helped, miss,' said Instox. 'But a part of me doesn't want to be helped. It doesn't even want to feel anything, anymore. I can only think of one thing which will make me not feel anything, ever again.'

There it was. It had been lurking around the corner.

'Where are you, sir?' said Ayingbi sharply.

Fortunately, unlike Mrs Elelem and Custard–Mustard, Instox did not attempt to withhold his location. 'The barrage in the deer forest, if you know where it is.'

'Yes, of course I do!'

'Well, my phone is about to die,' said Instox. 'If you have something to say, you might as well say it now.'

Ayingbi was annoyed by the sudden ultimatum. If Instox had planned to kill himself, he should've charged his phone first! Ayingbi was also not wild about attending to a call by a man in a desolate location at night.

'I don't think it would be right to rush things. Would you be alright if I counselled you in person, sir?' said Ayingbi. If Instox was receptive, maybe something could be worked out. They could arrange for a more public place to meet. 'Sir? Sir?'

There was a pause, and then, the beep of an ended call.

Oh, for fuck's sake, thought Ayingbi, angrily slamming Barney's receiver down.

*

It was a long ride to the deer forest in the forested city outskirts. The old barrage was a popular picnic spot by day, and secluded by night. A suicide-cum-picnic point, if you will. In the rainy season, the spillways would be barely holding back a churning white deluge. If you fell in then, you would likely drown. In the lean season, even with the sluice gates fully open, the water flow was so weak, jumpers would snap their knees on the riverbed itself. Right now, the water flow was probably somewhere in the middle.

Still enough to drown a non-swimmer.

Yes, yes, this was very dangerous. Meeting up with a man in the middle of nowhere in the dead of night. Ayingbi would have to be extra careful. She needed to work with an escape plan in mind, executable on a dime.

After parking her Scooty at the edge of the trees, Ayingbi followed the sound of falling water down a dirt path, eventually arriving at a compound, protected by chicken wire. A long walkway ran along the top of the barrage, with steps leading down to a one-room powerhouse on the opposite end.

Squinting, Ayingbi could spot someone shuffling at the edge of the water on the downstream side. But it did not appear to be her quarry. Probably some homeless fellow.

Partially concealed in the tall grass behind him was a shanty with light flickering inside, and a tiny wooden raft moored to the riverbank.

'Hey!' Ayingbi called out. 'See anyone come up here?'

There was no reply, so Ayingbi proceeded through the chicken fence, the gate lock of which had been broken. She clambered up a flight of stone steps and a short ladder to get to the grated walkway.

A woman came into sight, standing tall on the edge, twenty feet away. She looked in her mid-to-late thirties, rather attractive, and wearing makeup—her mascara and lipstick were both smudged. She was wearing a red satin cocktail dress that trapped crescents of moonlight in every fold.

Even if this was not the person who called, the signs were all there.

Cocktail-Dress noticed Ayingbi, and seemingly unfazed, continued puffing on a cigarette.

'Hey,' said Ayingbi.

'Hey yourself,' said Cocktail-Dress. Her voice was flat and raspy.

'Um, were you the one who called?'

Cocktail-Dress seemed confused. She flicked the cigarette over the edge, following the glow from its tip all the way down into the water. 'Called?'

'Us. The suicide hotline.'

Cocktail-Dress burst out laughing. High and tinkling. She held up a finger to nuzzle the underside of her nose; her false fingernails were very long and bright red. Ayingbi could see several tentative cuts along her left forearm, already beginning to scab.

'No,' said Cocktail-Dress. 'You see, I do not require help from any suicide hotline. As it so happens, I have every intention of killing myself. I look forward to it immensely. My will to live ricochets around the world and then withers—as if it can't suit an oxygen-rich environment. Now, if you'll excuse me.'

She neatly removed her shoes—the glittering, glassy, Cinderella-type, placed them side-by-side, as if outside a temple, and prepared to climb the walkway's parapet.

'No,' said Ayingbi, rushing forth and grabbing Cocktail-Dress's wrist. Cocktail-Dress gave a spasm of pain and wrenched her hand free.

Ayingbi stared at her own hand and was startled to find blood.

The cuts on Cocktail-Dress's other arm were fresher.

Ayingbi swore. 'You're really going to do it, aren't you?'

'Because obviously, until now, I've been saying I won't.'

'Let's talk about it,' said Ayingbi. 'What is it? Is it guy trouble?'

'None of your business.'

'I'll call the police,' said Ayingbi, pulling out her phone.

'Go right ahead,' said Cocktail-Dress, gazing towards the drop. 'But after you press dial, you better hope for a response time of about two and half seconds.'

Ayingbi put the phone away. 'Fine. I won't. But let's talk, please.'

'Madam,' sighed Cocktail-Dress. 'Let me die, for pity's sake. I did not call so much as a pizzeria. Are you sure you're at the right place?'

'Yes! I'm sure!' said Ayingbi. 'But I know it wasn't you . . . it was a man's voice . . . unless . . .'

Cocktail-Dress raised her eyebrows. 'Unless what?'

'Unless he's still out here.' Ayingbi looked left and right. 'This is really weird, but I have a request.'

'Polite decline.'

'I'm not going to ask you to not do . . . whatever!' cried Ayingbi, waving a hand at the drop. 'I got a call from someone, saying that they were here and that they were going to kill themselves.'

'It wasn't me.'

'I know. It was a man.'

'Well, there you go.'

'So, if it wasn't you . . . that means there's someone else out here . . .'

'Looks like they've already done it, then,' said Cocktail-Dress, peering down the length of the barrage. 'I don't see anyone else out here.'

'I can't believe that,' said Ayingbi. 'I need to find them.' She started to march off, but then she did a double take. She couldn't leave Cocktail-Dress alone, either.

'Why don't you come with me?' suggested Ayingbi.

'Who, me?'

'Yes. Let's find this guy, and see if we can convince him not to jump.'

Cocktail-Dress gestured at herself. 'Do I look like I'm in any position to tender that advice?'

'Listen,' said Ayingbi. 'If you help me find him, I won't bother you anymore. I'll even charter a plane for you to jump off.'

Cocktail-Dress peered at her. 'You really think there's someone else here? You're not just saying that as a stalling tactic?'

Ayingbi nodded vigorously.

Cocktail-Dress sighed. 'Alright. I'll help you. But you keep your word on that.' She gingerly stepped off the parapet and put her shoes back on. 'Fuck, that took a lot of courage. I had no plans of stepping back.' She looked around. 'So, which way, chief?'

'That way,' said Ayingbi, pointing at the direction opposite from the ladder. 'Thanks for doing this, by the way,' she added breathlessly, as they strode across the walkway together, Cocktail-Dress's heels clattering noisily on the grates.

'Think nothing of it,' said Cocktail-Dress. 'I'd rather save a stranger than myself.'

'Really?'

Cocktail-Dress smirked sideways at her. 'You've clearly never known what it's like.'

Ayingbi supposed a suicidal person was low on a lot of things, but perhaps never empathy. She released her grip on Cocktail-Dress's arm. They continued walking, Ayingbi peering nervously into the darkness. And then . . . sure enough . . .

'Over there,' whispered Cocktail-Dress in a hushed whisper, seizing Ayingbi's arm. Together, they stared, like tourists on safari, having spotted a rare and exotic animal.

A man was idling on the parapet at the far end of the walkway. He was wearing a dark business suit; his necktie was fluttering in the breeze.

'That's him!' whispered Cocktail-Dress. 'It's gotta be him, right?'

'Yes, I think so,' said Ayingbi.

'Well, there's your man. Go to him.'

'No, wait . . .' said Ayingbi slowly. 'There's someone else there, too!'

'Where?'

'Down there. Look at the staircase.'

Sure enough, there appeared to be a second figure at the bottom of the stairs leading down from the powerhouse.

'What, is everyone trying to kill themselves tonight?' grumbled Cocktail-Dress.

'Compound Peril,' muttered Ayingbi.

'What?'

'Nothing,' said Ayingbi.

'So, what's the plan, missy?'

'I don't know,' said Ayingbi quickly. But just as quickly, the most marvellous little idea came to her. 'I've got it.'

She peered at Cocktail-Dress, a broad smile spreading across her face. Cocktail-Dress was, for lack of a better word, sexy.

Very sexy. And if she knew anything about men—

'He'll listen to you,' said Ayingbi. 'You're hot.'

'What?'

'You pretend to be me!' said Ayingbi excitedly. 'Say that you were the suicide hotline operator who got a call from him!'

'Huh?'

'Look at you!' cried Ayingbi. 'Instox—that guy—is going to be way more receptive to anything you say!'

'You're crazy,' said Cocktail-Dress.

'No, no, this is a good plan! Look at it from a guy's perspective. You're depressed, you're up on a bridge and right before you do it, a buxom woman comes and chats you up. It's the stuff guys' fantasies are made of!'

Cocktail-Dress looked down at herself. 'Buxom, huh?'

Ayingbi shrugged. 'Well, you know.'

'And what will you do in the meantime?'

'I'll check out that other person, the one on the stairs. But I think yours is the guy. The one down there might just be a . . . worker, or something.'

Cocktail-Dress thought about it. 'Fuck. This is nuts. Alright, I'm in.'

Ayingbi grinned. 'Yes! Thank you!'

'Don't thank me yet.'

'Hang on, just a coupla things . . .' Ayingbi fluffed up Cocktail-Dress's hair.

'I got this,' interrupted Cocktail-Dress. She reapplied her lipstick, applied a dab of roll-on perfume to her neck, sniffed both armpits and adjusted her dress. As if, having recommitted herself to the land of the living for a few minutes longer, she had briefly reassumed its social etiquette as well.

'Shit,' she muttered, as her heels got caught in the walkway grating, for the sixth time. She kicked them off and went barefoot. 'So, what do you think?'

Ayingbi smiled and made an okay sign. 'Very girl on the edge.'

'So, if I'm pretending to be you, I'd have to know some stuff about him, right?' said Cocktail-Dress.

'Oh, yeah . . . I have notes . . .' Ayingbi hurriedly fetched them from her handbag. 'So, this is the stuff he told me over the phone . . . He works in the stock market, he's lost a lot of money—'

'He's killing himself because of money?' snorted Cocktail-Dress. 'Fuck that! I'll throw him over myself! What else?'

'He's sad,' offered Ayingbi.

'Wow, aren't you a perceptive one.'

Ayingbi flipped pages. 'That's basically it,' she finished lamely. 'Look, we didn't talk much. He just told me he was suicidal, what he did and where he was.'

'Does he know your name?'

'He knows nothing about me apart from my voice, and I doubt he'll be in much of a state to differentiate between two women's voices.'

'Cool,' said Cocktail-Dress. She gave a little jog on the spot. 'So . . . what do I say to him?'

Ayingbi tried to look like she was more experienced than she actually was. 'Just try to get him to find a reason to live. Mainly, work the womanly charm.'

'Reason to live, hah,' said Cocktail-Dress. 'Good one. Anyway, alright, I'll give it a shot.' She continued jogging on the spot.

'You okay?'

'I am, I am, just psyching myself up. I must say, I haven't felt this excited for anything in months.'

'Good,' said Ayingbi. 'Well, all the best to you. Now go to him.'

'Alright. Just one last thing.'

'What's that?'

Cocktail-Dress frowned at her. 'Don't ever put yourself down like that. You're a queen, got it?'

Ayingbi rolled her eyes. 'Yeah . . . yeah . . . I was just trying to make a case why you'd be better . . . anyway, go on, we're losing time.'

Cocktail-Dress pouted at herself in a compact mirror, fluffed up her hair again, as if unhappy with how Ayingbi had done it, batted her eyelashes, then began walking towards the man dawdling on the ledge.

Ayingbi, meanwhile, set her eyes on the fellow at the bottom of the stairs. She had no doubt that was not Instox. She kept low as she went round the powerhouse, finding the stairs. It was cool and misty here, a relief from the summer heat.

Her footsteps clip-clopping down the stairs were masked by the sound of falling water, and the dark figure sitting at the bottom of the stairs did not look up until the very last moment.

The smell of marijuana hit Ayingbi's nostrils. She wrinkled her nose. No, wait. Not marijuana. There was a difference. She, as a drug counsellor, knew.

Hashish.

It was a teenage boy, sitting with a bunch of paper crumples. A limp, leaky joint was dangling out a corner of his mouth. It looked like he wasn't a very good roller, and had only just managed to get one to light.

Ayingbi was rather put off. It didn't look like he was here to kill himself. More likely, just do drugs in peace.

'Hey,' said Ayingbi. 'What are you doing here?'

'Uhm, recuperating,' grinned the kid. 'I have a medical prescription for arthritis.' He was wearing a brown shirt, with some rock band name on it. Ayingbi had just the name for him.

'Since we're on the topic of not minding our own business, what are *you* doing here?' said Hash-Brown.

'I'm here for work,' said Ayingbi. She was sure this was not Instox, but even so, Hash-Brown's voice had already cracked, and she had to make sure. 'So . . . by any chance, did you call a crisis hotline a couple of hours ago?'

Hash-Brown frowned. 'Nope.'

'Yeah, I didn't think so,' said Ayingbi, looking back up the stairs towards the walkway. So that must mean Instox was the man upstairs, after all.

'Why?' said Hash-Brown. 'Did someone call a crisis hotline?'

'They did, yeah,' said Ayingbi, still looking up the stairs. She wanted to go up and monitor the situation. 'And they said that they were here.'

Hash-Brown exhaled a thin, smelly puff. 'To kill themselves?'

'No, to fish. Of course to kill themselves!'

'Jee-zus. And you're here, what, to stop them?'

'Take a guess.'

'What're you, his mother?' said Hash-Brown. 'Let people make their own choices.'

'Like . . . those choices?' Ayingbi jabbed a finger at the little crumpled-up joints. The guidance counsellor in her simply could not resist. 'Anyway, I gotta go help them. They're up there.'

'No, no!' cried Hash-Brown dramatically. 'It's me! I'm the one! Goodbye, cruel world, and all that!'

'Listen, man, I don't have time for this,' said Ayingbi, and she began to trot up the stairs.

'Nah, I really want to kill myself!' said Hash-Brown, standing on the first bar of the railing. 'Woo! Look at me! Woo!'

Anxiety spasmed through Ayingbi, but she suppressed the urge to reach out and grab him, knowing he'd get a kick out of it. 'Keep it up, you little shit,' she hissed. 'Watch what happens.'

Hash-Brown slowly lowered himself, looking very pleased with himself. 'So, there's a suicidal person up there, huh? I wanna see!'

And he began to accompany Ayingbi up. 'Suicidal people are disgusting. They have no will to live. We need to Auschwitz these assholes.'

Ayingbi knew this sentiment was not unheard of, yet she still found it offensive. 'You're not going to egg him on or anything, are you?' she said quietly.

'Nah. But it'll be fun if he jumps.'

Ayingbi wanted to slap him.

'It's a pity it's so stigmatized,' said Hash-Brown. 'If we were in medieval Japan, they would've cut their stomachs open. Or yeeted themselves over a cliff, like the Vikings.'

Irritating idiot.

'Hey look!' said Hash-Brown, as they walked around the powerhouse. 'That must be him!'

Ayingbi was relieved to find Instox still conversing with Cocktail-Dress. She began a purposeful, Let-A-Professional-Take-Over march towards them, but stopped when she noticed that Instox seemed receptive towards Cocktail-Dress, who, at that moment, let out a shrill laugh.

Ayingbi smiled. Things were going well.

'Who's the bimbo?' piped up Hash-Brown.

'Let's hang back,' said Ayingbi instead, and she tugged Hash-Brown back towards the powerhouse.

'So, what does this guy do?' said Hash-Brown. 'What's his deal?'

'Works the stock market. Like a broker or something.' Ayingbi wasn't exactly sure how shares worked.

'Pathetic. I have zero respect for these cowards. You need to develop a backbone to deal with life's problems,' said Hash-Brown forcefully.

'Kid, give it a rest, will you?' said Ayingbi wearily. 'You have no idea what it's like to be going through shit. Well, I guess you're still too young to understand.'

'Is that other woman with you?'

'Sort of.'

'Oh my god! He jumped!' cried Hash-Brown, pointing wildly behind Ayingbi.

Ayingbi spun around; both Instox and Cocktail-Dress were still there. Hash-Brown was laughing to himself.

'Haha! Oh man, that was great!' Seeing the look Ayingbi was giving him, he desisted. 'Okay, okay. Sorry, won't do that again.'

Ayingbi stepped up on the parapet and peeped down, wondering, if worst came to worst and someone jumped, it would mean an instant death.

'Don't kill yourself, dear lady!' came a cry from behind them.

Ayingbi and Hash-Brown turned. To Ayingbi's delight, Instox and a triumphant-looking Cocktail-Dress were rushing towards them down the walkway.

'You have so much to live for!' cried Instox. Up close, he was revealed to be a messy-haired, Vitamin-D deficient individual in his mid-thirties. His tie was dangling like a scarf around his neck.

'Oh . . . I wasn't going to . . .' began Ayingbi, looking at Cocktail-Dress, who gave her a surreptitious thumbs-up. 'I mean, I was going to, but . . . er . . . this kid talked me out of it. Convinced me that no matter how bad things seem, there's always a tiny chance they'll get better. Seems like good logic to me! Enough to make me, uh, not kill myself and stuff!'

Everyone looked at Hash-Brown.

'Huh?' said Hash-Brown.

'Didn't you?' said Ayingbi, smiling with her teeth slightly bared, a gleam in her eye.

'Oh . . . yeah . . . totally,' said Hash-Brown quickly.

'Well, that's great . . .' said Instox. 'So, you're all fine here, then?'

'Oh, yes,' said Ayingbi. 'Absolutely.'

Instox frowned. 'Your voice sounds familiar.'

Ayingbi immediately gave a cough. Then she grunted. 'Oh, um, it must be the adrenaline.'

'I see. Well, good luck,' said Instox. 'Hang in there, I s'ppose.' He held out a hand for Ayingbi and Hash-Brown to shake, as if they had gotten acquainted over a work lunch. Behind him, Cocktail-Dress was standing with a half-smile on her face.

It was a very strange moment.

Instox then looked at Cocktail-Dress. 'Shall we?'

Cocktail-Dress nodded at him. 'You go down to the car. I'll be there in just a minute.'

Instox nodded and walked off, a bit of a grin on his face. Ayingbi anxiously followed his movements, but it did not appear like he was in the mood to jump off anything right now. Jump on, maybe.

'What did you say to him?' said Ayingbi.

'Not much,' said Cocktail-Dress, absently fidgeting with her dress, which appeared to have slipped two inches lower than before. 'He's a really nice guy. We're just going to grab some dinner.'

'Er . . . he won't be drowning himself, will he?'

'No, he's more into being choked, apparently,' said Cocktail-Dress. Then she blinked. 'Er . . . I mean, no, he's sorted. For now.'

'And you?' said Ayingbi warily. 'You won't be killing yourself now, will you?'

Cocktail-Dress considered it. 'Nah. Not today. I'm not feeling it.'

'Saving lives feels good, doesn't it?' said Ayingbi heartily. 'Now just imagine how bad someone would feel if you—'

'Zip it, sister,' interrupted Cocktail-Dress, raising a long, manicured finger at her. 'Don't overplay your hand.'

Knowing to let a win be a win, Ayingbi shut her mouth, nodded tightly, and did not argue further.

'Toodles,' said Cocktail-Dress, brushing past Ayingbi. 'Not gonna do it! Relax!' she added, raising a lazy arm over her head as she walked away.

Meanwhile, Hash-Brown was watching with his mouth hanging open.

'That was . . . incredible,' he said to Ayingbi. 'You played that beautifully.'

Ayingbi, however, was pensive. 'I don't get it.'

'What?'

'I thought that guy had lost money in stocks. But he was wearing an Audemars Piguet watch. That's fuck-you money. Rich people never put their eggs in one basket.'

'What's your point?' said Hash-Brown.

'Maybe he just wanted to vent without telling other people the real reason. The stock market fall was just a cover, easily accepted as legitimate grounds for being suicidal.'

'What d'you think the real reason was?'

'Dunno,' said Ayingbi thoughtfully. 'Maybe there wasn't any.'

Hash-Brown seemed puzzled. 'Then why'd he try to kill himself?'

Ayingbi shrugged. 'Sometimes, kid, there isn't a reason. People just have had enough. It's not something you can pin down to this or that.'

'Hmm.'

'And it's not all lived in loneliness, either. Sometimes, you can spend all the time in the world with someone and not realize they were depressed. People can be incredibly skilled at hiding it.'

'I think the bimbo noticed the watch, too,' said Hash-Brown.

Ayingbi was sure she had.

'You think he's going to lay pipe?' said Hash-Brown suddenly.

'Pardon?'

'You think they're going to have sex?'

Ayingbi privately thought it certain, but she did not want to discuss sexuality of all things with a minor. 'Er, I don't know.'

Hash-Brown's eyes were glazed over. 'You were worried about him drowning. I can tell you he's drowning himself in those jugs right now.'

The teacher in Ayingbi was intolerant of impudence in older children. 'Enough!' she cried. 'Aren't you glad they didn't jump? How awful would that have been? Now, if we're all done here, let's move.'

They set off together down the walkway.

'And not that it's any of my business,' mumbled Ayingbi, 'but you probably shouldn't smoke.'

Hash-Brown grunted.

'Up, I mean.'

Another grunt.

'So, that's it, then,' said Ayingbi. 'You're going to disregard this, like every other bit of advice you've ever been given?'

'Like you said,' said Hash-Brown, through gritted teeth, 'it's none of your business.'

'Well, don't say I didn't warn you,' said Ayingbi huffily.

After another two minutes of walking, Hash-Brown suddenly said, 'd'you think he was good at studies?'

'Who?'

'That man in the suit? He was rich, right? So he must've been good at studies to get rich.'

'I guess? Unless he inherited it.'

'Yeah, but regardless—he was rich, right? But he was still depressed.'

'Rich people get depressed like everyone else, kid,' said Ayingbi. 'There's not much correlation.'

'So, it's not a guarantee, right? That if you're good at school, you'll be happy?'

'No, man. Far from it.'

'Are you happy?'

Ayingbi could not recall the last time she'd been asked that. 'Sort of. Doing my best, like everybody else.'

'Were you good at school?'

'I was, yeah.'

Hash-Brown looked Ayingbi up and down. 'So . . . being good at school is not a guarantee of success, either.'

'Very funny.'

But it did not look like Hash-Brown was joking.

'Well, so long, Hash-Brown,' said Ayingbi, once they reached the other end of the barrage again. 'This is where we part. It's been an interesting night.'

Hash-Brown shook hands, his head somewhat lowered. 'Well, goodbye . . .' he said. 'And . . . thanks.'

'For what?' said Ayingbi.

Hash-Brown opened his mouth. Then he closed it. Then, still hanging his head, he stuffed his hands deep in his pockets and walked away.

Cheered with how the night had gone, Ayingbi left the dam and set off clopping down the muddy path towards where her Scooty was parked. The route brought her in proximity to the hobo from earlier. This time, he did speak.

'They *did* look rich, hahaha,' he wheezed. 'You denied me a full belly's meal.'

'What?' said Ayingbi.

'Night-time. Sad time. I hear the splash. I wait a few minutes. I go in, I pull them out. I take out their things. I push them back in.'

Ayingbi looked back at the barrage. 'What? Like when people kill themselves?'

'Exactly!'

'You steal their stuff? Like a grave robber?'

The guy lived beneath a bridge. He waited for splashes to steal from suicide victims. Ayingbi knew the perfect name for him, too.

'Come, girl, I show you.' The Splash Troll held up one edge of the tattered maroon cloth that was his shanty's door. 'Don't be scared. Come closer.'

Ayingbi took a couple of steps down the riverbed. Her heels sank slightly in the soft sand, and the dark water, recently denied tribute, gulped accusingly at her.

The Splash Troll pulled out a dustbin, tipping it towards her so she could see the treasures inside—watches, wallets, mobiles and jewellery. 'I never take ID. Otherwise, cannot tell who was who. Body recovery one kilometre away. All who jump off here, end up there.' He paused. 'Not all. Some fish take. Some dissolve into nothing. One time, body stuck right there—snagged in branch.' He gestured towards the opposite riverbank. 'Should've jumped in the middle. When crane pull out body, all inside things come out. Stomach hole thiiiiis big.' He widened gunky yellow eyes, and held his gnarled hands two feet apart. 'Where eyeball, now fish tail. Wiggle, wiggle, wiggle.'

Ayingbi shivered. She'd heard enough.

'Tonight, girl, I wait for three splashes,' said the Splash Troll, when Ayingbi began to step away. 'But I get none.'

'Three splashes?'

'Splash, splash, splash!'

'No, two splashes. The woman in the red dress, and the man in the business suit.'

The Splash Troll peered at Ayingbi. 'No, girly. Three splashes. You weren't paying attention.'

Ayingbi stared at him for a moment. Then, she slowly climbed back up to the walkway, all the way to the powerhouse stairs, to where she had met Hash-Brown. She found nothing at first, scanning each step from left to right. She tried following the smell of hash, but it had gone. There was something else—kicked to the bottom of the stairs. Ayingbi chased after it. Balled-up paper. Ayingbi unwrapped it to reveal a bunch of crumpled exam answer sheets. Different subjects.

The name had been torn off, as had the grade, but from the rampant red crossings and strike-outs on every page, the performance was apparent. A couple of joint roaches were lodged like seeds between the pages.

Ayingbi looked up as realization dawned.

Hash-Brown too?

Fuck.

She scratched her head, recontextualizing her entire conversation with the boy. Ugh, why hadn't she picked up on it? A teenage boy had no business being here by himself . . . but he had perked up when the idea of Instox being rich and still depressed had come up . . .

She could still hear the Splash Troll's laughter, even after she had left the barrage and walked back into the forest.

'Splish, splash. Splish, splash. Beautiful nights like these belong to the splish-splashes. Three splashes I was denied. But no matter, others will come.'

Ayingbi shivered as she switched her Scooty on. The Splash Troll's cackling saw her off.

'You cannot stop the splashes, girl. You cannot stop the splashes.'

SIX

KITTY DITTY IN THE CITY

On the ride back to office, Ayingbi's post-audit of her own performance grew more critical.

There was nothing to suggest Cocktail-Dress and Instox were in the clear. A relationship of two unstable people—based on a passionate encounter when they were both at their most vulnerable—was a ticking time bomb. Worst of all, Ayingbi had totally missed the signs of Hash-Brown being suicidal. The kid had obviously researched the topic—he seemed familiar with the cultural discourse surrounding it.

She wondered whether Hardy would've made a similar mistake, and it made her feel insecure.

The idea of suicidal children was deeply distressing, even though teens often were. If suicide had to be a thing, it might as well be the preserve of those who had lived and seen enough of life's vagaries.

Ayingbi was suddenly filled with words of comfort, things she wished she'd said, courses of action she could now never take. She found herself revising the entire conversation in her head, looking for more hints and giveaways, more fingers to point at her own failures.

Miserable, she made a call on Phoenix first thing when she got back.

'Hello, Ayingbi,' said Rastogi, taking the call. 'You were gone for a while. All well?'

'Grhhgrm.'

Rastogi seemed to understand. 'Hang on. I'm coming down.'

Moments later, he was outside her cubicle, carrying a two-litre bottle of club soda. Ayingbi wildly thought he was going to pour her a drink, but then he uncapped the bottle, pouring it into a nearby daffodil pot, filling it up to the brim.

'Thought I'd take a leaf from my own book,' said Rastogi. 'Some things, you just can't handle over the phone. Now, tell me.'

'Sometimes, I just feel, aren't we only paying lip service to the cause by talking to callers in person? It's like we're taking one extra step, but not two.'

'We can never know for sure, Ayingbi. A perfectly happy person today could encounter a storm of unhappy circumstances that could see them up on a ledge within a month.'

'So, you're saying that it's okay if the person kills themselves, even if we tried to talk them out of it?'

'Um, why don't you tell me what happened just now? Tell me everything.'

Ayingbi did. Rastogi's eyes grew wider and wider, and by the time she was done, he looked part bushbaby. 'So, you went to save one person, but wound up saving three? Ayingbi, that's incredible! You should be proud! What are you upset for?'

'I'm not sure if my solution was sustainable.' Ayingbi sighed. 'I wish I could just . . . keep them safe forever. Like . . . deliver an anti-suicide vaccine with my words.'

'I know the feeling, Ayingbi,' said Rastogi. 'Believe me, I do. And yes, by meeting and interacting with people in person, we do get attached. It can't be helped. But here's the thing, if we dwell on what people might or might not do, in post-op, we may not be able to give our all to the callers whose calls are just around the corner. We need to be cheerful for them, too.'

Ayingbi nodded glumly.

'But if it means anything to you at all,' continued Rastogi, 'the way you told me the story, I think they'll probably be fine, all three of them.'

'You think?'

'Definitely. You engaged the kid intellectually, and for the other two, you found, er, let's say . . . a mutually agreeable solution.'

'But what if we're both wrong?'

Rastogi pottered over to another daffodil plant and watered it too; the glub-glub-glub of the draining soda filled the room. 'In this business, we need to celebrate the little victories, Ayingbi.' He looked at her significantly.

'Since there's no way of knowing about the big ones, they're all we've got.'

*

Ayingbi decided to take Rastogi's words to heart. Her new-found confidence, as well as her adjustment to nocturnal living, both reflected in her work, and a whole two weeks passed without her having to leave the office. She took a total of twenty-two calls during this time, all resolved successfully, the longest in under fifty-five minutes.

By the end of the first week of June, Ayingbi was raring for another challenge.

Things were getting too quiet in the office.

Maybe today, she thought, putting on her helmet as she strode down the stairs of her apartment building, feeling a bit like a gladiator suiting up in the Colosseum.

As Ayingbi was emerging from the tight lane in front of her flat, a black cat skittered across the road, cutting her path. She brought the Scooty to a halt, staring at the chow-mein stall dustbin the kitty had vanished behind.

She debated crossing, feeling unpleasantly superstitious. But it wasn't superstition. Her brush with she-did-not-know-what had not been forgotten. Ayingbi decided she wasn't going to take an unnecessary risk just to prove a point.

She waited patiently for a few moments for an autorickshaw to cross, and then felt guilty for letting the poor man take the fall.

Either you choose to be rational. But if you want to be superstitious, you commit to the superstition without being a coward about it.

Next time a black cat crosses my path, Ayingbi thought, I'm going to drive straight through. She thought that might be months away, or probably years.

But no, it was mere minutes.

This time at a zebra crossing, where Ayingbi had hit a red light. This black cat was fatter than the first, and it even looked back at Ayingbi after crossing. One of the black cat's eyes was yellow, the other green.

The traffic light too turned yellow and then green.

As a car began to honk behind Ayingbi, she rode on, being the first to cut the cat's path. Ayingbi was relieved. Hopefully that evened things out.

Cats did seem to be everywhere today. She could see them nosing about in bins or tripping across fences. Tabbies and street cats of every colour, even a glossy Persian with a collar around its neck, that looked like it had never left its house before.

They all seemed to be going in the same direction as her.

More of them appeared the further Ayingbi rode. Far too many—she was soon crossing entire herds of them, travelling like antelope. Cats weren't pack animals, were they? There were so many of them, it had caused a small traffic jam close to the office.

Ayingbi could hear the noise before she could see the cause—from far away, it sounded like a broken factory siren.

It was the cats, all right.

Not one or two.

Not ten or twenty.

They were there, swarming in thousands. It was as though Noah had decided to fill his ark entirely with cats, and release the lot on top of the old complex with Rastogi's office. Hundreds more were scrambling up the piping, leaping from ledge to ledge like video-game characters, hissing for space on the cornices or nuzzling each other on the window hoods. All of them had their tails raised and twitching. They seemed excited. With all the cats peering down over the edge, it looked as if the roof itself was yawing to a side.

Up close, the sound was infernal. The thousands of mews blended together into an orchestra of out-of-tune violas trying to warm up. On top of it all were screeches and honks from the traffic jam.

Still looking at the roof, a mystified Ayingbi dismounted and began to weave through the onlookers towards the building.

It was as if a great citywide call had been given, and every cat had answered.

The office building had begun to evacuate as shop owners came hurrying out, wincing as this Siamese cat brushed between their legs or that Sphinx cat used their shoulders as a pad to hop onto a transom.

Ayingbi began to wade through the little cat-Mecca, feeling her nose twitch. The air was thick with cat hair. But the cats themselves did not scratch or hiss, nor meow or rub themselves against her. They seemed oblivious to the publicness of the place, to their own staggering numbers, oblivious to all save getting to the roof as quickly as possible. Ayingbi wondered if Mrs Elelem's cat was here too.

'We can't work up there,' said someone, who, by the look of his shirt, worked in the mobile store below Rastogi's office. 'It's too damn noisy.'

Ayingbi realized it might be difficult for call operators too.

Fortunately, that was never to be an issue, for right then, as if awaiting her arrival, the cats already on the roof began to jump off. The first lot jumped directly down, bouncing off the air-conditioners, making none of that biologically wired effort to fan their bodies, attain terminal velocity or land on all fours. They all seemed to be striving for maximum injury, and without fail, they all twisted their bodies forward at the last moment, ensuring they landed on their necks.

Ayingbi's mouth fell open, but it was only several seconds later, when bloodstains began to blossom across the pavement, that her throat finally managed to push forth a croaked 'What . . .'

All the while, the cats continued to blithely topple to their doom: willingly, voluntarily and, within seconds, the pavement began to resemble a wet market. The stream of falling cats was steady—it was as if they had all queued up and were waiting patiently for their turn.

'Cats!' someone yelled. 'It's raining cats and, er, cats!'

Now the cats were vaulting far, spreading their limbs like flying squirrels, as if they didn't want cushioning from the other heaps of lifeless fur.

MEOWWWWW!!

MRAWWWWW!!

MAOWWAWW!!

The little cracks from their necks were horrifying—like hundreds of children dancing on a bed of twigs. The moans of the cats that had jumped but failed to enjoy instant deaths rose the loudest.

Unable to bear the scene for a second longer, Ayingbi ran inside and upstairs to the office, still hearing hailstones—like thumpity-thumps outside.

Her own cubicle wasn't empty. There was yet another skinny black cat in here.

Relaxed on her desk, eyes half-closed. It squinted up at Ayingbi. Then, almost in slow motion, it turned towards the cooler, which was on—the slats were bobbing gently with the drafts of cool, wet air.

The cat blinked at the corners of the cooler, as if scanning for an opening.

Then it puffed itself up and began to skitter diagonally towards it, paws criss-crossing over each other.

'No,' whispered Ayingbi. 'No!' And she moved to pick up the cat and maybe take it outside, but the cat hissed. Out popped the claws.

Ayingbi stopped.

The cat winked at her and resumed moving towards the cooler, hovering one paw in the air and turning back mockingly, as if waiting to see what Ayingbi would do.

Ayingbi took a step towards the cat.

The cat took a step towards the cooler.

Ayingbi took another step towards the cat.

It took another step towards the cooler, moth to flame. Now, the kitty appeared to be testing the very thing that Ayingbi was wondering about—whether or not it would be able to fit through the cooler slats. And it wasn't a particularly fat cat—it did seem like it would.

It was already trying. The head was in . . . and now the front legs had squeezed through . . .

'No,' croaked Ayingbi.

The blades of the cooler were just a few inches away from the cat's face.

'Stop, please,' pleaded Ayingbi.

The cat looked back at her through the slats one last time. Its pupils were fully dilated, it was purring and its rump was in a gentle wiggle. It really looked quite adorable.

Ayingbi closed her eyes as the hind legs bent fractionally, and the cat jumped.

There were a couple of noisy clunks, and the cooler's blades wedged shut.

Ayingbi opened one eye.

The cat was twitching and flailing.

It hadn't been decapitated. But its neck had clearly been broken, and was bent at a weird angle. One of its eyeballs had half-come out of its socket—it looked like the eye of a goldfish. The cat had lost a tooth, which could be seen floating in the cooler water.

'Oh God . . .' whimpered Ayingbi. The cat's tail was still vibrating. It was revolting, but she couldn't bring herself to look away. She continued to watch, transfixed, until the twitching had stopped, and the cat's body flumped downward for good, still hooked by the neck to the cooler's blades. It looked like it had hanged itself.

Ayingbi realized what she should've done in the first place, and, feeling foolish, she turned the cooler off, which brought silence to the cubicle, and Ayingbi realized the jollities outside had concluded as well.

Footsteps approached. A thin, dark-skinned, bespectacled man entered the office, peering into Ayingbi's cubicle. 'Damn. In here, too?'

'Are you . . .' began Ayingbi.

'Chatty. Hi.'

'Oh. Yes. Hi.'

They shook hands.

'Could've met in better circumstances, I know,' said Chatty. 'Hardy's coming in late, so I didn't have a reliever.' He wore a silver bracelet, and moved his arms a lot when he spoke. Ayingbi watched the bracelet slide up and down his forearm as he edged past her and tried to poke the cat. 'Schrodinger's cooler. I can't tell if the cat's alive or dead.'

'Did you see what happened?' said Ayingbi.

'No, I was on a call. Missed the fun.'

The fun??

'They were jumping off the roof on their own.'

'That's messed up,' said Chatty mildly.

'They were killing themselves. Committing suicide.'

The use of the word 'suicide' seemed to have alerted Chatty as to what she was trying to convey. 'Well, they didn't have our number,' he joked.

'Where's Dr Rastogi?' said Ayingbi.

'I don't think he came out of his office. Anyway, is it okay if I take off? I was waiting for one of you two to come in.'

Although Ayingbi found Chatty's nonchalance bewildering, she nodded. After he'd left, Ayingbi sat, not at all wanting to share office room with a near-beheaded cat.

A phone started ringing.

Ayingbi, in no mental space to be taking calls, either, let out a tch. She reached for Barney.

Only, Barney wasn't ringing.

Ayingbi looked from right to left. Wasn't Phoenix, either.

The ringing was coming from the black phone—Tuxedo.

Ayingbi lifted Phoenix's and Barney's receivers to her ear just to make sure, but the ring persisted.

She stared at Tuxedo.

The dead phone.

Ayingbi ran her fingers along its cord, which was covered in black velvet, before picking up the receiver.

She lifted it to her ear.

Not all silences are the same.

This was not a static silence. It wasn't quietness she heard. It was different—it was the sound of bated breath.

Ayingbi squeezed the receiver. 'Hello?'

Silence.

'Hello?!' said Ayingbi, more forcefully.

Unexpectedly, there came a voice from the other end. A child's—clear and cheerful, and too young to distinguish between male or female.

'HAPPY HOLIDAYS, BING-BEE MA'AM! HAPPY HOLIDAYS, BING-BEE MA'AM! EEEHEEHEEHEE!!'

Then there was a click, the line went dead, and there it was again—that noisy silence, like air being slowly exhaled out of a yawning mouth.

SEVEN

PERSONAL ERRAND

Ten seconds later, Ayingbi was pacing a tiny circle in the office lobby, swearing under her breath, her heart booming like a subwoofer in her chest.

Finally, she gathered the courage to peer inside her cubicle. Tuxedo's receiver was on the floor, the velvety receiver cord pulled taut, wobbling like a plucked guitar string from having been dropped. Ayingbi clasped and unclasped her left hand, which had, moments earlier, been holding the vile thing.

'Fuck,' whimpered Ayingbi, squeezing her eyes shut. That was horrible!

What a cruel trick to play on someone!

Dead phone indeed!

That scoundrel Rastogi had not told her the full story! He'd been outside Mrs Elelem's house as well that night! Whatever was going on, he was privy to it. He had to be!

On the subject of privies, Ayingbi could feel a very slight warmth between her legs, and she realized she'd peed a little.

Now, more than afraid, Ayingbi felt indignant at having been infantilized. Between this and the voice in her ear, the whole thing almost had a violation-like quality to it. It had touched her most intimate parts.

Cheap and underhanded.

Using a child's voice to frighten me. I'll show them.

After getting cleaned up, Ayingbi picked up Tuxedo's receiver, tapped the switch-hook, then pressed the receiver to her ear.

'Go fuck yourself,' she whispered into the telephonic void, before slamming the receiver down.

Outside, a municipal team, masked and gloved, was working through the carnage, scooping up the casualties into large white bags. Some of its members were sprinkling what looked like sand over the blood puddles.

Perhaps that whole gladiator metaphor had over-delivered on itself.

Rastogi emerged from his office a few minutes later and headed straight to the window. He peered all the way out of it, so all Ayingbi could see of him were his slightly raised heels and protruding bottom. Then he straightened himself up, hands on hips. His frowning eyes took in the rest of the office, apparently seeing what else was out of place. Finishing their scan, they finally came to rest on Ayingbi.

'Why don't you take the night off, Ayingbi?'

'Huh?'

'Go on. I'll take any calls that come your way. You look tired.'

'But my shift only just started—'

Rastogi waved it all aside. 'No matter. Take the night off. Get some fresh air. I'll handle things here.'

*

Ayingbi left the office without protest.

She had meant to confront Rastogi earlier. Tell him exactly what had happened. That she had got a taunting call on the phone she had been informed was dead. But when he asked her to take the night off, it no longer felt necessary.

What was the point anymore?

In dismissing her like that, after blatantly lying about the supernatural qualities of Tuxedo, Rastogi had forfeited all rights to retain her services.

This whole business was not merely shady, but downright sinister.

Tomorrow I will quit.

It already felt like a load off her chest. She didn't need this at all.

Ayingbi was, and always had been, open-minded when it came to the paranormal. She already knew something was at play. She suspected there may have been a spirit of some kind, back at Mrs Elelem's, that she had antagonized. But was it worth losing her mental peace over? Not in a million years! This open-mindedness, if anything, had been a liability.

Almost as if to get a taste of the perfectly good summer she could be having, Ayingbi did not go home but instead headed to a large mall nearby.

The mall was crowded—Ayingbi didn't realize it was a Sunday, and seeing people in such large numbers was startling. It had only taken her a couple of weeks of night shifts to get unwired from her own species, from the hoosh and swoosh of regular society. Ayingbi wandered, drinking in the easy fragrances of materialism—diffusers, perfumes, new clothes, coffee, cinnamon, caramel popcorn . . . it was a world removed from the one she had just decided to vacate.

After window shopping extensively through the showrooms on the ground floor, Ayingbi headed up to the first floor. She loved escalators—in the way children love bits of moving environment. She was always fond of the jewel-like green light under the silver steps.

On a confluence of corridors on the first floor, she found a free bench, where she could sit and observe people. If someone were to make a time-lapse video of human life in motion, this would be the place to do it.

Ayingbi studied each laughing, chatting face that walked past, imagining them at their lowest, wondering how close they had ever come to ideating. She did not take what she saw at face value. She'd spent too much time on the flip side to not suspect a grand façade. They all had to have a dark, twisted, sad side—one that wouldn't be revealed in fifteen minutes of small talk. Or maybe even fifteen years. Ayingbi felt a strange desire to shamelessly ask about it.

It's very nice that your son got a placement in Big Tech Company, Mrs Custard–Mustard, but did your nudes wind up on the Internet thirty years ago, by any chance? Does the world know how high up you shave your legs?

It was also possible, thought Ayingbi glumly, she was merely overestimating the extent of everyone's depression. This led to a prick of resentment—a sort of mortality chauvinism, as if they were silly for not fretting about it all the time.

To distract herself from her own thoughts, Ayingbi impulsively decided to watch a movie. This was what impulsive actions should look like. Not other things.

The witless gender-swap comedy did nothing to improve her mood, and she left the screening midway. After grabbing dinner at the food court, Ayingbi headed home, where, in a scrutiny of her own symptoms, she took an Internet quiz: 'How happy are you?'

At the end, a mortar board-wearing cartoon grapefruit informed her she was 65 per cent happy.

Somehow, that cheered her up.

Maybe not 65 per cent, but still, somewhat.

*

The next morning, Ayingbi decided to quit over the phone—a subtle middle-finger to the Rastogi method. However, Rastogi himself beat her to the punch by calling first.

'Hi, Ayingbi. I've been meaning to call you.'

'As have I.'

'What's on your mind?'

'No . . . you go first.'

'I was wondering if you'd consider taking a few days off the hotline.'

Ayingbi blinked. 'Why?'

'I believe there's been a slight error in judgment on my part.'

'What error?'

'I don't think having you in the night shift is working out all that well.'

Excuse me?

'Not working out all that well?' Ayingbi slowly repeated.

'I know we discussed it earlier . . .' said Rastogi. 'But seeing it in effect, seeing you running all around town in the middle of the night . . . I realized it's unfair. Unfair on my part. This is not a fair expectation to have from you so soon.'

'I don't have a problem with it,' said Ayingbi promptly. 'Did I ever complain?'

'Well, no,' admitted Rastogi.

'So, surely the same rule applies to Hardy! You wouldn't want him running around at night, either, would you? You've grounded him too, right?'

'Uh . . .'

'So, when all is said and done,' said Ayingbi triumphantly, 'it really is just a matter of sexism, isn't it?'

'These misgivings aren't new. I had them in the beginning, too, if you remember.'

'Okay,' said Ayingbi, quickly changing tack. 'So that means I can move to the day shift! Right? Right?'

Rastogi was quiet.

'Come on!' said Ayingbi. 'Having me in your hotline was all your idea, wasn't it? Now, you're basically telling me I'm done?' Her eyes began to burn with anger. 'I saved three people in one night, Dr Rastogi! Have *you* ever done that?'

'No,' said Rastogi quietly.

'You don't think I've been doing a good job?!'

'We both know that's not the case. You've been doing a tremendous job.'

'Then why am I being grounded?!'

'Nobody's grounding anyone! It's just that . . .' Rastogi hesitated. 'Well, maybe I've . . . given you too much to do, too soon. I was thinking . . . maybe a change of pace . . . Take a few days off, get rested, find your feet and then we'll talk? See if you feel up to it again?'

Get rested? Find her feet?! Really? After all that she'd done?! The prospect of quitting had all been very well when the decision was hers to take. But how dare Rastogi imply that she wasn't good enough?

'I am in perfect health and eager to continue work,' Ayingbi heard herself snap. 'My feet don't require finding, thank you very much! If I'm not being fired or grounded, then I will see you tonight, same time as usual. I don't know about the rest of you, but I have lives to save, Dr Rastogi.'

Ayingbi felt a rush of savage glee as she cut the call.

This rascal Rastogi would rather insult my work than reveal his secrets. The truth about Tuxedo. The truth of what happened at Mrs Elelem's house. Everything.

Sure as her Scooty was pink, she'd get to the bottom of all this.

*

Outside Rastogi's office complex, there was nothing left to indicate what had happened last evening. Sure, there was the occasional hint of bloodstain here or there, dried in a swiping shape, and there hung in the air a slight lime-like smell, but that was it. As Ayingbi learnt from the lady who ran the kitchen-supplies store on the ground floor, it had taken five garbage trucks and almost two dozen workers to get the job done.

Although she'd been too preoccupied elsewhere to delve deeper, yesterday's incident—with its potent mix of morbid spectacle and cats—had found Internet virality. All kinds of theories, ranging from black magic to mobile-tower radiation, were being kicked around, occasionally with the hashtag 'JonesMeown'. The papers, meanwhile, putting up a pretence of scientism, had merely stated that the possibility of a very elaborate and cruel prank was being enquired into. Ayingbi privately thought that nothing was too ridiculous anymore. They could tell her it was because Saturn and Jupiter had a stare-off, and she'd believe it.

Even when Ayingbi arrived, she found a small group of enquirers gathered outside the building, staring at the roof, as if hopeful for an encore. This might go on for a while, Ayingbi figured.

The enquirers seemed to sense that she worked there. Pre-empting requests for an eyewitness account, she skipped up to the office, where she found Rastogi waiting for her.

'You're angry with me, aren't you, Ayingbi?'

'No,' said Ayingbi shortly.

'I just wanted to reiterate what I told you over the phone. This isn't an evaluation of your performance.'

'You didn't tell the others to take a week off, did you? So, you'd know how I'd feel.'

Rastogi sighed. 'Well, maybe I was wrong. Some odd things have been happening, I'll admit.'

'*Odd?*' said Ayingbi. 'Just *odd?* A cat put its head through my cooler right there!'

'Yes, I saw. Well, what else has been odd?'

Ayingbi opened her mouth and closed it. If she wanted to confront him, now was the time. He knew about Tuxedo. He couldn't not know.

'Well, that's about it,' said Ayingbi.

But then, to Ayingbi's immense surprise, Rastogi himself popped the question: 'The black phone hasn't been giving you trouble, has it?'

Ayingbi was so sure he'd never bring it up, or skirt around it if she mentioned it, that she was utterly disarmed. 'No, it hasn't,' she heard herself mumble.

'Good. It shouldn't.'

'When you say shouldn't . . .' said Ayingbi testily, 'that means . . . it won't ring, right? It being a dead phone and whatnot.'

'Why? Has it?'

Ayingbi stared fiercely back as he locked eyes with her. 'Nope. It hasn't.'

'Well, then,' said Rastogi softly. 'It won't.'

The tense pause that followed ended only when Rastogi broke eye contact and began to walk out of the cubicle.

'Hey, Dr Rastogi?' Ayingbi heard herself blurt out.

'Yes?'

'Why do you think they did it? Why'd the cats kill themselves?'

'Curiosity, perhaps,' said Rastogi. And he left without looking at Ayingbi again.

Ayingbi slowly sat in her chair. She had sat here for so long she knew immediately something was off about the alignment of the three phones. In particular, Tuxedo.

She picked up the black receiver and put it to her ear.

There was a dialling tone now. Even the cord wasn't velvety. Ayingbi frowned as her gaze turned scrutinizing— the black phone was no longer weathered and chipped, but new and shiny.

It grew obvious pretty quickly that this wasn't Tuxedo. It was another black phone just like it. Rastogi had switched phone sets.

The little weasel. What's he playing at?

'Hey, Mayengbam. Want some nachos?' Hardy's arm snuck inside the curtain, clutching a family pack of tortilla chips.

'Um, yeah, sure,' said Ayingbi, pulling out a fistful.

Hardy presented the rest of himself inside. 'Nice we work here. Most places have a rule against chips because of keyboards and stuff. Weird what happened with the cats, huh?'

'Yeah.'

'I overheard you asking Doc. Why do *you* think they did it?'

'Beats me,' muttered Ayingbi. 'Is suicide even a thing in the animal kingdom?'

'I have no idea.'

'You don't think the cat incident could be . . . because of us? We're the suicide bureau, after all.'

Hardy laughed. 'The suicide bureau?'

'You know what I mean. Anyway, it's not like . . . this place is totally normal, you know?' Ayingbi glanced meaningfully at Tuxedo, knowing Hardy had three phones in his cubicle. He must have a Tuxedo-equivalent. If Hardy did not pick up on it, he was either thick or involved himself. Ayingbi decided to probe the chances of the latter.

'Listen, how long have you worked with Rastogi?'

'Three years. Why?' Hardy seemed eager. 'Are we gossiping about him? About his moustache? Man, what is *up* with that thing? He's gotta be a mouth-breather, right?'

'No . . .' said Ayingbi. 'Just . . . generally.'

She regretted bringing it up, but now, she'd have to say something to avoid Hardy getting suspicious. 'Uh, it's just that this kind of work must take a toll, right?'

'Oh, for sure. Just last night I was in a call with a lady. I've been thinking about what she said ever since.'

'What'd she say?'

'I was arguing that life is an equal mix of sweet and salty. We need to wait for the good times.'

'Okay?'

'She argued back that misery is the norm and happiness is occasional. Sadness is difficult to shrug off, while good times are fleeting. And we keep chasing these rare doses of joy while wading through a shit ton of crap. That's the terrible truth of life—it's not an equal mix. But people still carry on because they don't have a choice.'

'They *do*,' muttered Ayingbi.

A long, tense silence prevailed, with Ayingbi realizing what she'd said could have a very dark interpretation.

Sadder still, she'd bummed Hardy out. He eventually mooched off back to his own cubicle, leaving Ayingbi to eye the impostor Tuxedo with dislike.

After a while, Rastogi called from the lobby. 'Ayingbi? Hardy?'

Both of them stuck their heads out of their cubicles.

'I'm headed out for a personal errand,' said Rastogi. 'So, make sure at least one of you stays in.' And he left, whistling a forceful tune. Ayingbi's slightly narrowed eyes escorted him all the way out the door.

She waited until Rastogi had been gone a minute, before shouting out, 'Hey, Hardy! I'm going for a call!'

'Cool,' came the reply.

'I tried to avoid it because Rastogi is already not in the office,' said Ayingbi casually. 'But they're very adamant.'

'No worries, I'll be here. FYI, I've been thinking about what you said.'

'What's that?' said Ayingbi impatiently. She did not want to give Rastogi too much of a head start.

'Suicide in the animal kingdom. I looked it up. You know who else does it? Dolphins. Chimpanzees. I think it's very revealing that only the smartest creatures commit suicide.'

'That's only because I wasn't there,' quipped Ayingbi, flipping the silver switch and grabbing her Scooty keys.

*

Ayingbi had never tailed anyone before. But it was easy to keep up with Rastogi—he was a slow driver and his drive was through busy streets, so there was always some traffic between them.

The pursuit ultimately brought Ayingbi to the main city rail terminus.

Unlike Rahilgiri, it was still crowded with rickshaws and autorickshaws, taxis, lorries, hawkers and a bustling, brightly lit market. Ayingbi wondered if this was another case of prospective suicide by train, but then she spotted Rastogi's car parked in front of one of many grimy motels lining the main road in front of the station. After parking, she hurried towards the façade of a large, four-storeyed motel, which a vertical column of pink neon lighting had christened 'SPOTLIGHT'. There was a crown of yellow lights over the title.

From the street outside, Ayingbi could see a garish lobby, with dalmatian-print carpets and sofas, and gaudy golden chandeliers. Rastogi was currently making an enquiry at the reception. It would be safe to observe from outside, with a swarm of human traffic roving to and fro.

A couple of people left the motel as Ayingbi waited— one looked like a sleep-deprived college student, the other a very fat businessman, the back of his shirt untucked, like a little tail.

Ayingbi vaguely wondered if the place was also a brothel.

Rastogi was now staring at the elevator to the left of the reception desk. He turned back to make another enquiry from the receptionist, who already looked fed up of him. Finally, Rastogi elected to take the stairs.

After he had disappeared, Ayingbi swept in through the jerky, pressure-activated glass doors.

The motel had all the ventilation of a sarcophagus, and smelt strongly of cigarettes and curry.

A couple of well-dressed women were sitting on the sofas, staring expectantly at the door. Their gazes lowered to their nail polish when they saw Ayingbi. Ayingbi prayed that Rastogi, a married man, was indeed here on a call and not anything else.

She purposefully made her way across the lobby and up the carpeted stairs, eyes and ears primed for a sign of the good doctor.

The dimly lit corridors were all identical. Maroon and gold carpeting, dark brown doors at every ten paces, console tables with ashtrays. It was quiet—Ayingbi supposed noise-proofing was important.

There was no sign of Rastogi, or anyone else, on the first floor.

Ayingbi went up to the second floor. Here, a waiter crossed Ayingbi, carrying a tray of empty sundae glasses over his shoulder. Could it be that Rastogi was already inside somewhere and she had missed him?

But then, when she crept up to the third floor and peered down the corridor, she saw him at the far end, hesitating outside one of the rooms. He raised a hand to knock, then he stopped. Then he raised his hand again, scratched his head and then turned to the door opposite.

Was it because he was uncomfortable with the seediness of the place, or was it, as Ayingbi had begun to suspect . . . he didn't know what room it was?

It was Charter's Enclave all over again. By the look of things, Rastogi had arrived at Hotel Spotlight with an incomplete address. Was he certain about the floor, at least? Or was he simply going by trial and error?

Ayingbi did a quick mental count in her head, estimating ten rooms on each side, or twenty per floor, for a total of roughly eighty for the motel.

She hurried downstairs to the reception, where the receptionist was conversing with four hulking, bearded, kurta-pyjama-wearing men, all talking in raised voices. From what Ayingbi could make out, the men wanted to see the check-in register, a request the receptionist was point-blank denying. A bribe was also offered and promptly refused.

Ayingbi was unsurprised. Places like these sank or swam on confidentiality. They would cut the CCTV cables and blame it on rats, or burn down the room with the identity records and file an insurance claim the very next day. Establishments like Hotel Spotlight, ironically, thrived in darkness.

Finally, the receptionist managed to shake the men off. Grumbling, they lurched towards the ugly sofas, eyeing the two waiting women with something like contempt.

Ayingbi walked up to the counter. Maybe she could do better.

'I'm here to see someone.'

'Who?' The receptionist's tone was harsh and uncooperative.

'I'm not sure.'

The receptionist raised an eyebrow, the lines on one side of her forehead turning into full-blown wrinkles. 'You're not sure?'

Ayingbi shrugged. 'I've only seen the person. Very sad. Suicidal-looking. You have somebody like that walk in here?'

'Suicidal-looking?'

'It's like . . . they might just kill themselves, ya know?'

The receptionist frowned, her forehead lines turned into rows of deep Vs. 'Are they expecting you?'

'They sure are,' said Ayingbi. 'You see, they're my client.'

'What sort of client?'

Ayingbi looked around. 'I can't say . . . but you know.' She gave her a furtive nod.

'I'm sorry,' said the receptionist shortly. 'We cannot allow anyone room access without proper identification.'

Ayingbi could've kicked herself. There would probably be an established code word or euphemism for hookers to use. Hello, I'm here to sell showerheads, minus the shower.

Think, Bing-bee, think. If I were a suicidal person, what would I do? What telltale signs would there be of my presence?

Stress-eating, perhaps?

Ayingbi thought of the waiter who'd crossed her on the second floor with a tray of ice-cream bowls. Perhaps the person in question had downed a ton of comfort food as a final meal. Maybe she could find her way to the kitchen and find out which room had ordered the sundaes.

Yes, that was certainly an idea.

She wandered through a series of doors on the ground floor, looking for a 'Staff Only'-type area, and found herself in a corridor with trolleys of colourful towels and shiny bedsheets and linen. She was certain the place would look like a discotheque under black light and was careful to avoid touching anything.

She couldn't find the kitchen at all, but she did find an open storeroom. The first thing she saw in there was a stack of newly ordered toasters still in their boxes. Toasters! People were always taking them into the bathtub with them! Maybe she could find someone from room service and find out if anyone had asked to send a toaster up.

Ayingbi shook her head, appalled by the quality of her detective work. She returned to the lobby, where the four men from earlier were conferring in a corner.

Out of ideas, Ayingbi realized she would have no other alternative but to do what Rastogi was doing. Only, where Rastogi was being nice and polite, she would use a model of brute force. It would be shameless, but it would be faster.

She went up to the first floor, two floors below where Rastogi was, and pulled out her notepad. She drew two columns and wrote the room numbers on both sides.

First, she needed to figure out which rooms were empty and which weren't. Then, she needed to figure out potential candidates. All without Rastogi's plodding, painstaking method.

Ayingbi also decided that rather than ringing every bell and running away like a pranking five-year-old, she would sneak in a little message through the keyhole—like a musical Christmas card.

'I'm from the hotline, I'm here to help,' muttered Ayingbi, strolling to one end of the carpeted corridor. 'I'm from the hotline, I'm here to help . . .' she repeated it like a mantra, until she had whittled it down to its phonetic basics.

She stared the length of the corridor down.

Then she began to jog, ringing doorbell after doorbell, cupping her mouth tight over the keyhole and yelling, 'Um-frumtha-hotline-heyta-help!' before zigzagging over to the next door. The doors had begun to open before Ayingbi had reached the opposite end. Caught red-handed, she could not pretend to not be the offender, and she had to fend off some irate voices over her shoulder.

'Terribly sorry, sir, wrong room!' called Ayingbi, as one angry bald man waddled back into his room, his pants pooling around his ankles.

Someone else flung a racial slur at her. Ayingbi heard giggling and saw a slim white arm tug him back into the room. The door slammed shut.

She glanced at the people who *had* come out, making summary assessments of their grouchy frowns—on the basis of which she eliminated four rooms straight away, marking them with little X's. Two rooms had 'Make My Room' signs—she ignored those too.

'Um-frumtha-hotline-heyta-help!'

'Um-frumtha-hotline-heyta-help!'

'Um-frumtha-hotline-heyta-help!'

The words had already begun to lose meaning and sounded silly by the time Ayingbi hit the end of the corridor. She examined her notes.

Seven crosses. Thirteen doors still in question. There had been a couple of 'Do Not Disturb' rooms in there as well.

If it was a suicidal caller, they would *probably* not have a 'Do Not Disturb' sign outside their door. They would want to be disturbed. Right? Right?

Not necessarily.

Ayingbi began to amble towards the rooms she hadn't eliminated. The first one—Room 201—had a tray with two empty ice-cream bowls on the floor outside. She remembered her insight about stress-eating and paused. After some thought, she rang the doorbell.

In a moment, Ayingbi saw the fisheye lens of the keyhole darken. She rang the bell again.

'Room service!' she called out.

'No, you're not.' The male voice, though heavily muffled by thick wood and carpeting, sounded young.

'Uh . . . you're not the ones who called a hotline, are you?'

'Nope!'

'So, you're not in any danger?'

'No, we're not! Goodbye!'

Ayingbi sighed and began to trudge off. Behind her, the same door clattered open and a girl's voice, youngish, called out, 'Hey.'

Ayingbi turned. She could see a struggle to shut the door and to keep it open.

'No, don't—' said a male voice.

'She said danger—'

'Maybe she's talking about them . . . maybe she knows—'

'She's talking about something else!'

The girl sounded panicky and uncertain. The boy, presumably the party against further conference, managed to shut the door.

Ayingbi paused. A girl with a boy, speaking of danger—a charge the boy was vehemently denying. Hmm. Fishy. 'Sir, the lady said she was in danger,' she said, walking back to the door.

'No, she didn't!'

'I'm going to have to report this downstairs.'

'There's . . . nothing to report!'

'May I speak to her, please?'

Finally, the door, still chain-latched, opened three inches.

'Now, look, I mean no harm,' said Ayingbi. She could see the half-face of a very frightened-looking girl, and on top of it, the half-face of a very frightened-looking boy. 'But why did you react like that when I mentioned danger?'

'We didn't react!' said the boy. 'Did we?!' He glared at the girl, who, clutching at her cheeks, vigorously shook her head.

Ayingbi didn't believe it for a second. 'Hmm. Is there a telephone in the room?'

'No,' said the boy.

'Look,' said Ayingbi. 'I'm not here for you. I'm here for somebody else. Somebody who, I think, plans on killing themselves.'

'You *think* plans on killing themselves?'

'Long story. Now, it's kinda tricky for me to move around, but if you have room-to-room calling in your room, it'll save me bundles in time.'

'We aren't letting you in,' said the boy. 'Sorry.'

Ayingbi figured that it was a frightened young couple hiding out in a shady motel. They looked like they were still in school. An unpleasant realization struck her. 'Uh, there's no chance the two of you ran away together, right?'

The boy remained stony-faced, but the girl's face betrayed it all.

'Is that why you're scared?' said Ayingbi. 'That someone's coming after you?'

'Nobody knows we're here!' said the girl shrilly. 'Nobody!'

'Nobody? Are you sure? Because there are four big, bearded men downstairs, and they're making all sorts of enquires.'

The boy looked absolutely horrified, the girl slowly cupped her mouth with one hand. Tears welled forth from her eyes. Immediately, the boy moved to console her, then glowered at Ayingbi.

'Please,' said the boy shortly. 'Don't tell them. They will kill us.'

Hmm, thought Ayingbi. This could be serious. Ayingbi decided to temporarily stall her own mission, which she didn't even know was one for sure. Rastogi really could be booty calling here, for all she knew. He could've at least washed his face, first.

'Yeah, I won't tell. Can I come in, at least?'

Finally, they allowed her in. Ayingbi glimpsed into the open toilet door—there were no bathtubs. Well, there went the toaster theory.

There was no ceiling fan either or any dangly bits someone could hang themselves from. There were colourful bulbs and a tacky dresser. There was a painting of a maharaja and maharani behind the four-poster bed, and the floor tiles had peacock motifs.

Two colourful schoolbags, packed to bursting, sat in the corner of the room. Ayingbi felt sorry for them.

Obviously, the place couldn't afford to look too much like a bordello, so they had to have the constituents of a regular budget hotel room.

Like a telephone, thought Ayingbi, pleased to find it by the dresser. There were numbers for reception, laundry, room service, and . . . yes, room-to-room!

It was a regular phone with a three-by-four button grid, not like the hotline Holy Trinity. The boy, meanwhile, had double-locked the door again, and the girl was clinging to him and staring at Ayingbi.

They both looked undernourished. Was the cause of dispute a caste thing or religion or something else? The severity of the repercussions might depend on it.

Ayingbi looked at the extensions and referred to the list of rooms she hadn't yet eliminated. She noticed two more ice creams still sitting there, and she realized how famished she was.

'Anyone eating this?'

They shook their heads. Ayingbi grabbed one of the bowls and began to spoon tutti-frutti into her mouth while making the first call.

'What if there's caller ID in the other rooms?' said the girl nervously.

Ayingbi indicated the phone. 'This phone doesn't have a bar for caller ID, so why would the others?'

When the girl still looked unsure, Ayingbi said, 'Watch this,' as the call was taken. 'Hello sir, we have a suicide levy we'd like to impose.'

'Suicide levy?'

'Yes, it will be added to your room tariff, should you kill yourself, and your breakfast will no longer be complimentary.'

'Fuck off!'

Entertaining as this was, it was also time-wasting, and thereon after, Ayingbi began directly asking the receivers if they had called a crisis hotline, gauging from their tone of reply whether they were being honest. She was waiting for that little tell, for someone to be caught off-guard.

The boy and the girl looked perplexed.

'What are you doing?' hissed the boy.

'Um, so they're really downstairs then?' said the girl, in a small voice, several minutes later.

'Yes, I'm afraid so,' said Ayingbi, mentally striking out Room 306 and proceeding to Room 307.

The girl showed Ayingbi a succession of photos on her phone. They were indeed all men, in some rural setting. Tractors. Guns. Pictures with politicians. Ayingbi, distracted with room-calling, couldn't honestly tell if they were the same men she'd seen downstairs, even if she wouldn't put it past those chaps to be the honour-killing type in general.

'Maybe,' she said.

'What do we do if they come up here?'

'I'll pretend this is my room. You two can hide in the loo.'

The children liked that suggestion, and Ayingbi continued with the calls.

'Hello,' she said, as Room 309 took the call. 'You did not call a suicide hotline, by any chance, did you?'

'Pardon?' came a male, slightly panicked reply.

Ayingbi's suspicions rose. 'Um, we have received word from a suicide hotline that you are going to commit suicide here. Is that correct?'

Mister 309 began to flub. 'No . . . no . . . quite preposterous . . . absolutely not . . . which hotline? Who called?'

'I am not sure, sir.'

'They can't do that!' said Mister 309 loudly. 'They are supposed to be confidential!'

And he hung up. Thrilled, Ayingbi hurried towards the door.

'Where are you going, miss?! You said you wouldn't leave us!'

'I won't,' said Ayingbi. 'Just give me time for a quick errand, okay?'

'You don't understand, miss,' said the girl, and when she took Ayingbi's forearm, her hands were cold with sweat. 'They will kill me, and then they will kill him, too.'

Ayingbi gently pried her arm free and looked at both of them. 'Look, I said I'd be back, didn't I? You two hide and keep the door locked till then.'

She returned to the corridor, silently making her way up to Room 309, keeping her eyes peeled for Rastogi. He was still on the top floor by the looks of it, going painfully slowly. Ayingbi suspected he might have interrupted one too many couples during sex, by now.

What was so special about Mister 309, anyway? Why did Rastogi feel the need to personally take this call? Ugh, she still didn't know what was going on.

Ayingbi rang the bell and waited.

The voice seemed to come from right on the other side of the door, as if the speaker was leaning against it. 'Please, dear. Go home.'

'Open the door!' Ayingbi cried, pummelling it with her fists.

The door did not open; Ayingbi worried her phone call might have instigated him to do it. This little time could make all the difference for Mister 309.

She got an idea.

'Hey!' she said to the receptionist, after returning to the ground floor. 'Are you supposed to report cases where people are in danger?'

'What?'

'In case there's someone in a very difficult situation, are you supposed to report the matter to the police?'

'Ugh, not again. Who?'

For her latest trick, Ayingbi had to do a little exercise in voice modulation. She had to keep her tone conversational, as if she wasn't trying to attract attention, but also loud enough for the closest member of the honour-killing party to listen.

'Upstairs, in Room 309.'

'I told you not to go up there,' the receptionist scowled. 'Please leave.'

'No, you don't understand,' said Ayingbi, with the loudest hiss she could muster. 'A couple who eloped together is staying there. They say there are people coming to kill them!'

Ayingbi was staring firmly at the receptionist, willing herself not to look around.

'Ssh!' hissed the receptionist.

'They're in Room 309!' said Ayingbi. She winced, wondering if she'd gone overboard. 'A BOY and a GIRL! THEY'VE RUN AWAY FROM HOME TOGETHER!'

'Madam, please, keep your voice down!' said the receptionist loudly. Ayingbi kept herself planted over the counter, but she could see the receptionist's gaze nervously move leftwards, and out the corner of her eye, she could see the party of four leave the lobby and quietly slink towards the stairs.

The receptionist sat back in her seat and put a hand to her head. 'What've you done?'

Ayingbi tiptoed back up to the second floor, ensuring that all four men were there, zeroing in towards Room 309. Then she hurried down to Room 201.

'Hey, it's me!' she whispered into the keyhole. 'The escape route's clear,' she whispered, as Honour Girl opened the door.

'How do you—'

'Shut up, get your stuff and follow me!' hissed Ayingbi.

They obeyed. Moments later, the three of them were tiptoeing back down the corridor when they heard a great bang from above. It sounded like a door was being broken down.

Honour Girl squealed. 'What was that?!'

'Ignore it,' said Ayingbi. 'Come on, we gotta keep moving.'

In the lobby, the receptionist was staring at the ceiling, a hand on her chest. There were still little bangs coming, making dust shake off the ceiling. Ayingbi silently guided Honour Boy and Girl outside.

The smell of the crowded street felt like freedom after the suffocating curry stench of the hotel. Without loitering, Ayingbi pulled the children into the railway station.

'You kids have money for a bus or train?'

'Yes,' said Honour Boy.

'Get out of here. Once you're far enough away, find the police or a lawyer or something. Or maybe like an NGO.'

Honour Boy and Honour Girl looked at each other. 'What?'

'Look, I'm just thinking out loud, okay!' snapped Ayingbi. 'My point is—don't hang around here! Go!'

Honour Girl looked like she was going to cry. 'They'll find us again! They'll kill us, miss!'

'No, they won't,' said Honour Boy, stone-faced. Honour Girl's hand squeezed in his own, he looked at Ayingbi solemnly, a look of pitiful manufactured maturity. 'I'll make sure of that. Thanks for your—'

'GO! NOW!' barked Ayingbi.

The kids, caught off-guard, jumped, turned the other way and began to run, their backpacks bouncing behind them until they had disappeared into the crowd.

Meanwhile, there was commotion outside Hotel Spotlight, as the four men came marching outside, shouting and glaring left and right, before storming away down the road.

Ayingbi kept out of sight.

A few seconds later, there was a shrill female shriek. And minutes later an ambulance drew up to the hotel, and a small group of people, Rastogi included, escorted a man out.

The man was chubby, middle-aged and balding, wearing leopard-print rimmed glasses and crimson wristbands. Ayingbi realized they weren't wristbands but handkerchiefs. Handkerchiefs soaked in blood. He had slit his wrists. The man appeared drowsy, and his head was lumbering from side-to-side as Rastogi helped him into the ambulance.

Yes, yes, it had worked. The four men had broken the door down, just as she'd hoped. They would've found Mister 309 with his wrists cut, panicked and fled. The receptionist would've gone up to check on the destruction they'd wreaked, and also found Mister 309. It would've been her scream Ayingbi had heard. It would've been her scream that brought Rastogi rushing to Room 309.

All according to plan.

So, this was it.

This was Rastogi's personal errand.

He had tried to ground her, failing which, he had switched her phone—Tuxedo—out, without telling her.

He'd lied about a personal errand to come to this hotel and save this fellow, for whatever reason.

But why?

Who was Mister 309 supposed to be?

What was even going on?

EIGHT

THE DAY SHIFT

Rastogi returned to the office a while after Ayingbi did, and soon upon his return, Phoenix began to ring.

'Ayingbi?' said Rastogi once she'd taken the call. 'Could you come to my office for a minute?'

Relaxed in his chair, he had put a pot of coffee on. If Ayingbi didn't already know what he'd been up to, she never would've guessed.

'Like a cup?' said Rastogi.

'Sure.'

He poured out two cups, passing her one. 'I've been thinking about what you said earlier, and I do agree that it's time to put you in the day shift for a bit. You will switch places with Chatty.'

'Hmm.' Ayingbi took a sip of coffee. Strong and chocolatey.

'Don't take it the wrong way,' continued Rastogi. 'This rotation system is quite common. You have it in hospitals, you have it in the army. A tough assignment followed by a relatively lighter one. Normally, we do it every month. But I think we should do it earlier for you. This is simply because you are *new*. No other reason. It's important for your mental health.'

Ayingbi glanced at the Teeterling statuette—it was facing the other way, so she was looking at the back of its smooth, round head. Maybe Rastogi conducted all his shady business by night, and he wanted to nudge her away from it.

'How long will you keep me on the day shift for?'

'I was thinking a couple of weeks.'

Ayingbi was still uncertain. But she knew that if she wanted to quietly investigate into Rastogi's doings, she needed to not come across as difficult.

She accepted the offer with what she hoped was a conciliatory smile.

*

Summer shone brightly for the next two weeks, and Ayingbi, who had been sleeping consistently through the larger part of the day, was surprised by how hot the days had got.

There was no doubt that she was happier. Daytime was life-affirming in a way darkness could never be. Nighttime was forgiving and accepting of unusual activity, for which sunshine acted as a kind of celestial disciplinarian.

Even the calls, and their problems, seemed easier to resolve. Though she now averaged three calls a day, most of the callers did not seem to be, as Rastogi might have put it, with a Teeterling sitting on their shoulder. Or, more likely, Ayingbi was simply getting better at the whole thing.

One evening, Ayingbi found Chatty had come in early. He was in the lobby, putting up posters. Unlike Hardy, who dressed smart and corporate, always matching his tie with his shirt, Chatty was generally in loafers and what looked like his grandfather's kurtas.

'We're doing a bit of redecorating,' said Chatty. 'It's too depressing here, so I got my old band posters from college.'

'Does Rastogi know?'

'He hates the posters, so of course I'm going to have to put them up.'

It was fun putting up the posters, both for the petty rebellion against Rastogi as well as the realization that she and Chatty shared musical tastes.

One of the posters was of the Mughal Antiseptics, a Euro-dance band rather close to Ayingbi's heart.

'I remember these guys, they were cool.'

'Yeah, shame about the drummer, Yorkie.'

'What about Yorkie?'

'Killed himself a couple years ago, don't you remember?'

'Oh!' The blow landed sharply. 'You don't think it's inappropriate, putting that up in here?'

Chatty scratched his forehead. 'Actually I never made the connection. Let it be. We can put up others, without Saddies in them.'

Chatty called depressed people—Saddies. 'No, no,' said Ayingbi quickly. 'It's fine.'

'Better *we* decorate the place than Hardy,' said Chatty seriously. 'The place will be swimming with Rumi quotes.'

They were still putting up posters when Chatty got a call.

'Good luck,' said Ayingbi, as Chatty retreated. She lingered outside his cubicle, trying to overhear how he handled calls and comparing it to her own style.

It was different. Chatty's business voice was deep and reassuring. He seemed to be using logic in his arguments. Hardy, she recalled, always opened with a cheery, sing-song hello, like an old friend trying to get the other to guess who was calling. He kept things light.

Chatty—logical. Hardy—cheerful. They each had a hook. Maybe, she, Ayingbi, was nurturing and compassionate. That was probably how Hardy and Chatty saw her, too.

Matronly.

Ayingbi wasn't too pleased about it.

She retired to her own cubicle.

When there were just ten minutes left in her shift, Barney began to ring.

Ayingbi welcomed the ringing as a distraction from her thoughts. She planned to take the call on the third ring as always. She frowned when the ringing did not stop when she lifted the receiver, and then she realized it.

It wasn't Barney that was ringing—it was Tuxedo.

Ayingbi was taken aback. It was the second time this had happened. The first time . . . well . . .

She frowned at the black phone, remembering that Rastogi had switched it out a couple of weeks ago. Seeing

that the velvety cord was back, and the phone's slightly run-
down condition, she figured it was the original Tuxedo.
At some point, Rastogi must have switched it back. She'd
been ignoring it determinedly all this while; she had only
just noticed it.

A part of her wanted to drag Chatty here and make
him see what was happening. Another part, while not
exactly intrigued, wanted her to stand her ground. If she
fled now, there'd be no end to it.

'Ayingbi? You taking that or what?' came Chatty's call.

She slowly picked up Tuxedo's receiver, holding it an
inch away from her ear, as if it had invisible spikes.

'Hello?' said Ayingbi, her voice steeled, tentatively
waiting for something . . . not necessarily a child's voice,
but something . . . She did feel braver attending to the call
in broad daylight and with Chatty in the office.

'Hello?' a female voice whispered back.

'Yes?'

'Um . . . is this the hotline?'

Ayingbi cleared her throat, took a quick gulp of
water, and flipped her notepad open. 'Yes. How may I
help?'

'Uh, yes. Things are not well with me . . .'

Hmm. It seemed legit. None of that creepy nonsense
from last time. Maybe Rastogi had made some changes to
Tuxedo's line before restoring it.

'I'm here to help,' said Ayingbi. 'Would you like to tell
me about it?'

'It's not something I can say over the phone . . .'

'Well, you *did* call on one.'

'No, no, I cannot say . . .'

'Do you need emergency services of any kind, ma'am?'

'No . . . no . . . no . . .'

'Are you alone?'

'Alone?' The caller said it loudly, and the details of her voice emerged, as if stepping out of the shadows.

Ayingbi recognized her at once. 'It's you! Cocktail-Dress!'

'Pardon?'

'I . . . we met, remember? On the barrage? We saved Inst—er, the gentleman in the suit—together.'

'Oh, oh, yes . . . it's you, is it?'

'Yes, yes! This is me!' Cocktail-Dress sure was damaged goods, but it was a relief to hear her voice again. It told Ayingbi that Cocktail-Dress was still alive. 'How are you doing?'

'Um, not too well, actually,' said Cocktail-Dress. 'Do you think you could come over?'

'Are you suicidal again?' said Ayingbi. Last time, Cocktail-Dress had been very sure she wanted to kill herself, and had no intention of being talked out of it. But this time, she was calling. Something was up.

Cocktail-Dress began to sob. 'I don't know . . . I mean . . . I thought I was better, but here we are again . . .'

'Hey, hey, hey, I'm here . . .' whispered Ayingbi, cupping Tuxedo's receiver in both hands. 'Tell me everything.'

'He left me . . .' croaked Cocktail-Dress.

'Instox?'

'He's gone . . . said it was just a fling . . . You know, I was starting to believe fate had . . . some kind of plan . . . for me to . . . find him . . . but, alas . . .'

'Where are you? You're not back on the dam, are you?'

'No . . . I'm at home . . . I didn't have anyone else to talk to . . . but I remembered you . . . saying . . . you worked at a suicide hotline . . . and earlier he'd told me . . . which hotline he'd called that night . . . so I knew it must be . . . the one you . . . worked at . . .'

'You haven't done anything yet, have you?'

'No, I haven't . . . but I can't do this anymore, I really can't. What's the point if it's just gonna be this way, each time?!'

'It's not! Come on, you couldn't expect the relationship to last forever! It was . . . borne out of immense stress . . . which was . . . you know, the foundation of the . . . uh . . . thing,' Ayingbi's voice petered out.

'Can you come over?' said Cocktail-Dress again.

Ayingbi's heart sank. She really didn't want to. It was the third time Cocktail-Dress had asked, and each time, Ayingbi had tried to gently deflect it.

'I can't hack it,' sobbed Cocktail-Dress. 'Please, come over, as a friend, for a little bit!'

A friend? Hardly. Ayingbi knew her and had sympathy for her, but to come over?

'You know I'm at work, right? Why don't we speak once I'm free?'

She had not the slightest desire to call Cocktail-Dress from her personal number.

But then Cocktail-Dress said, 'I don't mean to pressure you. I haven't done anything . . . yet. But if you need me to stand on a cliff again . . .'

Ayingbi groaned. She didn't want to be blackmailed.

'Look,' she said unhappily. 'That's not fair. If you aren't actively suicidal, I can't make a personal visit.'

'No, I'm not . . . I'm not . . . yeah, you have other people to save . . . I get it . . . okay, bye.'

'No, hang on!' cried Ayingbi. She squeezed her eyes shut. Regardless of what she was saying, Cocktail-Dress had been suicidal before. And, technically, she was calling on the hotline. This would very much qualify as work. 'Maybe I can come, you know, for a little bit.'

'You will?' gasped Cocktail-Dress. 'Really?'

Maybe Ayingbi had become complacent sitting in office all day. It had been a while since she'd done a follow-up. As good as the day shift was, handling matters over the phone was not quite the same.

Ayingbi tapped Tuxedo on the side, still puzzled. Could a distress call coming on Tuxedo instead of Barney be a consequence of Rastogi having fiddled with the phones?

'Yeah, of course,' said Ayingbi, already getting to her feet, checking her watch and promising herself she'd wrap this up in an hour. 'What's your address?'

*

Another bungalow.

This one was in the oldest part of the city, with large, untended ancestral properties, meandering roads and maroon brickwork that appeared unchanged in decades. Old business communities, mainly. For some reason, Ayingbi had been expecting a ritzier locality for Cocktail-Dress.

She had coached herself on the ride, deciding that she did not need a clingy basket case on her personal time. No private details would be shared, no phone numbers exchanged. This would be a regular visit. Hopefully it wouldn't take too long—after all, she'd counselled a hysterical Nimmi after half a dozen break-ups since high school.

No car stood in the bungalow's driveway.

Ayingbi rang the doorbell next to the gate, and moments later, a crooked maid came shuffling out. She was small and dusky, dressed in a tatty purple-and-yellow sari, nibbling on her *pallu*. Her skin was rather thin and stretched over her skull, making her eyes look bulging and strained.

Ayingbi frowned and rechecked the address. 'Is this . . . um . . .' She realized she didn't know Cocktail-Dress's name. 'Is Madam inside?'

The little maid frowned. 'Madam? No, no, I am Suggi.' She pointed earnestly at herself.

'Madam! Madam! Tell her a friend has come to see her.'

'A madam?' Suggi seemed perplexed.

'Yes, the madam who lives here.'

'Oh.'

'Well . . .?' said Ayingbi, a few impatient moments later. 'Is she in?'

'Yes, yes, yes!' said Suggi. 'Yes, yes, yes!'

She floated over to the gate—it was impossible to see her feet scuttering underneath the sari—and unlatched it, opening it just enough for Ayingbi to inch through sideways.

'So, Madam *is* inside, yes?' said Ayingbi, as Suggi led her up a path of crushed clay.

'Inside, yes, inside,' said Suggi. 'Waiting. Waiting for you.' And she threw open the front door and let Ayingbi in.

The inside of the house was as warm and breezy as outdoors, as if every door and window had been thrown open.

'I am Suggi,' said Suggi.

She led Ayingbi into a living room, which had a couple of sofas pushed against the wall to make way for a portable dance floor. The windows were all open in here, too. There was a home theatre system, plugged up to an old VCR, which had two crooked pillars of cassette tapes standing next to it. Ayingbi tilted her head to look at the VCR tapes—they all appeared to be home workout videos.

Maybe Cocktail-Dress is on a self-improvement spree.

Suggi picked up the topmost cassette, which had a freckled white woman with an afro, dressed in a glittering purple swimsuit.

'This is January Valentine. She is bodacious.'

She held up another one.

'And this one, you can even do with a slipped disc. Sir uses it all the time. Sir is quite keen on fitness.'

Maybe Sir was so keen on fitness, he didn't realize his wife was depressed. And probably unfaithful.

'Sir isn't here, is he?' said Ayingbi. She could guess he wasn't.

'What makes you think that?' said Suggi, a little loudly.

'It's just that I don't see him,' said Ayingbi. Maybe it was best to leave this Sir fellow out of it for now. If he was home, or even expected, Cocktail-Dress would probably have not called Ayingbi over. 'Could you please tell Madam that there's a guest?'

'Guest?' said Suggi blankly.

'Yes,' said Ayingbi, emphatically gesturing towards all of herself. 'A guest.'

This was getting frustrating.

'Okay,' said Suggi, and then, like a cat that had just spotted a mouse, she sprinted away at full speed, her bare heels thudding against the floor.

Ayingbi wondered about this Sir that Suggi kept mentioning. Was the marriage abusive? Was that why Cocktail-Dress was suicidal? Did Ayingbi need to be more careful here?

Ayingbi's gaze continued to rove around the strange living room, and she very nearly jumped when she saw Suggi back in the doorway, still munching on an end of her pallu.

'Did you tell Madam I'm here?' said Ayingbi.

Suggi kept her eyes squeezed shut as she spoke. 'Madam is taking a shower. She will be out soon. Please wait here.' Something about the delivery made it seem like a recitation, as if Suggi had committed it to memory with great difficulty.

'Fine,' said Ayingbi.

Suggi did not offer Ayingbi anything. She continued to stand there, occupying little more space than a coat-rack, staring at Ayingbi, then turning away and proceeding towards a counter, as if about to do housework, then turning back at Ayingbi, all the while still chewing on the sari. There was something deeply off-putting about her presence.

Finally, she pulled the pallu out of her mouth—it looked like a snake regurgitating a disagreeable smaller snake.

'We have a fridge,' she said suddenly. 'Would you like to see what's in there?'

'Uhhh . . .'

'It is right here,' said Suggi, pointing to another door, which Ayingbi presumed led to the kitchen. 'Please, missus. You will like it.'

The kitchen was blindingly bright, and it was several seconds before Ayingbi could see Suggi standing by the fridge, holding the door open, like a limousine valet waiting for Ayingbi to get in. Ayingbi felt her stomach clench as she approached it—she expected the contents to be unusual.

But the fridge was full of fruit.

Colour-coded in a rainbow gradient from top to bottom, with jamuns and blueberries on top, followed by guavas, lemons, mangoes, peaches, and plums and cherries at the bottom.

'Guavas,' said Suggi, and she pointed at them. 'They are rich in vitamin C.'

I don't give a shit.

'Right.'

'Oranges,' said Suggi. 'They are rich in vitamin C, but not as rich as guavas.'

From all these little fun facts, it would easily seem like Suggi was personally invested, but she was talking in a monotone, as if narrating from a boring audiobook.

'Sir doesn't like mangoes,' went on Suggi cryptically. 'But unfortunately, refrigerating bananas turns them black.'

The jars on the shelves all had marks from where stickers had been torn off. The entire kitchen, this fruitarian paradise, looked like it had been repurposed from something else. Suggi moved towards the cutting board. Ayingbi stepped to a side to avoid her, and caught a whiff of something that smelt like formaldehyde.

Suggi began to cut onions. She cut each one very slowly, with an up-and-down motion, as if they had the toughness of burnt steak. 'Sir says we must start eating healthy now. Our earlier diet was not good, not good at all.' She looked dolefully at Ayingbi.

The onions made her sob gently. She wiped her eyes with the chewed-up pallu.

Ayingbi could feel ants crawling up her back. 'Um, could you please check up on Madam? She's been in the shower for a long time.'

Too long? She didn't do anything stupid in there, did she?

Once again, Suggi set down the knife, took two steps, and then tore out of the kitchen at top speed. Then her head popped back into view. 'We have another fridge, too. Please come take a look.'

The other fridge, for whatever reason, was on the landing of the stairs halfway up to the first floor. Once again, Suggi had held it open for Ayingbi. It was similar to the last one, only this time, all the shelves, from top to bottom, were full of pomegranates. Even the freezer box seemed full of them.

Anybody would go nuts living like this, thought Ayingbi. *Probably what happened.*

She considered leaving a message with Suggi, but was worried about this very long shower. She pressed for Cocktail-Dress's whereabouts a third time.

'Madam is out of the shower,' mumbled Suggi. 'You can visit the bedroom and check.'

Ayingbi finally went upstairs alone, and found absolutely nobody there. She tried to listen for sounds of a shower, or maybe a shower that had just ended—maybe a hair-dryer, or drawers being pulled open, or music or the squeak of flip-flops.

She found an empty bedroom, with a bed for two, immaculately made. The dresser had only men's cosmetics, and the cupboard had only men's clothing.

Maybe they were living in separate rooms?

Ayingbi checked the rest of the corridor. There was no other bedroom.

Yup. I'm being played for a sucker.

Ayingbi was forced, painfully, to again consider the fact that the phone call that had brought her here had come on Tuxedo.

She wondered if she'd been called by Cocktail-Dress at all.

Probably not. This was all a huge mistake.

With a look of determined calm, Ayingbi slowly walked back downstairs.

Suggi was back in the living room. She was copying the dancer on the giant TV. The TV was on mute, so it was essentially just the little housekeeper flailing around on the dance floor by herself.

Ayingbi quietly slunk past her to the front door.

It had been locked and bolted from the inside. Three sliding bolt latches, a chain latch and a rim latch. Ayingbi hadn't noticed this small ladder of security measures upon entry. She quickly unlatched the bolt and chain latches, and began to tinker with the unfamiliar rim latch, when—

'Madam.'

Slowly, Ayingbi turned.

Suggi was standing behind her. She had worked up a sweat from dancing. It was outlining her underarms, her collarbones, her nipples, her navel. The corridor reeked of it. Remembering it had been airy when she entered, Ayingbi realized the windows across must have been shut during Suggi's frequent excursions in and out of the living room.

'It's all right, Madam,' said Suggi slowly. 'Madam is showering. She will come down shortly.'

'Uh, I'll come back later,' said Ayingbi, in a voice that was 90 per cent wispy dry air.

'We have a third fridge, too,' said Suggi, and a shadow crossed her face. 'Would you like to see what's in there?'

It felt as if someone had injected ice into the veins of Ayingbi's feet. 'Open this door,' she croaked. She could feel the adrenaline rush kick in.

Suggi said something in reply, and then something peculiar happened. The adrenaline rush was so strong, it really did seem like time had slowed down.

Ayingbi watched, as if in a dream, Suggi lunge towards her, pulling the onion-chopping knife from her hip. She raised the knife, her eyeballs widening almost entirely out their sockets, even as she continued to lisp words of assurance.

A simple, stupid gasp left Ayingbi's lips.

'Oh.'

Now, she could see Suggi's eyes popping madly, the knife stiffening in her fist, veins hardening in her arms. The bone of her elbow bulged as the forearm reared for attack.

Time caught up to real speed, and Ayingbi realized she had raised her own hands, one to seize Suggi's forearm before it could bring the knife down, and the other, to Suggi's throat.

'Ackk . . . ackkk . . .' said Suggi, and Ayingbi could feel Suggi's larynx vibrating inside her clenched fist. She squeezed it like a stress ball, while pinning the hand with the knife to the wall. Suggi's struggle was soundless—she looked and sounded exhilarated—eyes rolling wildly and tongue wagging. Like a dog that was overwhelmed at being played with—it was terrifying, it was simply the *wrong* reaction to have in a fight. Ayingbi's grip leapt from Suggi's throat to her forehead, and she pushed it hard, mashing Suggi's head backwards into the wall.

Suggi crumpled where she stood, and Ayingbi tore off down the corridor, looking for an escape. All the doors and windows had been locked *from the outside.*

'HELPP!!!' yelled Ayingbi. 'HELPP!!'

Hide.

She would have to hide.

Behind her, Suggi had gotten up again.

Rotating frantically, wringing her hands, Ayingbi reached the stairs again. Suddenly, Suggi barrelled in from a side door at top speed, brandishing the knife.

Ayingbi screamed and dove aside, so that Suggi barrelled past, straight into the kitchen. Ayingbi lunged for the kitchen door, banging it shut and latching it, locking Suggi inside.

'HELP!' she yelled, with all her might.

No way out. The windows that had been open earlier were all locked.

The fridge on the landing.

Ayingbi ran upstairs to the pomegranate fridge, and clicked the switch off. She gripped it from the top with both hands, and pulled. It wouldn't budge. It was two tonnes of plastic and sheet metal, not so easily moved.

Ayingbi gripped the back edge of the fridge and pulled as hard as she could, till her shoulder joints were almost popping, and yet, the fridge still would not move. She tried to move it from the bottom, first by pulling, then by pushing. Still nothing. Ayingbi tried to jerk it forward from one side, making a jerk with her hip, while gripping the edge of the fridge two-thirds the way down. The fridge jerked forward an inch. Ayingbi did this a few more times on one side, and then on the other to even things out. And repeat.

'Yes . . .' breathed Ayingbi. 'Yes . . .'

Still so heavy. The fridge jerked forward with a sound of claws swiping against a chalkboard. There were little black C-shaped drag marks from where it had inched forward. Ayingbi tried to slip behind the fridge, but the condenser coil was hot, and she had to jerk the fridge out a little more before she had two feet of space to comfortably slip into, with wiggle room.

There was still no sign of Suggi, who, with any luck, was still stuck in the kitchen.

Ayingbi was now well-concealed behind the fridge. She gripped the sides and pushed.

'Move . . .' she muttered.

She flattened her spine against the wall, and raised one foot against the back of the fridge . . . and then another. She was completely off the floor now, knees bent, feet on the back of the fridge, back flat against the wall. Ayingbi began to put all the potential energy stored in her thighs into it. It still wouldn't move.

With her back still flattened against the wall, she began to slide upwards, walking on the back of the fridge, until her feet were near the top. Now, it was easier. She began to straighten her legs.

'MOVE!'

There was a sound of a window sash opening somewhere.

Suggi came noisily, and Ayingbi waited for the sound of her bare feet to thud up the stairs, before putting her entire might into the back of the fridge, straightening her legs out and tipping the fridge fully over, collapsing to the dusty floor as she did.

There was a flash and spark as the old fridge was yanked free of its socket, and it began to cartwheel downstairs, thudding heavily on every third step. It did a backflip, catching Suggi straight in the face. Suggi was cut away mid-yell, and a second later, both fridge and maid smashed to the floor at the bottom.

Ayingbi rose to her feet, vigorously massaging the bumped back of her head, ears still ringing from the crash.

Below, she could see Suggi's limbs spreadeagled from underneath the fridge. They weren't moving, not even slightly. The pomegranates had all come tumbling out, many had been crushed under the weight of the fridge. Ayingbi squinted at the maroon-purple puddles. She would never forget the exact shade of fresh bloodstains from her sojourn at Mrs Elelem's, and this didn't look like it.

Ayingbi ran downstairs, skipping nimbly over the fridge, when—

'Ow!!'

One of Suggi's hands had managed to grab Ayingbi's ankle with a pincer-like strength. The other was still waving like a car wiper, searching for the knife, which was inches out of reach. The little maid was still alive.

With her free foot, Ayingbi stamped hard on Suggi's hand, freeing herself.

The window in the living room was half-open—Suggi must've gone out through the kitchen window, and come in through here.

Tyres screeched in front of the house. There was a click of a car door opening.

Ayingbi stopped dead in her tracks.

Sir.

Fuck.

Ayingbi wrenched the window sash all the way up and clambered through, bumping first her knee and then her head, before toppling into the garden.

She lay low for a minute, moving only when she heard the front door slam, after which she began to move sideways, until she hit a corner. Peeping around it, she could see a purple hatchback parked imperfectly in the driveway, with the gate wide open. Sir's car had a red learner's licence sticker and a bright blue roof carrier.

Behind her, there was a grunt of another window being hefted opened.

Ayingbi ran as she had never run in her life, not looking back as she pulled out the Scooty's keys, and she rode away without her helmet on, her loose hair flying everywhere, like a shredded parachute in free fall.

NINE

ANOMIE LINES

So Ayingbi had been set up.

But *why*?

Did someone want her dead? Did they think Sir would do it? Was Sir's house a spiderweb of some sort and Ayingbi the fly?

There was no doubt it had been Cocktail-Dress she'd been speaking to—her raspy, under-modulated drawl was unmistakeable. But what harm had Ayingbi ever done Cocktail-Dress for her to send her there?

It wasn't Cocktail-Dress.

That's why the phone call had come on Tuxedo. It wasn't a mistaken redirection from Barney.

But then, if it *wasn't* Cocktail-Dress, who was it?

The consequences of all that had happened were only now becoming clear, and things looked dire.

Ayingbi was, by the time she reached home, confident that Sir was some kind of murderer or deviant and Suggi his partner-in-crime, and that she had been sent there to die.

For Tuxedo to presume he would've bumped Ayingbi off,
Sir must've been comfortable with the act of killing.

That entire house anyway gave off serial killer-y vibes.

The more time she spent thinking about it, the more
imagined clues she seemed to have left behind.

Was there a camera in front of Sir's house? Did Sir
manage to catch a glimpse of her Scooty? She'd lost her
hairband in the scuffle with Suggi—could some hair samples
have come with it? Could they be used to identify her?

Hell, was Suggi even alive? Ayingbi was sure (and she
felt bad for wishing the alternative) she was—the strength
in her fist when she had grabbed Ayingbi's foot had been
unfading. An alive and coherent Suggi was bad news—
she might give Sir a good description of their visitor,
notwithstanding the slight possibility that someone like
Suggi might not be good with descriptions.

All it really boiled down to was, was the episode with
Sir over?

I don't know. That's the worst thing. I just don't know if I'm
in the clear or not. I don't even know what that whole thing was.

She also didn't understand why her enemy had chosen
the voice of Cocktail-Dress. If they wanted to lure Ayingbi
over with a trusted figure, there were a dozen other names
that would've gotten the job done quicker.

She'd still fallen for it, though.

Maybe, like the cats, she'd been curious.

Ayingbi suddenly felt very exposed. She thought of her
Scooty, parked in plain sight on the road. It might be the
only thing Sir had to remember her by.

She had to get it out of sight.

It was very difficult, clunk-clunking the Scooty upstairs, and by the time she'd hauled it up to her flat, the rubber from the handlebars had left deep impressions on her fingers, and her shoulders and back were aching.

Ayingbi quietly stood her faithful steed by her bed. Then she fetched a broom and swept away the little dirt marks on the staircase, so a trail of wheel dirt wouldn't be traced to her door.

A stinging pain on her left forearm revealed a very fine cut. Until now, adrenaline had dulled the pain. She could also feel throbbing pain from the back of her head, which had hit the wall when she'd kicked off the fridge. Ayingbi paced around the Scooty, wincing as more and more minor injuries revealed themselves, unease and dread ebbing and flowing through her veins.

A bath?

She wriggled out of her jeans and then shrugged off her shirt. Her clothing was smelly and disgusting, and her undergarments were darkened and heavy with sweat. She took them all off, then regarded herself in the bathroom mirror.

She did not like what she saw.

She had lost weight. The shadow under her bosom looked more pronounced, but that was from sag, not some windfall gain in size. The weight appeared to have sloughed off in the worst possible parts.

Ayingbi was crestfallen. She used to be fond of her butt. But now, it looked like balloons that had lost half their helium two days after a party.

While the bathtub filled with hot water, Ayingbi took her time with her own nakedness, examining random crimps and crevices of her limbs, turning like a chimp that had just seen its reflection for the first time.

Ayingbi lit a black raspberry vanilla scented candle, then plopped a yuzu bath bomb into the filled-up bathtub, creating a sudsy stew for her to gingerly descend into.

Her glistening knees rose from the sea of fragrant suds. Ayingbi wagged her knees and whistled water. She wasn't comfortable. The back of the bathtub was hitting the bony nub of her neck, and her big toe kept coiling around the drain chain. She freed a clump of her hair that had gotten stuck to the shower curtain.

She noticed the pattern on the shower curtain. A horned purple beetle.

A thing that's purple. Better than brinjal.

Ayingbi silently fumed in the bathtub for a while before conceding she wasn't getting a morsel of therapy.

She plucked the chain out with her toes and waited till the water had drained. She rinsed herself under the shower, admiring how very like a telephone receiver a showerhead was. Then she shuffled out of the bathtub and towelled herself dry.

I have made so many mistakes.

So far, in all the shenanigans she'd gotten into, there was always a risk of other people getting hurt. But for once, she herself was in the line of fire. It already felt bizarre to think she'd been in a life-or-death situation just a few hours ago.

She couldn't even go to the police because of the whole Mrs Elelem situation.

Ayingbi got dressed and peeked out the window. Even though it was eight-thirty, the sun had only just set. Ayingbi blinked when she realized it was the summer solstice.

To cheer herself up, Ayingbi tried focusing on the people she had helped so far, but even that did not feel like strong motivation. This kind of sacrificing work was supposed to be a bottomless aquifer of courage to keep her going, and it troubled her to find the well empty.

Saving kids not enough for you, Bing-bee ma'am?

At that moment, disturbingly, it wasn't. Ayingbi felt resentful at other people for not taking care of their own problems, for optioning the drastic step far too quickly.

You numpties really need to call a hotline to be told that better times will come? The reason we are involved is because if we don't help them, we'll have their blood on our hands. Rastogi's system isn't benign or humanitarian—it's fucked up to the hilt. Every time we leave the office, we risk exposure to whatever they dosed up on. It's Chernobyl out there.

Ayingbi's mood got worse with the passage of time.

She really hoped Sir wasn't after her.

She was also distraught by the notion that she was secretly wishing Suggi dead.

Nobody should live like this.

By eleven, Ayingbi felt physically sick. The noodles she'd ordered sat uneaten after two bites. She felt in no shape to return to the office in seven hours, so she called Hardy and Chatty, asking if she could do a nine-to-nine shift tomorrow, instead of the usual six-to-six. Neither of them had a problem with it.

Whatever little sleep she managed that night was disrupted twice by the urge to pee. Both times she bumped into her Scooty in the dark, having forgotten it was there.

By next morning, Ayingbi had two beautiful purple bags under both eyes. Her bruises from yesterday were purple too.

More purple things. My luck must be changing.

She twisted a grey cotton shawl around her head like a scarf and put on a pair of winged sunglasses before taking a taxi to work. En route, she kept low in her seat.

'Nice look, Ayingbi,' grinned Chatty, as she walked into the office. He and Hardy were in the lobby with coffee. By the look of things, they'd been waiting for her to relieve them.

'I'm not late, am I?' said Ayingbi, looking at the clock. She'd lost track of time with the disguise and cab. Even after rescheduling shifts, she was fifteen minutes late.

Not done.

Ayingbi's irritation with herself increased.

'Not at all,' said Hardy. 'How was yesterday's call? Nobody died?'

Ayingbi thought of Suggi's arms flailing around from under the fridge.

'No. Hey, how common are crazy axe-murderers in India?' She had blurted it out before she could help herself.

'Crazy axe-murderers?'

'Like . . . psychopaths. Serial killers and such.'

'Uh, not very, I think,' said Hardy. 'They'd be more common in individualistic societies, where there's scope for anomie.'

'Anomie?'

'Yeah, like social disconnect. Less community, less social support.' He looked at Chatty. 'What do you think?'

'I concur,' said Chatty. 'Why do you ask, Ayingbi?'

'Oh, no reason,' said Ayingbi. She cleared her throat. 'The point being, it's quite unlikely there are serial killers living here in the city, right? The sort that hunt you down and stalk you, should you cross their path?'

Hardy and Chatty looked puzzled.

'Uhh . . . I guess?' said Chatty.

'So *assuming*,' said Ayingbi, 'someone happened to stumble across a very weird house where there's an unstable person who works for another person . . . it's unlikely that the second person is a serial killer, right? Right?'

'Huh?' said Hardy blankly.

'Ugh, chuck it. Listen, you guys have three phones, right? Both of you?'

'Yeah.'

'Come with me real quick.' Ayingbi led them into her own cubicle. 'One phone's for Rastogi to call, the other's the hotline,' she said, pointing in turn at Phoenix and Barney. 'Same for you?'

'Yeah.'

'Then what's this?' said Ayingbi, pointing at Tuxedo.

'The dead line,' said Chatty.

'We don't know what it's for,' said Hardy.

'Well, didn't you ask Rastogi when you joined? You must know by now that this thing is dangerous.'

'Doc said it's not to be touched. It's pretty creepy.' Chatty shivered.

'Has it ever rung for you?' said Ayingbi.

'Not for me,' said Chatty. 'It did ring for Hardy a few times.'

Ayingbi looked at Hardy. 'What did it say?'

Hardy opened his mouth and shook his head. 'I . . . I can't say, Ayingbi.'

Ayingbi's temper rose at once. 'You can't *say*?'

'Did someone call you, Ayingbi?' said Chatty. 'And you think they were a serial killer?'

'Why do you still work here?' said Ayingbi loudly. 'Come on, guys! What's Dr Rastogi hiding?!'

'We can't really talk about it, Ayingbi,' said Chatty gently. 'You'll have to take it up with Doc.'

'Where is he, then?' bellowed Ayingbi. 'Not in the office as usual! He's never there when the blasted thing rings!' Suddenly, she was shouting. 'You assholes! Get the fuck out of here! This is *my* office! This is *my personal space* right here!'

And she shoved them both outside the translucent plastic curtain, back into the lobby.

'Ayingbi?' Hardy was trying to peep over the cubicle wall. Chatty, shorter, was jumping up and down.

'Leave me alone, you jerks! I thought we were friends!'

'We are!' said Hardy. 'But we're telling the truth! This is all we know!'

'You won't even tell me what you heard, Hardy!'

'It's . . . personal.'

'Personal?!' Ayingbi didn't even know what to say to that.

'Doc means well, Ayingbi,' said Chatty.

'Does he now?!'

'Yes, he's looking out for you. He didn't want you to get in trouble.'

'Hah! Bit late for that!'

'What do you mean?' cried Hardy in alarm.

'What do you care?!'

'We do, Ayingbi! We do!' said Chatty.

'Are you in danger?' cried Hardy.

'No, I'm FINE! I'm probably not in any danger!' snapped Ayingbi. 'I just wish you would be more transparent about what's happening!'

'Look, we can't really—' began Chatty.

'Just . . . go away, both of you. I don't want to talk.'

'But—'

'GO!!!!!' bellowed Ayingbi, brushing away angry tears.

She was upset when they actually did go away.

Grumbling and restless, she began to take her anger out on the phones. She fiddled with the cords of Barney, Phoenix and Tuxedo, angrily tangling and disentangling them, banging the receivers together, winding them between her fingers and biting them. There was absolutely nothing displeasing about physically punishing the phones, especially Tuxedo.

She ran the three receiver cords between her fingers, lingering longest on Tuxedo's velvety one. Then she moved to their cables, chasing them to the hole in the desk, inside which they twisted into one and vanished in a hole in the wall. Ayingbi grabbed the bunched-up cables and gave a firm tug. Nothing happened—the three phone wires appeared to have the strength of a tree trunk together.

Frustrated and beaten, Ayingbi sat down, glaring at each phone in turn, saving Tuxedo for last.

She picked up the receiver and listened.

That airy whoosh again.

God, she hated it.

How much she hated it.

She imagined what Sonal from Merry Euphrosyne might do if she was left alone with Tuxedo, and immediately stopped imagining what Sonal might do if she was left alone with Tuxedo.

Sonal and Ribs. She'd forgotten about them.

Her thoughts once again strayed to Custard–Mustard.

And to Cocktail-Dress and Instox.

She thought about how much Barney's receiver looked like a brinjal, because it really did. All these phones were phallic. The blue, the purple and the black.

Enough of all this smutty thinking, Ayingbi firmly told herself. It was pointless.

It wasn't like Tuxedo was the shifty one.

The real thing was, all the phones were shifty.

Rastogi was unreliable, which made Phoenix unreliable.

Barney was unreliable too. Or maybe it wasn't. Ayingbi fixed Barney's wiring, hoping she hadn't messed up calls from coming through.

I'm the idiot in all this.

'Ayingbi?' came Hardy's soft call, from behind the curtain.

A wrapped submarine sandwich and butterscotch ice cream in a cup were lowered from a string over the wall.

'We'll take it up with Doc when he comes back, okay?' said Chatty. 'All of us. It's his thing to tell.'

'No need,' said Ayingbi. 'I'll take it up with him. You guys go. You've already been here way past your shifts.'

She wasn't angry at them anymore. Maybe they hadn't had any bad experiences with the third phone. Probably because they weren't dumb like her. Not having a bad experience with Tuxedo could have been as easy as simply ignoring it when it rang.

Ayingbi hoped they would understand her acceptance of the food as a peace offering.

It's Rastogi that owes me an explanation, not Hardy or Chatty.

There was an inherent comedy to all this, even if it took Ayingbi a while to see it.

She was potentially being stalked by a nutjob, she was probably being lied to by Rastogi and she most definitely had encountered a malevolent entity that wished her harm.

And here she was, unwrapping a sub like her life depended on it.

I'm going to sort out my own problems, starting right now, thought Ayingbi, munching on the meatball footlong.

Rastogi—she was going to confront him the moment he turned up. She would grill him from top to bottom about all of it—no exceptions.

The thing following her—if it cared enough—would reveal itself, and she would deal with it once it did. Perhaps, if her business with Rastogi concluded tonight, it would just leave her alone.

And like Hardy had said, there were hardly any psychopathic killers in India. Because there was no anomie and stuff.

Suggi was fine, they were all fine, and she'd gotten away just fine. There was nothing to identify Sir as a weirdo, per se. Ayingbi would officially stop being paranoid right away, because the evidence was sorely against it.

Which wasn't exactly true.

If Ayingbi had still been worried, she might have cared to look outside the window one last time.

And she just might've spotted a small purple hatchback car parked outside in the sea of vehicles, with a red learner sticker on the rear windshield and a blue carrier on its roof.

TEN

FLOOP

The whole day went by and Rastogi did not return.

By evening, Ayingbi's boredom and frustration had turned mildly self-destructive, and she impulsively decided to create an online dating profile for herself.

She made the profile as wilfully unattractive, needy and pathetic as possible, with a dreadful selfie to chase away the last man on Earth. Then she uploaded it. Ayingbi Mayengbam, aged twenty-nine, five-foot-four, was officially live on the singles market. Could the trade handle the heat? Could the local louts resist her bling?

She stood up, wiggling her bum triumphantly.

And a phone began to ring.

Dammit, thought Ayingbi, quickly dropping the whole act.

But it wasn't Barney.

Once again, the call was on Tuxedo.

Fuck that. I'm not picking it up again.

The euphoria of creating a silly dating profile shielded Ayingbi from a burst of panic. So, quite calmly, she began to pace around the empty office.

Tuxedo echoed dimly no matter to which corner of the lobby Ayingbi strutted. Its ringing seemed to fill the place up with unnatural stillness—as if the micro-movements of the real world had come to a halt.

Tuxedo rang for one . . . two . . . three whole minutes before stopping. It had rung for so long Ayingbi could still hear its phantom. Ayingbi casually helped herself to a Diet Coke from the fridge. As she was gulping it down, Tuxedo started to ring again.

Stubborn motherfucker, aren't you?

This time, Tuxedo rang longer than before. Four minutes . . . five now . . . six . . .

Give it up, homie. I'm not taking the call.

But Tuxedo persisted. Seven minutes . . . eight . . . nine . . . This test of wills was giving Ayingbi a headache.

There was no point in waiting. Unless Rastogi got back soon, which seemed unlikely, she'd be the only one in office for another couple of hours. She'd go mad if she had to listen to Tuxedo ringing for so long.

Ayingbi took a deep breath and took the call.

'Hello?'

She knew at once that this was it. It may not have been first contact, but it sure felt like it.

'Could've taken the call the first time, too, Susan.'

Cocktail-Dress's voice was light but sharp. Not quite the tone of a showdown Ayingbi had been expecting.

Breathe.

Just breathe, Bing–bee ma'am.

Ayingbi made a tense fist around the clenched receiver—her own little show of strength. 'What do you want? Who are you?'

Laughter in Cocktail-Dress's voice.

'Don't be scared, Susan. I'm a friend. You remember me, don't you?'

'Are you the thing that's been pursuing me?'

'*Pursuing* you? Pin-up girl that you are.'

'What do you want?'

'I don't want anything. Just saying hi.'

'It was you that called before, wasn't it? Why did you send me to Sir's house?'

'You want to save people, don't you, little Susan? Well, there was at least one soul in there worth saving. I don't think you helped them very much.' Then Cocktail-Dress's voice turned harsh. 'Nice account. I can tell you've been feeling lonely. I'd swipe right, not gonna lie. But if a great big cock in your pants could solve all your problems, I'd still be alive, you know what I mean?'

'What . . .' croaked Ayingbi.

And then the voice began to change.

The voice in transition was like nothing a voice ever was, or ever had been. It was like the words had been stitched together. A spoken version of a ransom note cut together from bits of newspaper, with a membrane of familiar voices glued on top.

'Hello!'

Ayingbi's hand cupped her mouth. It was the first voice Ayingbi had heard on a hotline, ever—Mrs Elelem.

Ayingbi's hand was now clutching Tuxedo's receiver so tightly her fingers felt chilly from lack of blood circulation.

'No time for further chit-chat, little Susan! I'm here for work. Now . . . another friend will call,' said the voice of Mrs Elelem.

'Custard–Mustard?' said Ayingbi stupidly.

'Not here. Over there. On the purple phone. Take the call, Susan. Take the call.'

Ayingbi wouldn't. Never in a million years would she come near this phone, or any of its ilk again, much less heed what they said.

'You will take the call, Susan. I know it,' said the voice of Mrs Elelem, as if reading her mind.

'Why?' whispered Ayingbi.

'Because if you do not, she's going to do it. And if you do not take this call, she will not ring again.'

Mrs Elelem's voice began to giggle. The sound was foreign to Ayingbi, because she had never heard Mrs Elelem giggling before.

'Don't feel lonely, Susan,' said Mrs Elelem's voice. 'You're not alone.'

Then the line went dead. Immediately, Barney began to ring on Tuxedo's right.

Take the call, Susan.

Ayingbi had not wanted to take a call less in her life.

People die every day, Ayingbi told herself forcefully. This is going to be another hoax. Another wacko in the city they're going to lead me to, and leave me there to die.

She considered the still-ringing Barney.

She will not ring again.

Fuck me, thought Ayingbi wearily, as she took the call. Just because she was taking the call didn't mean she had to act on it.

On the other end of the line, she could hear soft party music and distant chatter.

'Hello?' said Ayingbi warily. She could already feel her sense of responsibility towards the hotline, and Rastogi, withering away.

'H-h-h-h-hello . . .?'

Woman again. Voice thick with tears. Sounding drunk, too.

'Hello ma'am, thanks for calling. How are you doing this evening?'

'N-n-not too well, actually. I-I-I-I just need somebody to talk to.'

'Yes, that's why I'm here, ma'am.' Ayingbi was, of course, deeply mistrustful of the call and had every intention not to follow up on it once the receiver had been set down.

'I . . . I . . . can't keep doing this . . .' the woman snivelled.

Join the club, lady.

'It's my husband . . .'

'Your husband! What about him?' said Ayingbi dismissively.

'He . . . he . . . he . . . he . . .'

'He . . . yes? Yes?'

'He . . . he . . . I can't say it!' And there was a loud, elephant-trumpet of a nose being blown.

Ayingbi was so certain it was a trap that she fought the temptation of ridiculing and belittling the caller, if that, on the other end of the line. But, as always, the irksome professional in her stayed her hand.

'Go on,' she managed to say, more kindly this time.

'He . . . he . . . he . . . he . . .'

Ayingbi was supposed to avoid leading questions. But the woman hung on to that 'he' like a sloth from a branch.

'He beats you?! He cheats on you?!' said Ayingbi, finally caving in and going for the process of elimination. 'He's a drunk!'

'No, no, no,' moaned the woman. 'I'm stuck, and I fucking hate it, and I wish I would just fucking die. I've been doing this for eight years. I can't take another moment of it.'

Unexpectedly, another, somewhat distant, voice chirped up on the other end.

'Hellew, hellew, hellew! Muah, muah, muah!'

Ayingbi was startled. It sounded like another female had come up and started speaking to her client. Ayingbi could hear snatches of small talk. The caller gave a trilling giggle. The interregnum was awkward for Ayingbi, who just stood there with Barney's receiver to her ear.

So, assuming this was a genuine client, she was in a crowded place. She'd be just fine. She wouldn't kill herself. Not as long as she was still at the party. Probably.

A minute and a half later, the caller was back on the phone. The party music had dimmed further. It seemed she had walked further away to avoid being accosted again.

'Everyone is selfish! They're so selfish! Even if I kill myself, they won't care! It'll just be an inconvenience! An embarrassment!'

'What happened, ma'am?'

'I feel like I'm living inside this hamster ball that hasn't been cleaned in a while. I feel dirty. I cannot respect myself.'

'Mm.'

'Fucking ant.'

'Pardon?'

'Sorry, there's an ant in my glass. Let me fish it out. Jesus fucking Christ. Have you had many ants in your glass, miss?'

'Uh . . . I can't say that I have.'

'I've had so many, miss. So many.'

Two minutes into the call, and Ayingbi still had no idea what was going on. She hoped her client might find someone to drunk-cry on the shoulder of, and leave her alone.

'Sometimes they do things to me,' whispered the caller. 'Things I don't like. But I don't have a choice.'

'Who does?'

'I usually get myself as drunk as possible. That way, I can't really remember. Sometimes, I roofie myself. Is there a word for it? For roofie-ing yourself?'

'I don't know. Self-roofie?' suggested Ayingbi.

It seemed to perk the caller up. 'Self-roofie! Good one!' she said, even though it wasn't. Then she sighed and whispered, 'Maybe it'd be better if I died, you know? Better for everyone.'

'Look, madam, can I come over?' Ayingbi innocently suggested. It was her little test. If the caller called her over immediately, it would confirm Ayingbi's suspicions about this being another trap.

She scoffed, actually scoffed. 'And what will that accomplish?'

'Um.' Ayingbi was caught off-guard. She hadn't expected that. 'Maybe . . . some things are better in person.'

'There's no need. Look, maybe I just needed to vent, okay? I've vented enough, I think . . . okay, thank you . . . thank you for listening . . .'

'It'll help! I swear!'

'No, it'll be awkward.'

'Not at all!'

'I can't tell you where I am, I'm very sorry.'

'Whoa! Whoa! Hang on!' cried Ayingbi. 'Don't hang up yet!'

'What?'

'At least tell me what's wrong?'

'I just did . . . didn't I?'

Ayingbi checked the notes she automatically made for every call. 'No, you haven't, actually.'

'Ah, too many cosmos. Look, miss,' slurred the woman. 'You're probably just doing your job, and that's great. Maybe you are compassionate too. But the thing is, with or without this call, I'll be in the same position next month. I've crossed the point of no return. There is no salvation for me.'

Could this be a genuine case, wondered Ayingbi. Or another of the Entity's cruel, manipulative tricks?

'Just give me your address,' said Ayingbi. 'I'll see what I can do.'

'No, I don't want you to come.'

This was certainly new. Maybe the Entity was trying some reverse psychology. But just in case she decided to go, Ayingbi wanted the client's address at hand.

She also reminded herself that the phone call had come on Barney.

Barney had been legit until now . . . hadn't it?

The shady call taking her to Sir's house had come on Tuxedo . . .

Everyone calling on Barney had been real . . . But then again, you never knew. Nothing was real here, anyway.

Still, it would help to have an address.

'Please give me your address,' urged Ayingbi.

'No! We'll both get in trouble if you come here!'

'No, we won't,' said Ayingbi. 'Look, you called because you wanted help, right?'

'Why are you so hell bent on knowing where I am?'

Maybe this wasn't a trick, after all. Maybe it's just a routine call and I'm making a big deal about it for nothing.

Then Ayingbi remembered what the Entity had said:

She will not ring again. She's going to do it.

Ayingbi growled. She really needed this address. There was a push-and-pull of two voices in her head.

You're going to get yourself killed. And this time, you have nobody to blame but yourself.

'Look,' said Ayingbi. 'I won't call the police or do anything that embarrasses you. I'm just gonna drop by. It seems to me that you're in a crowded place, correct? You don't need to identify yourself or anything. And it really seems to me like you're upset about something.'

There was a long pause at the other end. 'Ah, what the heck. You're not going to be allowed in here, anyway.'

And then she gave Ayingbi the address, and she cut the call.

Ayingbi immediately picked up Tuxedo. Dead line again. Was that the call Tuxedo had wanted her to take?

Why did they think Ayingbi would take it for sure?

Fuck it, she thought. I'm not going.

She will not call again.

Nope, definitely not going.

She will not call again.

Ayingbi tilted her head back, and uttered a cry of despair.

Why? Why was she like this?

She patted her pockets and checked her handbag for her Scooty keys, before remembering she'd left it at home.

Maybe another reason to avoid going.

Ayingbi glanced at the address miserably.

Alright. She would go. And observe quietly from outside. Nothing stupid like last time. If there was a party in full swing when she got there, which was what it sounded like, she would quietly walk away.

In any case, this was Ayingbi's last night on the job. She would not retire cowering.

Ayingbi felt emotional on the cab ride over to the address the caller had given. She'd done well. She'd saved quite a few lives. Some good karma for when she died and was due for reincarnation.

The cab ride was not cheap—almost three hundred rupees! Ayingbi felt duped, but it was on the meter. She gnashed her teeth. She ought to charge Rastogi for this as well.

The taxi dropped her off by the gate of some new, very swanky apartments.

Ayingbi was sure the guard would terminate her quest then and there, but when she told him the address, he waved her in without any further questions.

Odd.

Ayingbi checked her watch. Eight-thirty. She wrapped her shawl round her head, put the sunglasses on, and walked in.

It was a plush colony. Expensive cars shone behind boom barriers. There was a swimming pool with a winding blue water slide, and a plexiglass gym. A park which looked like it had been carved out of a golf course. There were two symmetrical buildings—each fifteen or so storeys. Yuppie wealth, probably.

Even the apartment lobby smelt like a five-star hotel. Ayingbi thought of her own poor flat.

Even though there were many lifts, Ayingbi decided to take the stairs, wanting to retain full agency over her movements. The sound of tasteful Hindustani instrumental music grew louder with each floor.

On the stairs were well-dressed couples, smoking or holding drinks. Perhaps she'd been hasty on the yuppie wealth thing—most of these people looked in their mid-fifties.

Ayingbi grinned, putting on the expression of a resident trying to slink past as innocuously as possible. As part of her disguise, she'd worn jeans and a top, a bit of a change from the comfort wear she normally wore to work.

She found the apartment, and she knew it was the right one, because there was a relaxed dinner-and-drinks party going on inside. It was a mixed crowd, mainly, but not only, middle-aged uncles and aunties, and Ayingbi felt comfortable with the idea of walking in.

The front door was open, people were moving in and out. Nobody seemed to be checking who was going in. Maybe because it wasn't a large wedding—it would be absurd to break into a house party.

Maybe a quick pop-a-roo. In and out. Two minutes.

Ayingbi took off her shawl and sunglasses, walked inside, and was instantly struck with envy. Each square metre of the parlour was worth more than anything she owned. Beautiful statues, beautiful paintings, beautiful carpets, beautiful ottomans and divans, women in enchantingly lovely sarees. No waiters or waitresses—there was a self-service buffet counter and bar, behind which was a wall of frighteningly expensive-looking liquor. There were also colourful mattresses on the floor, on which people were playing board games.

There didn't seem to be a dress code. There were some people in casual wear, too.

Pretty strange.

Good for her, though, trying to blend in.

A middle-aged couple, rather well-matched, approached Ayingbi. The man was in a blue tuxedo, the woman was in a blue figure-hugging dress.

'You have your things, dear?' said the husband.

'Um, my things?'

'You know, the things in the invite?'

'Oh, I do!' said Ayingbi, loudly and confidently, and she was planning to make a show of rummaging inside her handbag, when another good-looking, silver-haired, grey-suited man swept in from the side and butted in—

'Of course, she has. She's my guest.'

The wife reached out and lifted Ayingbi's chin. 'Look at her, so pretty.'

The husband smiled at Ayingbi. 'Perhaps you and I will have a dance later.'

'Sounds good,' said Ayingbi, giving him double finger guns. The couple left. Soon, another woman in a lavender sari, also smelling of lavender, joined them.

'Hello! I am Mrs Wadhwa! This is my husband!' Mrs Wadhwa draped an arm on the shoulder of Ayingbi's rescuer. 'Welcome to our party!'

Ayingbi realized these were the hosts, and was startled to find herself welcomed without invitation.

'Isn't he handsome?' said Mrs Wadhwa, referring to Mr Wadhwa.

Weird question.

'You are a lucky woman, ma'am,' said Ayingbi.

Mrs Wadhwa pulled a picture from her phone and showed it to Ayingbi. 'This is us when we started dating.' The photo had what looked like Mr and Mrs Wadhwa as kids, both in grey-and-white uniforms.

'You started dating in school?'

Mrs Wadhwa looked at her husband fondly. 'We've been together since we were, what was it, darling—twelve?'

Mr Wadhwa grinned. 'Actually, it was more of a friends-with-benefits thing.'

Mrs Wadhwa burst out laughing, but Ayingbi found the joke so inappropriate she could manage no more than a weak smile.

Perhaps sensing her discomfort, Mrs Wadhwa placed a ring-encrusted hand on Ayingbi's shoulder. 'Oh, he's only joking, of course.'

Thank God.

'Yes . . .' said Mrs Wadhwa, suddenly going solemn. 'We were never really friends.'

'Please, help yourself,' said Mr Wadhwa. 'We'll meet again, later, I'm sure.' He winked at Ayingbi. 'Maybe we'll dance.'

'Uh . . . maybe we will,' said Ayingbi uncertainly. She looked around for a deejay or a dance floor, but couldn't find one.

Mr and Mrs Wadhwa walked away to another group of guests. Something hit Ayingbi on the cheek and bounced off. She caught it before it fell to the carpet—it looked like a small, bright red chip.

'Oh, sorry,' said a man in a billowy shirt and pork pie hat. 'Did I get you?' He'd just exploded a crab with a crab hammer. The buffet was fancy—this appeared to be the seafood counter, with oysters, crabs, lobster and all kinds of fish.

He took the crab shell from Ayingbi, put some crab on a plate and handed it to her. 'Here, try some.'

Not wanting to look out of place, Ayingbi tried it. The flesh was sweet and juicy.

'Tasty, right?' said the man. 'It's better with a dash of vinegar.'

'It is,' said Ayingbi. 'Thanks.'

'Maybe,' said the man, 'you and I will have a dance later.'

Ayingbi blinked. It was getting weird now. 'Uh, I'll have to think about it . . . Please excuse me.' She shuffled off to a side, crossing another row of strange snacks—gingko, ginseng, rocket leaves. Did anyone actually eat these things by themselves?

There were at least six empty bedrooms that Ayingbi checked before scoping out the balconies.

On one of them, she found her.

She was wearing a chiffon halter-neck with a ribboned lilac sash and purple sunglasses, raised into a headband.

'Hey,' said Ayingbi.

'Hey.'

Yes. Yes, it was her.

'You know who I am?' said Ayingbi.

The woman shook her head.

'We spoke on the phone . . . earlier?'

'Oh . . . jeez . . . ' said the woman. Her face crumpled slightly. 'You actually came here . . . oh, jeez . . . you shouldn't've . . .'

'No, it's okay,' said Ayingbi kindly. 'That's what I'm supposed to do.'

'You don't understand,' whispered the woman, taking Ayingbi's hand. 'You shouldn't've come *here*. Leave, please.'

'Why? What's over here?'

'My husband, for a start.'

'Which one is he?'

The woman led her inside, surreptitiously. 'You see that man? It's him.'

It was the gentleman in the pork-pie hat, now standing in a group.

'Him?' Ayingbi supposed abusers came in all shapes and sizes. The husband had a party face on, and he did seem charismatic, in a cut-up kind of way. The angle of the group was subtly positioned towards him, and the others looked entertained in his company.

'He's actually shot me before,' shrugged the woman, as though it were nothing. 'Or at me. He missed.'

'Were you going to kill yourself if I hadn't come?'

'I think so, yes,' said the woman. 'Four floors is plenty.'

The fuck?

Actually, as Ayingbi recalled, three was plenty if you were a cat.

'I wish people were kind and empathetic,' said the woman. 'I want to run away from this world. I wish society was better. It's a fool's paradise, and I don't want to live in it anymore.'

Ayingbi wished she didn't have to engage intellectually so many times. She felt powerless whenever that happened. Much philosophy around the final sin ultimately boiled down to a personal, unfalsifiable meaning of life, often developed over a lifetime to the point of ossification, leaving little scope for argument or rebuttal.

'I didn't think you'd be . . . ah . . . you know, Asiatic . . . Like a mongoloid,' said the woman, as if she was looking for a politically correct term, and this was what she had come up with.

Ayingbi shrugged.

'He makes me wear a halter-neck,' said the woman. 'You just pull this knot right here . . .' she tapped a knot at the back of her neck, '. . . and FLOOOP! My tatas fall right out. Saves time, you see. FLOOOOP!'

Ayingbi frowned at her. Tatas? Floop? What? It took her a moment to understand what the woman was probably talking about.

'I'm not wearing a bra,' said Floop.

You don't say.

Floop was very skinny. Her halter-neck showed quite enough of her stiff, teardrop-shaped breasts, separated by two inches of bony cleavage. Floop? She was flattering herself. Cocktail-Dress? Now there was a Floop, if Ayingbi had ever seen one.

'I hate it. I hate my life,' said Floop. 'I hate what he forces me to do.'

'What does he force you to do?'

'I don't like doing it. But he makes me take part in these things.'

Floop was being, in Ayingbi's opinion, extremely uncommunicative.

'Go seek a divorce,' said Ayingbi woodenly. 'Get help.'

'It isn't just that life is unfair. It's that it is so consistently, methodically, perfectly unfair,' said Floop. 'What's there to tell? These people anyway think spousal abuse is totes adorbs.'

Ayingbi, however, was no longer listening. She'd just noticed a car in the parking below.

A purple hatchback with blue carrier. She looked for the red sticker on the back and spotted it.

It was like the world had gone dim. Somewhere, Ayingbi could hear Floop still talking, but it sounded like it was from another galaxy.

The car was parked there. Right. There.

Terror, sheer terror, lit up her entire nervous system like a Christmas tree.

Sir was here.

Sir had followed her.

But . . . how . . . why?

'Oh . . . fuck . . . oh . . . fuck . . .' Ayingbi's legs gave way and she collapsed to the balcony floor.

'Hey, you okay?' said Floop, whose own mood seemed to have improved in Ayingbi's company.

Ayingbi clung to Floop's shins, feeling herself capitulating to her weakest instincts. She couldn't reply—she began to stammer. She had never known she could stammer like this, to be so out of control.

'You're white!' said Floop. 'Here, don't worry. I haven't roofied it yet.' She handed Ayingbi the drink she'd balanced on the handrail. Ayingbi drank. She was not herself. She needed support.

'I think . . . I think someone's here to kill me,' Ayingbi squeaked. She was used to being the supportive one, hero of the hour. What was this?! All her worst fears were coming true—Sir was here. He had managed to track her down, after all. In spite of all of Chatty and Hardy's assurances.

She heard Floop say, 'Do you need help? Do you want me to call somebody?' Immediately, Ayingbi felt small and feeble, with the roles reversed. She had no idea what Sir even looked like.

I'm never leaving this place alive.

This is the last place I'll ever know.

I'll be murdered in these apartments.

He can't kill me in here, thought Ayingbi, and she promptly crawled to her feet and tottered back into the palatial parlour. She had already forgotten all about Floop, who escorted her inside.

I'm not going down without a fight.

Ayingbi pilfered a steak knife from the buffet table and shoved it inside her handbag.

'Hey, do you want to call the police?' said Floop. Her concern for Ayingbi's situation was moving, but Ayingbi was still too scared witless to acknowledge it.

Does he know I'm in here? Does he have eyes on me right now?

Ayingbi felt sick. Feverish. She wanted to vomit.

I might be using that, she thought, regarding the knife. *Imagine.*

'Attention, attention! Everybody! Could you all step in for a moment? This is going to be fun, I promise!'

It was the host, Mr Wadhwa, who had spoken. The call was repeated, and the few people lurking in the balconies or bedrooms strolled back in.

Mr Wadhwa was grinning. 'It would seem, ahem, we have a bit of a situation on our hands.'

'I got extras in all sizes! B-Y-O-C!' someone chimed, and everyone, for some reason, laughed.

'No, no, we are sorted on that front,' said Mr Wadhwa. 'Thing is, there were fifty-five people on the guest list. But there are fifty-six of us here in total. It would seem there is a gatecrasher among us.'

Well, fuck, thought Ayingbi. Who even keeps tabs on numbers at a party? But it surprised her that they did not know she was the gatecrasher. Were these people also strangers to each other? Were some of them also strangers to the hosts? What kind of party was this?

She could feel Floop's reassuring hand on her shoulder. It was nice that Floop wasn't a snitch.

'Correction, dear,' said the Mrs Wadhwa. 'We had that one pull-out, remember?'

'Just the one? Dear me, we must be careful.'

And again, for some reason, there was laughter.

Mr Wadhwa, too, chuckled. 'Well, well, the plot thickens. So that means . . . fifty-four people on the guest list . . . and a total of fifty-six people present. This means that our gatecrasher friend brought a buddy.'

Ayingbi had heard the expression about people nearly soiling themselves in fear. It had always seemed like hyperbole—right until the point her host dropped that line.

Her legs began to quake.

Oblivious to her predicament, the host was still smiling.

'Naturally, these people thought they'd come in here for some fancy grub and high-end bubbly. Nobody was asking any questions.'

And Mrs Wadhwa slammed the front door shut. Ayingbi's heart was hammering so hard she thought it might pop the buttons off her shirt. She tipped against a sofa to steady herself. Floop gave Ayingbi an inquiring, what-do-you-want-to-do kind of look.

'I don't believe they plan on identifying themselves . . .' grinned Mr Wadhwa. 'So, I think . . . it's time to play a little game . . . to seek them out . . . maybe have them introduce themselves . . .'

Ayingbi's face swam from one guest to the other. They all looked excited. Eager at the prospect of games.

'Dark Room?' someone said.

An immediate clamour of ayes.

Ayingbi was not sure how playing Dark Room would help unmask a gatecrasher, and she certainly didn't think being in a darkened room with Sir would be in her best interest either.

'Noor?' said Mr Wadhwa.

Noor, a tube-dress-clad woman in her early-forties, was at the switchboard, one leg folded backwards, a hand covering her giggling mouth.

The light clicked off, and there was darkness. Giggles and rustles. Even the smacks of a few stolen kisses.

'The thing is,' came Mr Wadhwa's voice, 'they don't know what we do here. Noor?'

The light clicked back on. Everyone had removed their shoes. Realizing not doing so might out her, Ayingbi hurriedly slipped out of her own footwear.

'Oh, oh . . .' said Mr Wadhwa, after glancing around at everyone's feet. 'No matter, no matter. Let's try again.'

The lights went out again. When Noor turned them on fifteen seconds later, the men had taken off their socks, the women had undone their hair.

In spite of her terror, something about it unnerved Ayingbi. Exactly what the hell was going on? And as her eyes were flying from face to face, trying to fathom the cause of delight, she saw him, all the way across the room.

He'd made eye contact for a fraction of second before looking away. He was much shorter than she'd imagined, with hazel eyes, crew cut and a pointed chin.

The lights were off again, and this time, they stayed off for much longer. More jostling, more shuffling.

When Noor turned the lights on again, the floor was glinting. Everyone had removed their watches and jewellery and laid them at their feet. Some had tucked them neatly into their footwear.

Sir, meanwhile, had stealthily moved two places closer to Ayingbi. And then the lights were gone again, and she could see him no more. Nor anyone else. But she needn't have worried about not seeing the others well enough.

When the lights came on the next time, Ayingbi's jaw dropped. It was not the only thing to have dropped.

'They really didn't know what kind of party this was,' giggled the host, very hairy-chested and hairy-armed.

Everyone had taken their tops off and laid them neatly in a pile at their feet. They were grinning at each other, some shamefacedly, some lustily, some longingly.

Ayingbi realized she might be late and, hurriedly, tugged her top off too. The insanity of what was going on had only just occurred to her . . .

Meanwhile, Sir had moved three steps closer. He, too, seemed to have cottoned on to the game and taken his own shirt off, revealing a very lean and muscular torso that had already gained admirers, both male and female. Like some horrible horror movie monster, the character kept inching closer every time the lights clicked on.

Then the lights were off again.

Fuck.

Fuck. Fuck. Fuck. Fuck. Fuck.

Ayingbi willed herself out of her paralysis and began to gently move backwards through the pitch darkness, speculating what clothing they might be required to remove next.

That was the game.

It had to be the lowers.

It had to be.

She heard belts being unbuckled—a merciful giveaway—and slipped out of her jeans just as the light came back on.

It was gorgeous. It was absurd. The missing links of Floop's story finally began to fall into place.

There stood Ayingbi in her undergarments. As did everyone else. She could see erections rising in their tighty-whities, eye contact was made, partners were chosen. Sarees in different stages of being peeled off, some women were already working on their blouses—pins unpinned, buttons unbuttoned.

The smell of human flesh, sweaty and perfumed, began to permeate the parlour.

Ayingbi could not believe the situation. One moment, she had thought she was going to die. She had never suspected that in the next, she might be gamely participating in a geriatric orgy. This explained why the watchman had been paid off to not ask questions . . . this was obviously something that had been organized in secret . . .

The lights were off again, before Ayingbi could see how close Sir had gotten. Maybe she could shimmy to the other side of the room in the dark. What next?

There wasn't much left, to be honest.

Praying that she would be wrong, Ayingbi reached back and unhooked her bra. The lights returned, and all manner of nipples—protruding from all shapes and sizes of breasts and chests—were staring back at Ayingbi. Big ones, little ones, flat ones, pokey ones, all shades from orange to pink to purple to brown, like a second set of eyes below the first.

Heck, even back home at Manipur, it's not unusual for women to wander around topless all the time.

Ayingbi let her bra drop in front of a crowd of fifty-five other people. People were looking at each other without embarrassment.

Maybe there was something comfortingly human in communal nudity.

Ayingbi was blushing furiously.

Blushing?

Five minutes ago, she'd been scared to death.

My blushing itself is a tell, thought Ayingbi. Was this a cult? Would they tell her to leave with a pat on the bum if they caught her, or something much worse?

The light went off again. Ayingbi sighed. There was only one thing left to remove, anyway. More jostling. Ayingbi could feel hairy elbows moving against her, and she fought the urge to swat them away. Was it Sir? Was he already here?

Ayingbi wondered if she could cling onto her modesty one last time. She couldn't. She took her panties off, face burning with embarrassment, and picked her feet out of the holes. Even in the dark, Ayingbi could sense the anxiety to let it all commence. Perhaps all this was sexy. Fun detective games and the promise of intercourse. Who knew? The light came back on.

Only two men, excluding her father, had ever seen Ayingbi in a state of total undress in her life, and none in the past three years. This was traumatic. Ayingbi stared determinedly at her inward-pointed toes, crimson-faced, praying she wouldn't be asked to partner up.

Naked.

So naked.

Many eyes were on her. Penises, in various stages of arousal, some wilting already, others stiff enough to hang a purse on.

Ayingbi looked around frantically—Sir was nowhere to be seen.

Goosebumps rose on Ayingbi's flesh. A man, perhaps in his fifties, seemed to notice the goosebumps rise. He stared shamelessly, made eye contact with Ayingbi and gave a creepily paternal smile.

Ayingbi immediately backed away.

She had a sideways look at Floop, who had taken off her clothing most mechanically. Her tatas had indeed popped out, though Ayingbi might've missed the 'flooop!' in the dark.

Meanwhile, the rhythm of foreplay had begun, a concupiscent obstacle course for Ayingbi to weave through across the parlour. She kept bumping into calves and buttocks and shins—they were soft and pleasant to bump into.

Chosen couples had begun to kiss; through the window of their pressed open mouths, Ayingbi could see tongues squirming against each other. One short-haired woman had begun to massage a man's erection. Human scent was clearer without clothing, emanating from the folds and crevices of skin where the scent glands were now exposed. Inhibitions were unravelling, the veneer of gentility being cast aside as biology took over; women were tossing their hair and men were shrugging their shoulders . . . and there, in the middle of it all, stood Ayingbi.

She remembered they didn't have a dress code.

Quite the contrary.

Humans were easier to label as animals without clothes on. Different heights and patterns of body hair and shades of skin.

Ayingbi caught herself marvelling at how different people looked without clothes on than with, at how different breasts looked, how dissimilar penises were, and then she swore to look everyone in the eye. She could hear consent and boundaries being negotiated through the most primal grunts, coos and whispers.

Some had begun to take the tables, others the mattresses, drawers were thrown open and containers of condoms, drugs and who knew what else pulled loose. The Potemkin of upper-crust propriety tipped over in favour of the salacious. The synthetic smell of flavoured prophylactics joined that of sweat and perfume.

And before she knew it, as she wandered through the swirl of writhing bodies, her eyes met a hazel pair, and Sir was standing right in front of her.

This time, their eyes stayed met.

Sir raised a knife, sharp and serrated, as Ayingbi stood looking gormless.

Another hairy hand blocked the blow. Assailant and Ayingbi both looked sideways to see her saviour. It was him—Floop's husband. He appeared to be yelping something.

Sir whipped around and slashed the knife—plunging it into the man's shoulder. A tiny sputter of blood burst forth. But the husband was strong, too. His fist found Sir's jaw. Sir was knocked back, right into Ayingbi.

It took a while before others could tell anything wrong was happening—they supposed one of the infiltrators had been apprehended, that was about it.

Ayingbi fell, her spinning arms finding a sprig of long, coarse white pubic hair to break her fall.

'Ow!' yelled the much older gent.

One woman in her thirties, who had already wedged her face between his drooping buttocks, looked sideways.

First came a gasp, and then a scream. Some more lovemaking couples looked around, stunned as they finally noticed the blood.

Sir turned back to Ayingbi.

Two low bangs rang out through the parlour. Ayingbi looked around wildly for the source, and saw a grim-looking Mr Wadhwa holding a stumpy, smoking pistol. He looked furious.

Sir's end came, just like that.

The naked gathering jumped as a whole, and Ayingbi fell backwards into two or three people. She could feel the tangle of bare flesh, torsos and thighs. A mass of human flesh, still warm with lust, soft and oddly comfortable to topple backwards into.

Three people had been hit with Sir's blood.

Then the screaming began.

It was dit-dot-dash from there. Ayingbi saw the scene as though it were in five-frames-per-second: people yelling, screaming, dressing as quickly as they could, stampeding towards the exit. She saw Floop howling over her husband, who was lying in a pool of blood.

It was only in the mass exodus that Ayingbi realized she was still naked. Still numb from shock, she too dressed.

Before leaving the apartment, she took one final look at Sir. His hazel eyes had already glassed over. Blood was bubbling out of two bullet holes on either side of his chest. The man was as dead as could come.

Ayingbi stumbled out of the apartment and down the stairs. On the third floor she collapsed—overwhelmed by terror, by the sheer madness of it all, by joy and gratitude at her own survival, and she burst into tears.

ELEVEN

METHOD TO THE SADNESS

Ayingbi hoped she might have a little time on her hands before someone raised an alarm proper. The party hosts might want to clean the place up first, dispose of the contraceptives and aphrodisiacs, dress the scene of crime as a regular old party—not an orgy for middle-aged millionaires. But the gunshot would've been heard in the other flats too.

Ayingbi knew she couldn't stay. Already, she could hear the vroom of vehicles leaving the colony at top speed—it sounded like a street race had just been flagged off. She used the commotion to quietly slip out and call a taxi.

She would have to go back to the office one last time to get her things.

On the taxi ride, she quietly blocked Rastogi's number, and then, with some thought, Hardy and Chatty's, too. She was no longer curious—she was simply done with all of it. She also fretted about Suggi, who had seemed very devoted to Sir. How would she react if she figured he had died in his pursuit of Ayingbi? Wait, had Suggi come with Sir too?

Another spasm of fear jolted up Ayingbi's spine, and she reached inside her purse to grip the filched knife for reassurance.

It was numbing to realize her fears had not been an exaggeration.

Back at the office, even though the two-man night shift had begun, nobody was home. Rastogi still wasn't back, and perhaps Hardy and Chatty had both gone for follow-ups.

Without dawdling, Ayingbi scooped up her laptop and phone charger, and swept her hand around all corners of the drawers to check she'd left nothing behind.

And then, as she was on her way out, one of the phones started to ring. Ayingbi had enough experience now to recognize the ring as Barney's.

She closed her eyes, one foot literally outside the cubicle.

She was exhausted. She was in no shape or position to be taking calls.

But wait! It wasn't her shift! Why had the call come to her?! Ayingbi realized that when she'd gone for Floop, in her troubled state of mind, she'd forgotten to flip the silver switch. Which meant, for call purposes, she was still in office.

What the fuck are you doing? Take it! yelled a firm voice in Ayingbi's mind—the control centre of logic, reason and decency that never left her, even when matters were at their direst. In any case, she was quitting without giving notice.

And so Ayingbi took the call, careful not to let her weariness slip through. 'Hello! Thanks for calling. How are you doing right now?'

'Not too well, dear.' Male voice. Deep and rich. Baritone-y. 'Not too well at all.'

Wait til' you hear how my day was.

'Now, before you give me your spiel, your magician's patter, whatever,' said Barry Tony. 'Just know that I've heard it all. Every day is a blessing, blah, blah. Deep down, we all know it's bullshit. Most people aren't fussed about living. Life is a revolving door of twenty problems. They're holding on by a thread that has nothing to do with their own happiness.'

'If you called, sir, you must've known there was a spiel coming.'

'I didn't come for the spiel. I came for something else.'

'What's that, sir?'

'I'm taking a chance on you. You're my only way of knowing.'

'Knowing what?'

'That I still matter.'

'Of course you matter!' said Ayingbi, overcompensating lack of conviction with force.

'Well, you'll be able to prove it in just a moment.'

Ayingbi did not want to prove anything. She just wanted Barry Tony's assurance that he'd be all right, so she could put the phone down and go home. She decided to knock out the drill, or as Barry Tony put it—the 'spiel'.

'Have you contacted your—'

'Yeah, yeah, it's all the same to them. People pretend to care. Maybe they *do* care, but only up to a point. It's never not cosmetic.'

Ayingbi thought it was a relief Barry Tony had such a lovely voice, because he would probably be quite miserable to know in person.

'Tell me, dear,' said Barry Tony. 'Do these suicide hotline calls actually help anyone?'

'Yeah, loads of people.'

'What, do they call again and give you feedback?'

'Er . . . not exactly. They don't call back.'

'That could mean two things.'

'Well, we hope it's one, and not the other.'

'Pretty optimistic.'

'Um, we drop things off on a positive note, and if they're calling, it usually means they want help. It means they don't plan on doing it.'

Barry Tony was quiet. 'Is that so?'

'It is.'

'What about in real life? The people you know? Did it get better for them?'

'I don't know anyone else who's been suicidal.'

'What about for you?'

'I haven't been suicidal, either, sir.'

'No?' Barry Tony seemed surprised. 'Then how did you get this job?'

'Uh, you don't need to have been suicidal to work at a crisis hotline, sir.'

'Oh, I thought you'd have to. Wearer knows where the boot fits, that sort of thing. Anyway, I want to die. I'm on the verge of doing it.'

Ayingbi listlessly spat out the usual arguments, but Barry Tony kept batting them all aside.

Maybe you can SPITE your enemies by living.

'Please don't?' said Ayingbi, out of options. 'No reason not to. Just don't.'

'That,' said Barry Tony, 'I leave up to you. You get to decide if I live or die.'

'Well then, sir, you live.'

'No, not like that.'

And then, Ayingbi heard a gun cock, and all her fatigue and frustration vanished like a puddle on a hot skating rink.

'You hear that?' Barry Tony whispered. 'Nine-millimetre, Smith and Wesson. It has one round inside it.'

Ayingbi stiffened. 'What?'

'Who am I?'

'What?'

'Who am I?'

'I . . . er . . . you're the gentleman who just called.'

Barry Tony gave an impatient tch. 'What's my name?'

'Er . . .' Ayingbi pretended to shuffle papers. 'I'm sure you told me, sir, I think I wrote it down somewhere.'

'No, I didn't.'

'Um, are you asking if we have caller ID? We aren't tracing this call.'

'I haven't told you who I am, dear, and I don't think some call tracking app has, either. But I gather from your tone, you don't know.'

Ayingbi attempted a shifty, apologetic chuckle. 'No, sir. Ahahaha . . . You got me. I don't.' She relaxed her squeeze on Barney's receiver, praying that somewhere, the same was being done to a trigger.

Give me a break, dammit. I'm tired, I'm tired, I'm just so tired right now.

'Please don't . . .' she heard herself whisper.

Now Barry Tony was laughing. 'I am one hell of a narcissistic prick, aren't I? Putting you, an innocent girl, in this situation?'

'HINT!' bellowed Ayingbi. 'Give me a hint!'

No reply.

'HARDY!' yelled Ayingbi, to the office at large. 'CHATTY! DR RASTOGI! ANYBODY!'

Nothing.

'Oh God . . . oh God . . . oh God . . .' Ayingbi began to feverishly babble, feeling some of the sense leave her as it dawned that this might really be happening.

Then Barry Tony spoke. 'Sorry, I'd gone to get a sip of water.' He cleared his throat. 'Well then, you were saying.'

'Let's talk about something else, sir!' yelled Ayingbi. 'Tell me about your family! You must have kids! Friends! Imagine them! Imagine them learning about what you're doing!'

'Don't guilt trip me, dear. I'm divorced, drunk and my kids don't give a shit. There. I made mistakes. I can't take them back. I'd kill to take them back, but I can't. I can't live with them, either.'

'Talk about your divorce! What happened there?!'

'I don't want to talk about my divorce. I just asked you who I am, and you said you didn't know. That's all I wanted to know, really.'

'I'm sorry!' bawled Ayingbi. 'I'm really sorry.'

'Don't be. It's all right.'

'Please . . . Please . . .' sobbed Ayingbi. 'Please . . . don't kill yourself.'

There was no voice from the other end.

'Are you crying?' Barry Tony sounded surprised.

'Y-yes,' sniffed Ayingbi, surprised to discover that indeed she was. She gave a great hiccup. Could this possibly be a way out?

'Even though you don't know who I am.'

'Y . . . yes, sir,' said Ayingbi earnestly. 'Somebody cares, sir.'

'You really don't want me to kill myself, do you?'

'N-no. Not at all.'

'It would distress you if I pulled the trigger right now.'

'Yes, sir. Very much so, sir.'

'In that case,' said Barry Tony quietly. 'I would suggest you put the phone down.'

Ayingbi screamed as the sound of the gunshot pierced the room.

*

In the morning the day after the next, there were two news items of interest.

Ayingbi had barely managed to read them through the blur of her own tears.

One of them was about the murder of a businessman, right in the middle of a crowded dinner party in an upscale apartment. The perpetrator had apparently also been killed in the struggle. The police investigation had led them to the perpetrator's house, where his maid had been found dead, apparently of her own doing. A media storm had followed, and many facts revealed that the murder had come under the most suspicious circumstances. Nobody knew why the stranger had been allowed entry into a secure gated colony, or why the cameras happened to be off at the time. Nobody could establish any clear connection between perpetrator and victim. And more interestingly, it appeared the scene of crime had been heavily tampered with, before the police had arrived. More and more such details dropped over the next few days, ensuring the case stayed in the limelight.

With one sensational case capturing a bulk of the public consciousness, the other story would fly relatively under the radar—the suicide of a 1980s Bollywood playback singer. He had sung over two thousand songs in five different languages. His devotional tracks were still played on old PA systems at local festivals and fairs. His voice was regarded as utterly distinctive. One of a kind, really. The suicide had stoked the usual debates on mental health and the plight of washed-up entertainers, but Ayingbi had no interest in any of them.

Her bedsheets had been soaked with her own tears for the past two days.

No doubt, this was what the Entity had wanted all along—to get her like this, miserable and depressed.

It was not until five days later when Ayingbi, starving and sleep-deprived, finally decided to take a bath.

When she stripped and stepped in front of the mirror, it was like looking at someone else.

Her body had shrunk.

Somehow, dropping five kilos had given her an additional chin. She'd had an acne breakout on the neck and between the collarbones. Her purple eye bags appeared to be retracting inward, making her eyes look raccoon-like. There were stretch marks too, on her shoulders and bottom—non-parallel striations of cream and hazel that she definitely did not have earlier.

Ayingbi messed up her hair and bared her teeth in the mirror, trying to stretch this self-diagnosed unattractiveness to its limits.

She immediately opened the medicine cabinet and began rummaging for cosmetics she could haphazardly throw on. She emptied nearly the entire cabinet when she found something tucked away at the back.

A dried-up daffodil. Where did that come from, she wondered, as she threw it out the window.

When she stood in front of the mirror again, intending to dramatically scribble lipstick all over her face, something happened.

The brownish stretch marks on her shoulder began to wiggle . . . and shimmer . . . like a nest of maggots. Then they began to move around, braiding into each other, forming shapes—recognizable ones. A huge head . . . with horns . . . tiny torso . . . arms . . . legs . . . Or maybe, the stretch marks weren't moving at all, and she was only imagining it. Either way, moments later, the stretch marks had twisted and knitted into what looked like a very ugly birthmark. Squinting, Ayingbi could just about make out the form of the ugly Teeterling from Dr Rastogi's desk.

Ayingbi blinked at Stretch-Mark Teeterling.

Two stretch marks parted in a toothy smile. 'You don't blame yourself for Barry Tony's death, do you, Susan?'

'It wasn't my fault,' said Ayingbi squarely. 'I'm not responsible for that.' She didn't think it was really there; she knew a lot of it was hunger and insomnia, but she was just going along with it.

Stretch-Mark Teeterling scampered around the back of her neck to the other shoulder. 'I know you're hurting,' it said quietly.

That's what it wants, thought Ayingbi feverishly, remembering what a Teeterling was. *It wants me to be depressed and kill myself.*

The idea that someone wanted her to kill herself was not nearly as frightening as it was saddening. Maybe that was the devilish final trick to be pulled here. It wasn't going to happen—but Ayingbi had spent so much time guarding against it, it kept popping up in her head unhealthily.

'If you could choose not to exist, Susan, would you do it?' said Stretch-Mark Teeterling. 'If you were to snap your fingers, like—that—would you do it?'

Ayingbi knew she must not let the creature get inside her head, but the walls of her mind had been softened by pain and grief, and in spite of her better judgment, she found herself indulging it.

'I guess,' said Ayingbi. If ever there had been a time in Ayingbi's life when she felt like not existing, this was it.

'Then you could probably do it,' whispered Stretch-Mark Teeterling. 'It's just a chore to get through. Let me help you. I can list out all the painless ways . . .'

'Give it a rest, will you?' said Ayingbi loudly. 'I'm not going to kill myself. I just feel like garbage, okay? Lots of people feel that way, and they aren't fucking killing themselves!'

Stretch-Mark Teeterling dove from Ayingbi's shoulder, funnelling neatly between her cleavage, swinging pole-like from her navel, straight into her panties.

Then it reappeared over her left hip. 'Woof, that coochie cold. Like the lips of an Arctic cod. Didn't get many replies on hump-and-dump-dot-com, did you?'

Ayingbi had forgotten all about that dating-app account she'd made.

'Maybe you think you're a heroine,' went on Stretch-Mark Teeterling. 'But you really haven't saved anyone. You haven't even saved yourself. You just pushed them all back into misery. The ones you couldn't save . . . well, they're the ones thanking you right now.'

Ayingbi gave a dry sob. 'Shut up.'

There was no reply. Ayingbi looked around—Stretch-Mark Teeterling had gone—the brownish striations did not appear to be moving anymore.

Ayingbi looked at herself and shook her head.

Fuck this.

Fuck everything.

In the filled bathtub, Ayingbi closed her eyes, wishing she could just go to sleep and never wake up again. She felt her fingers joylessly caressing the valley between her thighs, looking for any form of physical relief.

'Ooh. Shiny. Are you thinking about the dead guy?' she heard a voice say.

Stretch-Mark Teeterling was back. It was on her knee now, grinning down.

Ayingbi swatted her knee, but Stretch-Mark Teeterling had already appeared on the opposite one. 'Bet using all those rotary phones is paying off now, huh?' He wiggled his spidery fingers with a wicked grin.

Ayingbi slapped the other knee, too. This time, Stretch-Mark Teeterling really was gone, and there were big red palm-shaped welts on both her knees.

Ayingbi sighed and listlessly finished her bath.

Chatty and Hardy hadn't tried to contact her at all—which was obvious, since she'd blocked the number of everyone at the office, but it hurt that there hadn't seemed to be a dedicated effort from their end.

As a small consolation, Ayingbi finally did find sleep that night.

She dreamt of humpback whales. She wasn't sure what they looked like or how to distinguish them from other types of whales, but she mumbled it to herself first thing when she woke up—'I dreamt of humpback whales.'

It also occurred to her, the following day, that she did not know the number of the hotline where she had worked for over a month. She knew Rastogi's number, of course, but she didn't know what someone might have to dial, for instance, for Barney to ring.

She looked it up. There was a barebones website for Good Morning Helpline, with an office address and a hotline number.

The hotline number given there was Rastogi's personal mobile.

So, for appearances, and perhaps legal purposes, it seemed like Rastogi had fronted his personal number as the hotline itself. So what number, then, would someone have to dial, for Barney to ring? Or the other hotline phones—the ones Chatty and Hardy were using?

It made no sense.

Ayingbi then looked up 'suicide hotline'.

A big number blared on the screen, assuring her that help was available. Ayingbi chewed on her lip.

This wasn't suicide ideation. She was merely becoming obsessed with the general concept and was worried that too much interest might become a slippery slope. But maybe mental health could be in the absolute pits without it being an emergency.

Ayingbi rang up the number. It was taken by a feathery female voice.

'Hello, thank you for calling. This is Suchismita.'

Ayingbi never used to identify herself by name on the phone. There weren't many Ayingbis. Moreover, she didn't want to confuse the caller on the very first beat with an uncommon name. You wanted to open with the comfort of the familiar, or so the Merry Euphrosyne handbook had advised.

'Hi,' said Ayingbi. She'd have to make up some lame story now. 'Um, I'm depressed.'

'I am here, ma'am. Would you like to talk about it?'

'Yeah, sure,' said Ayingbi. 'So, I signed up for a summer job, hoping to make a difference in other people's lives. But it wasn't what I was expecting—'

'What were you expecting?'

'Well, I knew it would be tough. But I didn't think I'd be lied to and deceived by the people I was working with.'

'How did they deceive you?'

'I won't get into that,' said Ayingbi. 'But because work was so emotionally gruelling, I allowed myself to be vulnerable around them. Big mistake. I almost died a few times, and these people probably had an idea that something like it might happen, but they didn't care to warn me at all.'

'Oh . . . have you tried to harm yourself?'

'No. Someone else has, though.'

'Who?'

'A shadowy wraith—a skinny maid—and her boss.'

'Sorry, a what?'

'A skinny maid.'

'And before that?'

'A shadowy wraith.'

'A shadowy wraith?'

'Yes.'

'Like a spectral, demon-type figure?'

'Precisely. Maybe it's still trying to kill me. I'm not sure.'

'Right. Right. And their boss?'

'No, only the skinny maid's boss.'

The shadowy wraith itself was self-employed.

'I see,' said the operator. She was being patient with her. No doubt, she'd been instructed to tolerate all kinds of nonsense.

Ayingbi realized she was wasting the nice lady's time, so she quickly said she'd be fine and cut the call.

Hearing a voice on the other line, for the first time, presented Ayingbi with another uncomfortable truth— something she'd known to be true, that she badly missed taking calls.

Yes, it was true that Barry Tony had died, but that objectively wasn't on her, and she wasn't going to punish herself for it any longer. Ayingbi had enough faith in herself to know that people could trust her. She had become quite good at it, too—she knew where Suchismita, during their brief chat, had faltered, and how her handling of Ayingbi's call could have been improved.

Most of all, Ayingbi missed the exhilaration of talking someone off the ledge, persuading them to give everything a second chance. But she couldn't admit it too emphatically either.

That moment, crossed between the limbo of the terrible things she'd gone through, and the realization she was missing them made Ayingbi feel worse than she ever had in her life.

There was a knock on the door.

Ayingbi opened it.

Her landlady.

Ayingbi's mind jumped to her rent date, but then her landlady pressed a steel tiffin box into her hands. Ayingbi numbly opened one end and saw the yellow humps of rows of laddoos, sprinkled with green pistachio bits. She stood there, trembling, as the landlady told her she hadn't seen her around in a while and just wanted to check if everything was all right.

This simple act of everyday human kindness was too much.

Ayingbi grabbed the woman, and she cried and cried. She felt herself being hugged back, that comforting warmth of human palms upon her back, and she cried even harder—the pain, fear, guilt, loneliness and grief exploding out of every orifice in her face, in rivers and streams.

'I want to go back home!' she blubbered. 'I'm feeling so alone! I can't take it anymore! I'm done! I want to go back home!'

TWELVE

THE AGONY

Ayingbi had never been good at paddy fishing. It was back-heavy work, and the very first session had divulged a teething lumbar problem.

I'm getting old.

She stood up straight in the paddy field, pyjamas rolled up in the ankle-high water, gazing past the prairie of green–yellow stalks, towards her parents' house. Its white roof was winking under a sun that had risen at four.

'Look,' said one of her nephews, aged seven, crouched nearby. 'This fish is dead.' He leaned down and picked up a muddy, greyish-white crescent. Ayingbi was transfixed by it.

The not-so-dead fish began to thrash. The kid hurled it with all his might, far into the field, with a yell of delight.

'No,' muttered Ayingbi, hearing a faraway splash, and thinking of the Splash Troll. 'Don't do that.'

And then the chills began.

Oh no.

It was happening again. But even recognizing the warning signs would not stop it from coming. Ayingbi's field of vision began to shrink. The misty paddy field suddenly held all manner of twisted secrets, weaving towards her like alligators. Terror rose as an invisible frost from beneath, travelling ice-like through Ayingbi's veins.

'No . . .' groaned Ayingbi. Breaking free from a moment's paralysis, she splashed towards the edge of the field, but could not muster the strength to climb up the ridge. She tried to puke, but there was nothing to throw up. So, she flumped onto her back and lay there, hissing air in and out through the teeth, eyes squeezed shut. Her heart was jackhammering as she gasped up at the sky, swiping at her face and arms for sweat that was not there.

That which she had thought was a dancing Suggi poked its head into sight.

'Are you okay, Ayingbi?' said one of her younger cousins.

Ayingbi looked hard at him, clinging onto his features to ground herself to the familiar. She raised a hand and stared at it, trying to get it to stop shaking, but it did not listen—it may as well have been someone else's.

She gave up, flumped back and sighed.

Third time this week.

The cousin produced from his pocket what he had determined, during Ayingbi's last panic attack, to be a home remedy—a dried red chilli. But all Ayingbi saw was one of Cocktail-Dress's false fingernails.

Is there no escape?

She was so sick of being afraid all the time.

Later in the day, Ayingbi finally unblocked Rastogi's number and called him.

'Afternoon, Ayingbi,' said Rastogi, and Ayingbi blinked. It was almost dark where she was. 'I've been trying to reach you for over a week.'

'Yes . . . the signal here is not very good,' said Ayingbi, somewhat lamely. A convenient lie—connectivity had actually improved exponentially since her last visit, but Rastogi wouldn't know that.

'Ah, yes. I see.'

From his tone, Rastogi sounded like he was suppressing breathlessness.

For a moment, Ayingbi hesitated. 'Am I in danger right now, Dr Rastogi?'

'Danger?'

'You must've known what you were putting me through.'

'You're right. I did know, and I went ahead with it anyway.'

'So, you admit it!'

'I do.'

'You know I almost died, right?'

'I'm very sorry, Ayingbi,' said Rastogi. 'But I had no choice. You'd walked into the house in Charter Enclave on your own. You saw it, didn't you?'

Ayingbi exhaled sharply. 'So, you *do* know about it.'

'It doesn't matter if you saw it,' said Rastogi. 'What matters is *it* saw *you*. From that moment on, you were never safe.'

'You could've told me this at any point. What good is telling me now, after everything's happened?'

'I don't suppose saying better late than never, helps?' said Rastogi. 'Tell you what—why don't you come to my place for dinner this Saturday? Say, eight o' clock. I'll tell you everything. Chatty and Hardy will be there, too.'

'They're liars, just like you!'

'Not Chatty and Hardy! I have not been fully forthcoming about my business, I admit it. But if you give me the chance, I can explain myself. What do you—'

Ayingbi abruptly cut the call. She could blame her rudeness on any number of things later, starting with the poor signal.

She thought matters over all evening, gazing upon the bluish mounds of distant hill, until the sun had vanished into them.

She obviously couldn't be here forever. Summer was coming to an end. Schools would reopen in a week.

Ayingbi eventually booked an early flight back to the city, deferring the decision to attend Rastogi's dinner to the very last moment. She was already dreading going back. The city felt sad and seamy. Her most recent memories of it were a haze of human flotsam, grief and, of course, the lurking terror that had no name.

Once again, Ayingbi was forced to confront her own stoicism about the supernatural and form an opinion. Was it really something she wanted to grapple with, knowing that it would be something she never fully understood?

Ayingbi felt queasy on the night-time flight back. As the descent started, she looked at the toy-block houses outside the window . . . wondering who might be making those grand, awful plans . . . and it was in that moment, scanning the city from the vantage point of an aircraft, that Ayingbi began to feel like a bit of a deserter.

Fuck this.

I should've taken a train.

After the flight had landed and she had mobile service again, she found messages from both Hardy and Chatty, whose numbers she had also unblocked, enquiring whether she'd come for Rastogi's dinner. She did not reply to either of them.

Back-to-school messages had started on the teachers' group chat. Some of her colleagues had posted pictures of their holidays. Ayingbi posted photos of her own hometown, and was swarmed with replies on how beautiful it looked, with inquiries about this tree or that flower.

It felt nice.

Her landlady had given her Scooty a wash and a top-up in her absence, which she found very touching. Ayingbi also learnt that Nimisha had been to visit twice, because Ayingbi hadn't been taking her calls.

Ayingbi spoke to Nimmi for four hours that night. It was a lovely conversation. Other things were going well enough for Ayingbi to feel like perhaps she needed closure on the project that had taken up much of the summer.

I'll attend, thought Ayingbi, at last.

Rastogi called on Friday night.

Ayingbi RSVPed quickly, without discussing other matters.

*

Saturday afternoon arrived. Assured that Suggi, too, was permanently out of commission, Ayingbi finally decided to take her Scooty back out onto the streets.

She could smell homestyle-cooking as she climbed the stairs to Rastogi's flat. Outside his front door, were two pairs of sports shoes and a pair of high heels.

Ayingbi wondered who the high heels belonged to.

She stepped out of her own wedge sandals before ringing the doorbell.

A squat, cherubic woman opened the door. 'Ayingbi! Finally! Please, come inside! Make yourself at home!'

Like her husband, Mrs Rastogi had nailed the pronunciation of Ayingbi's name.

Ayingbi stepped inside the threshold, and put on a pair of fluffy pink slippers she found on a rack. Chatty's laughter guided her towards the drawing room.

Lounging on the floor around a table laden with food and drink were Hardy, Chatty and a very attractive young woman who Ayingbi presumed was Hardy's wife.

Hardy's and Chatty's eyes widened upon Ayingbi's arrival, and with roars of greeting, they rose.

'Ayingbi! You came!'

'We were so sure you wouldn't!'

Hardy's wife also rose, with a smile. 'Hi, I'm Nandini.'

Ayingbi shook her hand.

The men's greetings, Ayingbi returned with stony stares—they were still untrustworthy in her book.

'Wow . . . you've, uh . . . been working out?' said Chatty.

Ayingbi, recalling she'd been five kilos heavier when they'd last met, simply glowered at him.

Rastogi, meanwhile, had also emerged from the kitchen. 'Oh!' Even with her RSVPing, he seemed stunned to actually see her there.

Ayingbi reserved the stoniest, most defiant stare for him.

Haha. Surprise, motherfucker.

'Ayingbi! Hello! You did come after all! Please, please, have a seat! Move, you lot!'

Looking flustered, Rastogi gave Chatty a bit of a kick to a side in a way Ayingbi resented. Even though she felt lied to and deceived, it still annoyed her that Rastogi appeared to have a bond with the men that he didn't have with her.

'Uh, I brought something,' said Ayingbi, holding up the casserole she'd brought. 'It's chak-hao kheer. It's made with black rice.'

Another thing that's purple.

Rastogi awkwardly said that she shouldn't have, and that it was very thoughtful.

'What'll you have, Ayingbi?' said Chatty, scootching towards the minibar. 'I make a mean whisky sour.'

'Oh, nothing,' said Ayingbi automatically. She sat on the sofa and looked around the drawing room—it matched the hobbyist décor of Rastogi's office.

'Rubbish,' slurred Hardy.

'Maybe something special from the kitchen, Ayingbi?' said Mrs Rastogi, wandering back into view.

'Just water, thank you, ma'am,' said Ayingbi softly, holding her knees together. She was finding it difficult to relay unhappiness or frostiness towards the sincere-seeming Mrs Rastogi.

'Lemonade? Cold drink?' pressed Mrs Rastogi.

'Yeah, okay.'

'Pfft,' said Hardy. 'She's like a college kid when they go to their friend's house. You ever wonder where those beers keep disappearing, Doc, have I the answer for you.'

Ayingbi was irritated by the teasing, however playful. As far as she was concerned, Hardy no longer had any right to it.

'So, Ayingbi, let's talk!' said Nandini, after the Rastogis had again retired to the kitchen. 'You teach KG, right?'

'Yeah.'

'What subjects?'

'Most of them. English, Hindi, Maths, Value Education.'

Chatty choked on a chicken leg. 'Value Education, really?'

Hardy shrugged. 'It makes no sense. Adults lead such amoral lives. What's the point, even?'

'I think the purpose of moral science is not to create moral adults,' said Nandini, 'but to make adults have a twinge of guilt whenever they commit daily amorality.'

Ayingbi was upset. She had slaved over the brightly-coloured, sparkly proverbs pinned up all over the classroom. All that for a twinge of guilt?

There was a laboured pause, and she felt somewhat compelled to make conversation.

'So, uh, how'd you and Hardy meet?'

'Couple of years ago,' said Nandini. 'Through friends.'

Ayingbi smiled, knowing it was insincere and with effort. 'Nice.' She had mentally checked out. This was not why she was here.

'It took her a while to realize what a creep I was,' said Hardy. 'But by then, it was too late. We were already married.'

'Hah!' said Nandini. 'Ayingbi was smarter! She saw right through you the first time! No wonder she ran away!'

Out of nowhere, Ayingbi's temper rose. The very audacity. The bullshit of sitting here with a pointed smile, making forced small talk, never felt clearer.

So, this was what Hardy had told Nandini, eh? That she'd run away? That she'd *fucking run away?*

Ayingbi rose. She kicked Hardy. Hard. As one might a stray football.

'OW! What the hell?'

'You asshole!' hissed Ayingbi, angry tears bubbling in her eyes. 'Do you even know what I had to go through?'

'Shit, Ayingbi!' cried Chatty, alarmed. 'They didn't mean it like that! It was just a joke.'

'Oh, haha, yes, we're all laughing! Jerks! You guys don't know anything, do you?! Did you even care? Did you even bother to ask, what made me quit?! You just called me here for your shit party, like it's all good, like nothing happened?'

'Yes, we called SO MANY TIMES!' protested Hardy. 'You'd blocked us!'

'You think I'm here to play games! To listen to your bullshit love stories, Hardy? Or your fucking cocktail recipes, Chatty?'

Ayingbi's voice was shaking from the effort of keeping it as inaudible as possible.

'We're . . . we're really sorry!' said Hardy. He jabbed a finger towards the kitchen. 'He made us promise not to tell you.'

'So, you two *do* know what's going on!' hissed Ayingbi. 'And you kept me in the dark! Do you know how much deep shit I got into? How many times I almost died? That I haven't slept in weeks!'

'DIED? WHAT THE FUCK—'

'Okay, I SWEAR we didn't know!'

Hardy and Chatty looked absolutely terrified. Nandini looked bewildered and ashamed, as if it had all happened because of what she'd said.

'STOP PRETENDING LIKE EITHER OF YOU GIVE A FUCK! You don't care! You never cared! You're . . . you're . . . just horrible . . .' Ayingbi was blabbering.

Now, both of them were gasping about why she didn't tell them what she'd gone through, etcetera, etcetera, wringing their hands, denying everything. It was a furious, three-way argument, entirely in gasps and hisses.

'Don't tell me Dr Rastogi told you not to!' said Ayingbi fiercely, as Chatty threatened to bring it up again. 'I'm sick of hearing it!'

'All okay, kids?'

Mrs Rastogi had finally popped her head in.

Ayingbi attempted to compose herself as quickly as possible, while Hardy hurried to help with the fries. Listlessly, Ayingbi lifted a chicken drumstick, peeled off the foil, and gnawed it down to the bone. Then, hiccupping, she flumped back on the sofa, while Chatty and Hardy stood there, hanging their heads.

Nandini, who had been sitting motionless for a while, reached inside Hardy's pocket and pulled something out of his wallet. She showed it to Ayingbi.

It was a passport-sized photo of a turbaned Hardy, from his much younger school days.

Ayingbi frowned. 'So? That's Hardy—from school, or something.'

'That's not Hardy.'

'Hm?'

'Not Hardy. That's Mandeep,' said Nandini. 'Hardy's brother. He's no longer with us. Mandy . . . bleeped . . . himself when he was nineteen.'

'Bleeped?'

Nandini widened her eyes at Ayingbi significantly.

'Oh,' said Ayingbi. 'Oh.'

It felt like a blunt hit to the back of the head. She blinked. It took a while to process. Hardy had a weak smile on. He bunched his lips up, as if it was an awkward thing to talk about, and he didn't want everyone looking at him.

It hit Ayingbi again, this time in the lower belly. 'Oh . . . fuck,' she said, unhelpfully. 'Your twin?'

'Yeah.'

'Is it true?'

'I mean . . . yeah . . .'

One of Nandini's hands reached across and began to scrub Hardy's arm.

'I'm sorry . . . about Mandy,' murmured Ayingbi.

'Yeah. Thanks, Ayingbi.'

'But . . . why didn't you say something? We've talked about stuff before.'

'It's not easy, I guess. Actually, not that it's not easy, it's just . . . there's always something else to talk about.'

Ayingbi fell silent, suddenly feeling robbed of any right to stay mad.

'Could you all not stare?' said Hardy, giving a toothy grin as his eyes began to glisten. 'I kinda start crying whenever people look at me like that.'

Unsure of what to say, Ayingbi returned the photo, and Nandini carefully tucked it back.

'Um, I only showed it to you because I wanted you to know that Hardy's intentions are pure,' said Nandini. 'He never wanted you to get hurt. He really does this thing to help people.'

Ayingbi half-glanced at Chatty, perhaps unwittingly. She did not want him to think that his explanation was owed next. But Nandini noticed, and she explained on Chatty's behalf anyway.

'Chatty couldn't get into medical school.'

Chatty gave a limp smile, too. 'Physics. Physics was the problem. Can you imagine?'

'Oh,' said Ayingbi, again. Was she not going to be allowed to be angry with Chatty as well?

'But I wanted to save lives anyway. I didn't want people to die. I really, really wanted to do this.'

Ayingbi almost felt guilty now. Chatty looked awkward and embarrassed, and Hardy's eyes were brimming with tears; Nandini was still massaging his shoulder vigorously.

'Dr Rastogi asked us not to tell you, Ayingbi,' said Hardy thickly. 'I know it's terrible, and we wish that you hadn't been kept in the dark this whole time, but it really was for your own good.'

'But why?'

'Because I didn't realize how much danger you'd be in.'

The soft voice had come from behind them, where Rastogi was standing by himself. He walked into the room, holding a tray of galouti kebabs in one hand and a large black holdall in the other. 'Ayingbi, a quick word, if you please? The rest of you, get it while it's hot.' The drawing room seemed tense. 'Please,' said Rastogi, and he gestured Ayingbi towards the balcony. 'Carry on, you three.'

Ayingbi followed him outside. She peered down. They were on the second floor, much lower than Floop's balcony. She gazed at the cars parked underneath—none of them were purple.

Rastogi set the holdall down. 'There's so much to tell, Ayingbi, I'm not sure where to begin. All I ask for is your indulgence. A lot of what I'm going to say now is going to sound very strange. I know you have no reason to trust me, but please, humour me. I swear I'm telling the truth.'

'Hmph,' said Ayingbi. 'Okay, whatever.'

'Let's get the obvious out of the way first, I suppose. As you obviously know by now, the rotary phones you use are not normal phones.'

Ayingbi nodded.

'Can you tell me what you think they actually are?' said Rastogi.

'Well, there's Barney—the purple phone—that's where I get distress calls from. Except I don't know what the hotline number even is. Only that people do seem to wind up calling.'

Rastogi nodded.

Ayingbi continued. 'Phoenix—the blue phone. That one's regular. For you to call me and for me to call you.'

'Good. And finally?'

'Tuxedo,' breathed Ayingbi.

'The black one.'

'Yes. It hardly ever rings. And when it does ring, well . . . I don't know who it is on the other end of the line.'

'What do you hear?'

'The first time it rang, it taunted me. The second time, it lured me to a house where someone tried to kill me.'

Rastogi lowered his gaze. He seemed agonized when he spoke. 'I'm so sorry, Ayingbi. I swear on my kids, I had no idea this would happen.'

'Sometimes,' said Ayingbi. 'I wonder if I was too good at my job. That I'd been annoying someone on the other end of the line for too long.'

Rastogi exhaled. 'Well . . . this is not a job you can ever be too good at. Your performance is nothing to apologize for.'

'But was that what got me in trouble?'

'I don't know. Really, I don't. But I suspect it may have been.'

'I figured,' said Ayingbi, 'the thing on the other end of the line wanted people to die, and I kept getting in the way. But none of it explains your actions, Dr Rastogi.'

'I suppose,' said Rastogi, 'I had better start from the beginning. It all started many years ago. I was young, I was foolish. My curiosity about my craft had me poking about in places I really shouldn't have, and before I knew it, I was dabbling in the occult.'

'Like . . . supernatural stuff?'

'Maybe you won't believe me.'

'No, I do . . . I've seen enough.'

'Anyway, I won't get into the details, but I managed to come up with this little device that would pick up calls to other hotlines, all on its own, and redirect them to me. Like a little antenna, primed for a very specific frequency.'

Ayingbi frowned. 'Huh?'

'I know, I know, it's weird,' said Rastogi, raising his hands. 'Bear with me. You know the purple phone—what do you call it—Barry?'

'Barney.'

'Well, that's what I call a Phantom Router. What it does is . . . um . . . it tracks calls being made all around a given area—in this case, the city . . . and it detects which ones are being made by people who have death wafting over them.'

Ayingbi stared.

'Often,' continued Rastogi, 'these calls were being made to suicide hotlines. So, I adjusted the device, so it would poach those calls and redirect them to me. And I could attend to them personally.'

'That sounds illegal,' said Ayingbi. 'And unethical. You weren't who those people were trying to call.'

'I know,' said Rastogi. 'I understand the ethical dilemma fully. But I realized something, which made it feel justified.'

'What?'

'My Phantom Router had helped me thresh out, with the sharpest precision, the people in most desperate need of my help.'

'You mean the ones with death hovering over their heads.'

'Exactly. The point wasn't that they were on the verge of death. It was that many of them could yet be saved. That's why we don't get crank-callers or time-wasters on our hotline. It was this precise fine-tuning I was looking for. If anyone called, I knew they were all serious. I didn't think the cookie-cutter handling of a regular hotline would help them. Unlike those operators, I knew to give them proper and dedicated attention.'

'How'd you set the phones up? Don't you need technical expertise for this sort of thing?'

'Help from my wife, of course. She handled the screws-and-wires part of things . . . until the point science permitted, of course. Thereafter, we were swimming in telepathy and para-psychology. The mental vibrations emitted by a person about to die. Real freaky stuff.'

'Okay,' said Ayingbi. 'I'll accept that. Then?'

'Then . . . all was well for a while. I attended to the calls I got, rerouted from the Phantom Router, often in person . . . but then . . . the router began to pick up an interference of some kind. I was puzzled, because I thought I'd calibrated it to a tee. It was unintelligible. I couldn't do anything to stop it.'

'Then, what did you do?'

'With some wrangling, we managed to segregate the two signals. Of course, this required setting up another pathway, on another Phantom Router. This isolated the voice, although it was still garbled. We tried a number of coatings—rubber, cotton, paper . . . nothing worked. The solution came only months later, when we coated the wire with silver foil and then with black velvet. The velvet brought the second signal through, crystal clear. With time, we were able to convert the signal into comprehensible language. Finally, I could understand what was being told over the Velvet Hotline. It was a warning, Ayingbi.' Rastogi paused. 'Telling me to stop. Telling me not to meddle in affairs I did not understand . . . Saying that it was unnatural to interfere with people trying to kill themselves . . . Saying that it was being denied its due . . . It soon dawned on me . . . that the voice I was speaking to . . . was not of this world. And I realized how dangerous my little Phantom Router was.'

'So where was the voice from?'

'I don't know. But not from around these parts, so to speak.'

'But . . . what is it?' said Ayingbi. 'The Entity, the . . . whatever it is?'

'I don't know,' said Rastogi. 'But like you, I figured it wanted people to die, and for me to not intervene. And herein, I made my first mistake.'

'Which was?'

Rastogi sighed. 'For ten years, I had what I believed to be a working relationship with the . . . Entity. That it was my job to save lives, and it was the Entity's job to try to dissuade me. I thought since I was the pioneer in uncharted territory, the Entity was well within its limits to try and stop me. I was the outsider, so I would be the one begging, haggling, asking concessions, looking for the Entity's goodwill, trying to save as many people as possible. All the while, completely misunderstanding what I was dealing with.'

'Huh?'

'I used to think the Entity was a neutral ferryman, like a sort of Grim-Reaper, ensuring that those who wanted to go, could do so without obstruction. That perhaps it treated suicidal people as already dead and us, the preventers, as . . . needlessly disruptive.'

'Hang on,' said Ayingbi, annoyed. 'It took you ten years to realize what a twisted little creep that thing is?!'

'It wasn't like that earlier. Only recently had its behaviour changed. Of late, I learnt that it had been actively whispering to people . . . poisoning their minds . . . persuading them to do it . . . even the ones who hadn't planned on it.'

Ayingbi nodded. Now this sounded more like the Entity she knew.

'Sounds like the Teeterling,' she muttered, recalling her encounter in the bathroom, embroidered on her own flesh.

'Yes!' said Rastogi. 'I call it that myself! But I'm sure it looks nothing like the Welsh demon. I imagine that in our world, the Teeterling is formless and soundless. Invisible and impalpable. But it has a way of getting inside people's heads, making whatever was making them feel bad worse and nudging them towards the great inevitable.'

Ayingbi slowly exhaled, closing her eyes. This was bad. She had imagined it would be something like this, but it was different to hear it from Rastogi himself.

Rastogi grimaced. 'Now listen up close, because it gets much worse. A few months ago, I learnt that the Teeterling did not plan to merely goad. It has been planning something new. Something different. Much bigger. It never told me directly, of course, but I was able to piece things together in its little taunts and jeers.'

'It taunts you too?'

Rastogi nodded sadly. 'Generally, in the voices of the people I failed to save.'

Ayingbi's heart sank a little. 'Been there.'

'That's why I switched out Tuxedo, if you noticed,' said Rastogi. 'I knew you'd received a call. But the Teeterling didn't like that . . . it wanted a direct line to you. I had to eventually put it back and hope for the best, or it would've started targeting innocents ruthlessly. I thought putting you in the day shift might take some of the heat off, but alas.'

'Hmm.'

'When the Teeterling started contacting me, Ayingbi, I felt like I had a moral responsibility to pay attention.' Rastogi looked like he was sucking on something very sour. 'Anyway, I think the Teeterling's harvesting the people who kill themselves. Harvesting their pain.'

Ayingbi was sickened. 'What?'

'You've seen it yourself, haven't you?'

Ayingbi thought of her first run-in with the Teeterling, back at Mrs Elelem's house, when it had—

'Yes. I've seen it happening. I think.'

'Do you remember the lady in Charter Enclave had made two calls? The first, I received on the Phantom Router, when she was still in a grey zone, where she could still be saved. You got the second, by which time, her condition had deteriorated past the point of no-return. That's why that call went to a regular hotline, and the Phantom Router didn't pick it up.'

Ayingbi nodded. Things were beginning to make sense. Sort of. Going by the strange rules this world operated in.

'Recruiting you wasn't just about your bravery, Ayingbi, although it was a big part of it. After your encounter, the

Teeterling would've gotten inside your head and aggressively targeted you, too. I had to keep you safe. You've seen the daffodils around the office, right?'

'Yeah.'

'Every morning, I douse the place with spring water. Daffodils. Sunny things, bright things, the colour yellow. These are all totems of life—the daffodils, especially. The Teeterling doesn't like them very much.'

'What about back at my flat?'

'I'd broken in and planted dried daffodils all over your flat,' explained Rastogi. 'I'm good at housebreaking, as I've had to do it to stop people from . . . you know . . . You may even have found some of them. I've even taped a couple under your Scooty. I'm sorry for that, of course.'

Ayingbi shook her head. This was getting very weird.

'So . . . when I went home to Manipur . . . I was still miserable. Was it because I was being targeted by the Teeterling? I didn't have any daffodils there.'

'No,' said Rastogi. 'The Teeterling has lost interest in you. Normally, it would have enjoyed menacing you still, but for the past few weeks, it's been too close to its goal.'

'What goal?'

'The Agony.'

'The Agony?'

'You remember me telling you the Teeterling was harvesting people's pain, right? Well, it means to raise a monster, Ayingbi. A hellish creature, powered by the wrath and anger and hate of people that killed themselves.'

Ayingbi blinked. 'The Teeterling means to raise a monster . . . powered by the anger of people who killed themselves . . .'

'Yes.'

'It means to weaponize the dead?'

'Indeed.'

Even with all the things Ayingbi had already seen, it sounded bizarre, almost silly, to consider.

'I'd been negotiating with something evil,' mumbled Rastogi. 'I often wonder if I hadn't started talking to it, would it even have developed an interest in our world? Sometimes, I fear the Velvet Hotline is what gave it access in the first place. I tried shutting it off last year, but then the Teeterling started calling me on my personal phone.'

'But how?' said Ayingbi. 'You said it was very difficult to decipher what the Teeterling was saying, outside of the Velvet Hotline.'

'It seems that while we were figuring out the rules of the Teeterling's world, the Teeterling was busy figuring out ours. It can now come and go as it pleases. It has figured out human language. It continues to use the Velvet Hotline . . . for convenience. So that I know it's calling.'

Ayingbi's head was reeling. She was not sure what to make of this at all. 'What does the Agony look like?'

'I don't know,' admitted Rastogi. 'I imagine something huge, something monstrous.'

'And it will, what, like attack and kill people?'

'I suppose it will.'

Ayingbi sighed. 'Are you sure it will come?'

'Yes,' said Rastogi. 'I have no doubt. The Teeterling is going to raise the Agony very soon. I do know it has harvested enough people to do it.'

'It's not conjecture, right?'

'Don't think of it like that, Ayingbi,' said Rastogi firmly. 'Just because I don't have the details does not mean I am not confident about the rest. The Agony is absolutely going to come. The Teeterling may raise it tomorrow. It may raise it next month. And we will have to deal with it when it does.'

'We?'

'Me, Chatty and Hardy, that is.'

'Hmm.' Ayingbi tried her best to show her exclusion did not affect her. 'Do Hardy and Chatty know the whole story?'

'They do. They have Velvet Hotlines in their offices, too.'

'Does the Teeterling call them?'

'Oh, yes. Hardy more than Chatty. Sometimes in his brother's voice,' said Rastogi quietly. 'Though I daresay, the Teeterling has found you much more interesting.'

Ayingbi squirmed. 'I don't think it tried to kill either of them, though.'

'Like I said, it only began to reveal its malevolence recently, once it grew comfortable within our world and its rules. It is more confident. More interfering. A year ago, it wouldn't've dreamt of misguiding you.'

'You said you negotiate with the Teeterling. What does it ask from you?'

'There are some suicidal people it really, really wants to
see over the hill, for whatever reason. In return, the Teeterling
sometimes promises to delay the unleashing of the Agony.'

'And you let that happen?' said Ayingbi, her voice
immediately sharp.

'Oh, no, never, of course,' said Rastogi. 'But it doesn't
like that. That's when it taunts me about the Agony. Which
is good, in a way, because that's how I learn about it.'

'Right,' said Ayingbi. 'Right.' And now for the million-
dollar question. 'And . . . er . . . how does one deal with the
Agony, exactly?'

Rastogi finally unzipped the holdall, and took out—

'A sword?' It looked familiar. Probably from Rastogi's
office collection.

Rastogi shrugged. 'It's a monster. Swords probably
work on them, right? Chatty and Hardy already have
theirs.'

'Er . . . thanks. I think,' said Ayingbi, as Rastogi thrust
it into her hands. It was gently curved and had a golden
hilt, and a sheath of maroon velvet. She pulled the sword
out to catch a gleam of silver.

Ayingbi could not feel more at a loss about what was
going on.

A sword. Really?

'Are you all right, dear?' said Rastogi.

'I'm fine,' said Ayingbi. 'I think I need a drink.'

'Are you satisfied with the explanation?'

Ayingbi was satisfied with the explanation, but it had
left her with more questions than answers. 'I guess.' Then

she added, in a somewhat small voice, 'Uh . . . can I join in the fight against the Agony?'

Rastogi looked ashamed. 'I'd dare not presume, Ayingbi.'

'But *suppose* I want to join?'

Rastogi shook his head. 'It's your right to join. I don't have any say in that matter.'

Ayingbi glanced inside. 'I want to talk to them about it.' She paused. 'Thanks, Dr Rastogi, for giving me answers.' She went back into the drawing room. Chatty, Hardy and Nandini seemed a lot more drunk than when she had left them.

'Oh, hey!' said Chatty, brightening up. 'You got a sword! Sword buddies!'

'Did Rastogi tell you guys about the Agony and the Teeterling?'

'Yeah,' said Hardy. 'Fun, right?'

'Not exactly,' said Ayingbi, helping herself to a beer before she sat down. 'So . . . what's the plan?'

'Que sera sera,' said Chatty.

Somehow, Ayingbi didn't quite think the Agony could be fought with swords, spring water, and que sera seras. 'That's not a plan, Chatty.'

'We don't know anything about it, Ayingbi, so we'll deal with it when it comes,' said Chatty.

'In fact,' said Hardy. 'I don't even think there's going to be an Agony. It's just something the Teeterling is making up to scare Dr Rastogi.'

'Now why would it do that?'

'It likes to fuck with us. It's fucked with you too, right?'

Their relaxed attitude did fortify Ayingbi after the grim meeting with Rastogi. Perhaps the alcohol had helped. Ayingbi downed the rest of her beer in one go.

'I needed more than beer the first time Dr Rastogi told me what was up,' grinned Hardy.

Nandini giggled. 'He did. He did.'

'You know what I think is weird?' said Chatty. 'That Dr Rastogi hasn't figured out when the Agony will come.'

'That's because it's not gonna comeeee, you guys!' said Hardy. 'Get over it.'

Ayingbi shook her head, vaguely confused by all the flippancy. She finished three more beers in relative silence, feeling a pleasant rush to the head. 'So, we're going to fight this thing or what?' she slurred, playing with the sword. She'd never held one before in her life.

'You will, you will,' said Nandini. 'But first—' She gave a dewy smile and poured out four measures of whisky.

'Oh, that's nasty,' mumbled Hardy, as she began to mix every available drink on the table. 'That's really nasty.'

Finally, four glasses of some unholy tincture of whisky, store-brand vodka, wine and beer were passed around.

'To fucking up the Agony!' sang Nandini.

They all downed their drinks, and immediately, Ayingbi knew it was a bad idea. The mixed drink sloshed around her stomach, wiping out clear line of thinking. The drinks were anything but smooth on their own. Mixed, they were downright vile.

'Nope . . . nope . . . bad idea,' said Chatty, and clutching his mouth and stomach, he dashed for the bathroom.

Hardy and Nandini, clearly more experienced, shook their heads vigorously, eyes squeezed shut. Ayingbi could already feel the liquid fighting to come out the same way it had come in, but she suppressed the reflex.

Her head was swimming. The drink had fully dulled her senses. She resumed absently fiddling with the sword. Nandini had become giggly and touchy-feely with Hardy. Hardy himself had become contemplative.

He must be thinking about his brother.

Ayingbi lifted the sword up and tried to wave it around. Her wrists were weak. It was top-heavy, and the blade about three feet long. She imagined a big, scaly dragon. Would she really have to lop its head off? Swinging wildly like a hero?

Ayingbi found herself giggling uncontrollably at the idea, and she toppled onto Nandini, infecting her with the same condition.

'Quick, quick!' sang Nandini, pulling a notebook out of her purse and ripping out three pages, in a manner very reminiscent of Ayingbi's kindergarteners. 'Let's draw the Agony!'

Ayingbi, in her present state, could hardly conceive of a more entertaining game. 'Ooh! Let's!'

They each grabbed pens from the pen stand and slunk onto their knees on the carpet, and for five minutes, they scribbled like children.

Ayingbi really had no idea what the Agony would look like. But she was good at drawing—it was an essential part of the primary-teacher skill set. She drew a cross between the dragon she'd been imagining earlier and one of those muscular supervillains they had in comic books.

'Look what I made!' cried Hardy. His version of the Agony looked like a huge green alien, with a single eyeball and hundreds of feet for hair. It carried a ray gun.

'What's with the ray gun?'

'It vaporizes you.'

'And the feet on the head?'

Hardy scowled. 'Look at that abomination Ayingbi drew. Why's mine the one under scrutiny?'

Chatty stumped out of the toilet, looking annoyed at having missed a spate of laughter. 'What're you guys up to?'

'We drew the Agony!' said Hardy.

They each held up their drawings.

Chatty squinted at them. 'The Agony will look nothing like that. It'll probably be invisible, like the Teeterling itself.'

'Dinner!' called out Rastogi, from the kitchen.

Afterwards, when they had all gone to help with the wash-up, Mrs Rastogi placed a gentle hand on Ayingbi's shoulder. 'Everyone seems to want a private word with you, Ayingbi. I hope it's not too late for me.'

Ayingbi nodded, setting down a soapy plate, and Mrs Rastogi led her back to the balcony.

To her surprise, Mrs Rastogi scooped up Ayingbi into a tight, lasting hug. Then she leaned back, gazed into Ayingbi's eyes and gave a tch. 'Poor, brave girl. You've been through so much. And yet you came back.' She wiped a strand of hair off Ayingbi's forehead.

Ayingbi blinked. 'Sorry?'

Mrs Rastogi released Ayingbi. 'But why? After everything you were put through, why?'

It took a moment for Ayingbi to gather her thoughts. 'I think I needed answers. For . . . a lot of things.'

'You got them, didn't you?'

'I did . . . I guess.'

'Are you going to stay? To fight the Agony?'

Ayingbi honestly didn't know. It still felt weird to believe the Agony was real. 'Dr Rastogi gave me a sword. But I have no idea how to use one."

'Neither do they,' said Mrs Rastogi. 'But I guess a sword wouldn't hurt.'

A sword wouldn't hurt.

If this thing worked out, they should put that on matching T-shirts.

'You know why my husband sought you out, right?' said Mrs Rastogi.

'Yeah, to protect me from the Teeterling.'

'He could've stopped at mere protection. Why recruit you?'

'Because he thought the fact that I went to save Mrs Elelem . . . er . . . the first caller . . . made me . . . a good person or something.'

'That's right. But why do you sound like you doubt it yourself?'

Ayingbi sighed. 'Because I don't quite think I am, aunty. Full disclosure—when I went to attend to Mrs Elelem's call, I was too late. She was already dead. But my reaction wasn't disgust or horror. I mean, it was, but underneath all of it . . . there was kind of an exhilaration too, you know? Like I felt thrilled to see a dead person. The whole thing felt like an extreme sport. The slightest miscalculation, and someone would die. There was a power, and it was alluring.' Ayingbi closed her eyes. 'Sometimes, I wonder if that isn't why I took the job—to see some dead guys. There you go. I'm no hero.'

It felt like she was revealing some dirty secret.

'You didn't see very many, did you? Dead people.'

'Damn near none,' said Ayingbi, her voice shaking. 'I was good at my job.'

Mrs Rastogi began to tut. 'I know you don't think it's heroic, Ayingbi. Nobody wants the burden of heroism. We wind up making excuses for ourselves.'

Ayingbi gazed inside the window to the drawing room.

Nandini was now singing. Maybe in some parallel dimension, it would be considered good singing. But Rastogi's eyes were squeezed shut as if he was trying to recall a phone number—he was gently shaking his head and tapping his knee.

'Chatty and Hardy are in, aren't they?' said Ayingbi.

'Oh, yes.'

'I expect I will have to be, too.'

'Not in the least,' said Mrs Rastogi. 'But whatever you decide, I want to make sure that the air has been cleared between you and my husband.'

'It has.'

Mrs Rastogi nodded. She quietly touched Ayingbi on the cheek before leaving.

Ayingbi had, in fact, already made her decision.

For a moment, she thought she'd only made it right now, after her conversation with Mrs Rastogi.

But she knew, in her heart of hearts, that if she'd come all the way from Manipur just for answers, she could've gotten them over the phone too.

THIRTEEN

HOLIDAY HOMEWORK

'So, what's the plan now?' said Ayingbi, as they left the Rastogis' flat together. 'Will you two be going back to the office?'

'Oh no,' said Chatty. 'Doc's giving us the night off. He'll be taking calls on that earpiece of his. Heaven knows when the man sleeps.'

'Ah,' said Ayingbi. 'Right.' She slung the holdall with the sword over her shoulder. Rastogi had let her hang on to it, regardless of what she decided to do, not knowing she had already decided.

Now that her adversary had a somewhat clearer form, Ayingbi was raring for a confrontation. The liquor had probably helped, too.

She bid Hardy, Nandini and Chatty good night, and they parted ways on the road outside the apartment building.

But Ayingbi wasn't headed home, even though that was what she told the others.

The office, when she unlocked it with a hidden-hook key, felt like a familiar, home-like environment. To have missed it felt like a marker of competence. She walked around the lobby, trying to count all of Rastogi's protective amulets. She went to her own cubicle last, where she sat and swivelled side to side in her chair, gently fingering Tuxedo's receiver, before picking it up and putting it to her ear.

'H'lo?'

She put the receiver down. Maybe there was a number she could dial to get to the Teeterling. Like a 6-6-6, ring-a-devil type situation. After a while, she thoughtfully picked up Tuxedo's receiver again.

'Call me back,' she muttered.

Then she resumed pacing. She took the sword out of the holdall, waving it around, lunging and parrying, desisting only when she nearly put a hole in the wall.

'Do it,' she grunted into Tuxedo, an hour later, with the energy of a bar-brawl instigator. 'I know you're there. Call me back, I dare you.'

And she slammed the phone down.

This time, almost in sync, she felt a sharp, searing pain on her hips.

Ayingbi gasped; her first instinct was that she'd been stung by two wasps at the same time. But it wasn't that— it was a moving pain, already travelling upwards. Ayingbi shot off her chair, unbuckling her belt as she tore towards the toilet.

Maybe picking a fight was a bad idea.

It felt like she was being tattooed by invisible needles or some creature was crawling up her body, dragging its stinger like a plough.

She lifted up her shirt in the toilet to find the stretch marks on her hips moving. She rubbed her eyes. Yes, like little caterpillars, they were wriggling out of the waistband of her jeans, travelling upwards. Ayingbi rubbed at them—they did not stop. Finally, they spiralled around her navel, as if conducting a ritual.

Through blinked tears and little gasps of pain, Ayingbi saw the stretch-marks bending and twisting into letters . . . and the letters knitting themselves into words . . . branding themselves onto her skin . . . laterally-inverted, as if they knew there'd be a mirror.

H . . . O . . . L . . . I . . . D . . . A . . . Y . . .

Ayingbi wiped her eyes.
Holiday?

. . . H . . . O . . . M . . . E . . . W . . . O . . . R . . . K . . .

Homework? Holiday Homework?

. . . B . . . I . . . N . . . G . . . B . . . E . . . E . . .

No.
No way.

. . . M . . . A . . . A . . . M . . .

Ayingbi emitted a final squeak of pain, keeling over, her eyes squeezed shut. When she opened them again, the words were gone and only a palimpsest of the pain remained.

Back in her cubicle, a phone began to ring.

Ayingbi raced to take it.

Tuxedo.

'What good timing, Susan!' came Cocktail-Dress's cheerful cry. 'Hi hi hi! Did you miss me?'

'Listen, moron,' said Ayingbi, through gritted teeth, her free hand massaging her stomach. 'I'm done dealing with you over the phone. Why don't you face me in person?'

The Teeterling changed its voice. 'Don't have a face, Susan. I shot it off, remember? All because of you.'

Hearing Barry-Tony's voice almost punctured a hole through Ayingbi's resolve. But no. She must keep her cool.

'You've got a big mouth,' she said. 'Seeing as you're scared of me. You've been scared ever since I saved all those people during Compound Peril.'

'Ah-ah-ahhh, not all of them,' came the voice of Cocktail-Dress.

'Whatever, it was enough to freak you out at the time. And that's why you tried that stunt with the cats. You tried to get me to quit.'

Even as she began to talk these things out loud, matters began to fall in place in Ayingbi's mind.

'But you didn't quit,' said the Teetering quietly.

'And that's why the whole trick with sending me to Sir's place,' said Ayingbi. 'You needed people dead, to raise the Agony. I was getting in the way, so you thought you'd have me killed.'

'Top of the class as always, Susan.'

Ayingbi was squeezing her phone so hard her clenched fist was shaking. But fear was giving way to triumph.

'Listen, shithead, I survived that, too. I'm still standing. You know what gives me strength? Knowing that you're scared! So, it doesn't matter how many Agonies you raise, because I'm going to cut them all down!'

Cocktail-Dress's voice did not speak for a while. Until it did.

'It wasn't enough. You are a happy person, Ayingbi Mayengbam. It distresses me. I know you aren't going to kill yourself. But after what I do next, you will. Surely, you will.'

And the Teeterling's voice changed again.

This time, it was not one voice, but many.

The voice of many, many excitable children. Giggling laughter. It sounded like a creepy little game, with clapping after every other word.

'Bing-bee ma'am, Bing-bee ma'am, the bell has rung!

Bing-bee ma'am, Bing-bee ma'am, the axe has swung!'

The generalized babble of a group of children would sound the same to most, but never to a kindergarten teacher . . .

Ayingbi's mouth fell open.

No.

It wasn't possible.

It was more of the Teeterling's stupid mind games.

'No . . .' whispered Ayingbi. 'You can't . . .'

'Bing-bee ma'am, Bing-bee ma'am, there's still time!

'Although, Bing-bee ma'am, you'll have to climb!'

'STOP IT!' bellowed Ayingbi. She swayed and very nearly collapsed in her chair.

'Bing-bee ma'am, Bing-bee ma'am, what's taking so long?

Bing-bee ma'am, Bing-bee ma'am, we're running out of song!'

And then Tuxedo went dead again.

'STOOO-OOOOP!' howled Ayingbi. This was a profane and unimaginable transgression—to taunt her in the voice of her own kids.

Still reeling with new-found horror, Ayingbi did not realize, at first, that another pair of spiky words had been twisted onto her belly.

She lifted up her shirt, and read them upside down.

HAMELIN TOWERS.

*

A half-hour's Scooty ride brought Ayingbi to an under-construction industrial tower, within what a billboard promised would one day be a luxury industrial complex. The tower was still half-girders; construction had stalled because of a court case.

There was no gate, no guard quarters or labourer tents. Ayingbi rode straight inside, right up to the tower. Slinging the holdall over her arm like a giant purse, she allowed mobile torchlight to lead her in, where she found stairs. It was a dangerous climb—the stairs were still untiled and without banisters, and there was a huge, empty shaft for a future elevator.

A voice boomed out throughout the building, halfway up, informing her she had come to the right place.

'About time you got here.'

Cocktail-Dress's voice sounded as if it was coming on a public address system, reverberating across the walls and girders, magnified tenfold by the poor acoustics.

Indeed, as Rastogi had said, the Teeterling had learnt to come and go as it pleased—using the Velvet Hotline was purely a matter of convenience.

'Shut up,' grunted Ayingbi. She unzipped the holdall and pulled the sword out, letting it rattle and clang up the stairs behind her.

'Tell me, Susan, if you were shown every setback you would ever face, every loss, every trauma, every heartbreak, every failure, every little thing that chipped away at your heart, what would you do?'

'Shut up,' growled Ayingbi again.

'What would a child do, Susan? A child of five?'

Ayingbi slowed down.

What would a child do . . . when what? She hadn't been paying attention. Until now. But she could hear it. Dozens of little footsteps, pitter-pattering up the stairs, a couple of floors above. Entranced, Ayingbi ran the rest of the way up, until she could finally see.

It was children all right . . . half-a-dozen of them . . . and from the looks of it . . . her children.

'Shoot,' muttered Ayingbi under her breath, having subconsciously trained herself never to swear in front of children.

Although it did not look like the kids were in any position to understand. Their eyes were closed, they were shuffling like zombie sheep, ushered by an invisible force, huddled so close they almost stomped each other's shoes off.

'STOP!' yelled Ayingbi. 'STOP!'

Her heart skipped a beat as a couple of them cut corners on the unguarded flights with little leaps.

'It's me!' yelled Ayingbi, storming up the stairs as fast as she could with the sword. 'It's Bing-Bee ma'am! Wake up!'

But the little sleepwalkers could not, would not understand.

'SNAP OUT OF IT!' cried Ayingbi, too afraid to push past them and physically block the way, lest she accidentally shove someone overboard.

They reached the roof. It was still in the middle of casting, and TMT rods were sticking out everywhere. And there, the children began to fan out, slowly, inexorably waltzing towards the remotest edges, unwalled and unprotected.

'No . . .' croaked Ayingbi. She'd seen this happening before. The cats. They'd all gotten to the roof. And then, they had . . .

She fell to her knees. 'Please . . .'

'It's not coercive, Susan,' boomed the Teeterling. 'It's never coercive. I don't know what Doc told you.'

'Please . . . make them stop . . . I beg you . . .'

'You want to know how I'm doing this?' said the Teeterling, as the little children trotted away gaily towards the edge.

Ayingbi screamed, her hands on her head. 'Please! Make them stop! I'll do anything!' There were six of them—she could not stop them all, even if she tried.

'All I did was give them a glimpse of their own future,' said the Teeterling. It had switched to the voice of Barry Tony. 'A mental picture of all the problems they'll ever face. It seems six of them didn't think it was worth the trouble, after all!'

'Stop! Stop!' howled Ayingbi, pulling her own hair. 'Please, stop!'

'I wasn't sure the mental projection thing would work, though. That's why I had to test drive it with the cats first. That was a bit too easy. Brains like chewing gum. Turns out, it's very easy to bum them out.'

The six children had finally stopped. Another step, or even a strong gust of wind, and they would go over, twenty floors straight down.

One-by-one, like characters in a play, they began to squeal.

'Oh, golly! Suicide!'

'Breathing? Who needs it?!'

'I am thrilled at the prospect of taking my own life!'

'It seems like there's only disingenuous friendships and an unhappy marriage in store for me!'

'Whoops! Looks like my passion's gonna be squeezed outta me, drop-by-drop!

I'm getting that diagnosis at fifty anyway! Why bother waiting?'

'What do I have to do?!' yelled Ayingbi. She knew this wasn't about them. This was about her. 'Tell me what I need to do!'

'You already know, Susan. It's not that difficult.'

Ayingbi peered towards the edge of the roof. It couldn't be more obvious.

'Do it, and I'll spare them all,' said the Teeterling.

This was it. This was what this had all been about. Ayingbi closed her eyes. 'Promise?'

'Promise.'

Ayingbi bent her knees, but then she shook her head. 'This won't make you win, though. Suicide on gunpoint is simply murder.'

But the Teeterling, it seemed, was not in the mood for Ayingbi's stalling. The children began to chant in unison—

'Bing-bee ma'am, Bing-bee ma'am!

We all wanna be free!

Although Bing-bee ma'am!

You have the count of three!'

Ayingbi knew she was out of options.

'Bing-bee ma'am, Bing-bee ma'am!

No time for a queue!

Although Bing-bee ma'am!

You have the count of two!'

The tots all bent their knees as if they were on the highest diving board at some pool, intending to splash with style.

'Bing-bee ma'am, Bing-bee ma'am!

It cannot be undone!

Although Bing-bee ma'am!

You have the count of one!'

Ayingbi shrieked and barrelled towards the edge of the roof, cannonballing clean off. She squeezed her eyes shut and hugged her knees to her chest.

In a second.

It would all be over in a second.

Ayingbi didn't know that the Teeterling would keep its word.

But she knew that if she didn't jump, it would've made her kids jump.

However, Ayingbi's fall was broken almost immediately, and softly. Stunned, she cracked an eye open to find she'd been caught inside the safety netting a few metres below the roof.

Ayingbi clumsily sat upright, the net cutting into her hands.

The Teeterling was howling with laughter; it made the entire tower pulse like a gigantic boombox. 'You did it! I can't believe you actually did it!'

Ayingbi scrambled back onto the roof. She dusted her jeans down, reached for the sword, and stood up straight. The children had drawn back, and were once again huddled together. They were now looking at something at the other end of the roof.

Ayingbi looked too. She blinked stupidly. Something was off. The scenery had changed.

Then she realized she was looking too low.

'Have you jump?' cried the Teeterling. 'And have you miss our grand finale?! I could never!'

That which she hadn't been sure would even be—it was already here.

The Agony is absolutely going to come. The Teeterling may raise it tomorrow. It may raise it next month.

Well, it wasn't next month.

It wasn't even tomorrow.

Whether or not her goading had caused the Teeterling to do it was irrelevant.

Ayingbi's disbelieving gaze rose and rose, the smokestack-like red legs giving way to a gelatinous pot belly the size of a hot air balloon, which finally tapered away into a hideous head, crowned in dancing orange flames. Fifty feet from top to bottom, it looked Biblical, tongues of red fires licking its arms, and its mouth an infernal furnace, leaking white hot sparks from the gnashing teeth.

It did not carry a ray gun.

The Agony.

The kids appeared to be pleasantly hypnotized by it; they were looking without seeing.

'You really thought I'd have my friend scrape his first meal off the pavement?' said the Teeterling. 'Not after all the trouble he took to bring them here!'

'NO!' yelled Ayingbi, scrambling towards the kids with her sword raised, gaze fixed firmly upon the Agony, the numbing shock of its sudden appearance giving her something like bravado.

'Ah well, see you on the other side, Susan,' said the Teeterling. 'Been nice knowing you.'

The Agony reared its head and roared—a screech of drills and chainsaws; it was a wonder the tower remained standing. It leapt off the stair shed, landing with a thud in front of Ayingbi, lowering its head to peer keenly at the kids.

'Oh no, you don't!' yelled Ayingbi, and revising the drills she'd been practising in office, she charged and lunged, whirling her sword, skimming it across the creature's car-sized foot.

The Agony hardly felt it, but it was enough to make it tear its gaze away from the children, and towards Ayingbi, who was still busy hacking away at the foot like an inexperienced woodcutter.

Unreal.

This cannot be happening.

'That's right!' yelled Ayingbi, still swinging wildly, to absolutely no avail. 'There's a lot more where that came from!'

The Agony's eyes narrowed.

'Shit,' muttered Ayingbi.

And before she knew it, Ayingbi had been seized in the creature's vile fist. She thought it might crush her then and there, but instead, it smacked its hand upon its porous, gelatinous belly, thrusting her deep into its own body.

Ayingbi tried to scream, but she couldn't scream—the insides of the Agony were a white hot nothing, neither solid, nor liquid nor gas. She did not know what this place was, but she didn't have to—it itself told her. Inside, she saw it all, she felt it all. Countless anguished faces, the awful toll they had paid; their screeches sizzled around her, engulfing her in the blurry shapes and colours of their own despair. They were with Ayingbi, or maybe they were Ayingbi herself, for so much was being radiating and absorbed, she could no longer feel where she ended, and they began.

The voice of the Teeterling once again boomed out, this time inside Ayingbi's own head.

Nobody asked to be here, Susan. So, we hang onto the good times to make the bad times seem worthwhile. It's not worth it, they knew . . . they all knew . . .

It was the kind of pain that you couldn't guide or control or even comprehend, you could only surrender and succumb to, and even then, you would not have its mercy, a grief too powerful to be wielded for anything apart from total self-annihilation.

Hardy was right. We only make good times precious because of how fleeting they are . . .

The fiery little faces were swarming around Ayingbi like piranhas, as she thrashed and flailed through her purification.

You felt the thrill of it yourself, didn't you, Susan? When you jumped off? I know you did. I felt it within you.

Ayingbi heard a familiar voice, but knew it was hopeless—the chattering of misery knives was drowning out all remaining thought; she was already fighting on reserves.

'Hey, you're here too?' It sounded like Mrs Elelem's voice, although without the haughty veneer of the Teeterling commandeering it. 'Let us help you. It's not worth being here with us.'

Ayingbi opened her eyes. One of the fiery faces had cooled enough to reveal the face of Mrs Elelem—soft, misty and white, as if painted on a flower petal.

Another unfamiliar petal-face drew up beside Mrs Elelem, but when it spoke, Ayingbi recognized the voice.

'Oh, didn't I put you in a spot of bother. I feel so ashamed,' said Barry Tony. 'I was feeling low . . .'

'Sorry,' burbled Ayingbi. 'I couldn't save you.'

He wanted it.

'Think nothing of it,' said Barry Tony kindly. 'It's done. It can't be helped.'

He wanted it.

'I should've tried . . .'

'Shouldn't've put it on you.'

He wants it still. He's the brave one.

Ayingbi squirmed.

A third face was flying towards her. The streak of insanity was missing from what little of Suggi's features Ayingbi could make out.

'Sorry, miss,' said Suggi. 'Didn't mean to hurt you . . .'

'Sorry I chucked a fridge at you,' muttered Ayingbi.

Look at her. Look at the wretch. Tell me what she'd be doing if she hadn't done it.

'I told you not to put yourself down,' said Cocktail-Dress's petal-face, her expression severe as she flew in from underneath. 'Stop it at once.'

The faces began to grow agitated, like molecules in increased heat. They began to vibrate and zigzag around. This was it. Ayingbi would be cooked alive. She wanted to throw herself off the Hamelin Tower again. She wanted to throw herself off all the towers in the world. It was maddening, it was unbearable.

Finish her off, the cold voice inside Ayingbi's head commanded. She could tell the instruction was for the Agony.

And then, she saw it at last. It may have been invisible in the real world, but here, in whatever hell this was, she could see it.

Out of the rancid darkness, the Teeterling was swimming towards her like a crocodile.

Do it now!—growled the Teeterling.

It was a beast of such hideous design, a great warped creature of many planes, some glittering black, some grey; it looked like a serpent made of shards of dark steel; the light was bouncing off it most unnaturally.

DO IT NOW, I SAY!

The battle was between the two of them now, spiralling around each other, caught in each other's vortexes. Perhaps Ayingbi understood little about the nature of the Teeterling, but after a point, the nature of the little screeches it was emitting seemed to change. Once delighted . . . they now felt . . . and Ayingbi had no way to know this to be true . . .

frustrated. Its movement within the Agony, too, was becoming increasingly erratic.

Within the tranquillity of shut eyelids, Ayingbi found a thought to cling onto, and with it, she felt the tide turn.

Yes, yes. This place was the land of human suffering. It wasn't the Teeterling's world at all. It was the Teeterling that was the outsider, not Ayingbi or any of the petal-faces bobbing about. It knew *nothing*. It could not command, it could not do squat in here. She could feel the energy ripple out from the petal-faces, too. Their eyes were shut, and they were fighting with her. She knew their struggle on her behalf had a balming effect; it rippled out of them in veins of blue. Ayingbi was astonished to find the biggest spurt of blue emanating from herself, like a leaky fountain pen.

The screeching of the Teeterling was so shrill Ayingbi thought it might deafen her; it began to thrash about, the mirror shards jerking and snapping this way and that. The borders of red and blue began to swivel and blur. Purple shoots appeared and began to dance around like seaweed.

Ayingbi was crying so hard she felt like her insides might shrivel up. 'Hold on,' she muttered to herself, waiting for the worst to come. 'Hold on.'

And so, Ayingbi held on.

She had nothing to hold on to, so she held onto herself.

The convulsing Teeterling's shrieks approached a terrifying crescendo, and there was a pop, the curtains of Ayingbi's tightly shut eyes flashed white and, finally, she was spat out. She felt her feet hit solid ground, back-pedalling a few steps and falling on her back, rolling into a backwards somersault she did not quite finish.

Ayingbi, groaning, raised herself on her elbows, opening her eyes to find the Agony in metamorphosis.

It was like watching a slow chemical reaction. Or maybe an enormous werewolf de-transforming.

Infernal red as it had been minutes ago, the Agony was already turning purple (Ayingbi's brain wildly noted the existence of yet another purple thing), and now, a beautiful midnight blue. The mouth had shrunk, teeth blunted, eyes had become large and soft. The size of the belly, however, remained conspicuously intact.

The angry fiery faces inside the belly had calmed down too. They were no longer zooming around, but like Cocktail-Dress and the others, had settled into misty, moon-like white petals. They were presently floating serenely up and down the Agony's belly like soda bubbles.

As of now, the Agony stood there, a lame, fifty-foot gorilla, with a face like a guinea pig.

And then, unmistakably, this bright blue gelatinous grotesquery began to cry. Cry, like a baby, with basketball-sized tears.

Ayingbi watched, frozen, her mouth slightly hung open.

The creature raised one long arm and carelessly wiped its face. Then it fell backwards onto its bottom—its legs were so short and stumpy; its torso so long.

In a summer full of them, this was the strangest thing she had seen.

The creature did not look scary at all. It seemed . . . well . . . in agony. Ayingbi decided to risk it.

'Hey,' she said gently.

The Agony tearfully looked at her. 'Wua-hah-haha,' it sobbed.

Ayingbi slowly got to her feet and retrieved the sword she had dropped earlier.

'WUA-HAH-HAHAHA!!' The Agony jabbed an accusing finger at the sword, and Ayingbi apologetically hid it behind her back.

'Sorry . . . I won't . . . I won't use it . . . promise!'

'WUA-HAH-HAHAHA!!   WUA-HAH-HAHAHA!!'

Tenderly, the Agony began to poke at its side, like a child that did not know when to stop picking its scabs.

Ayingbi was close enough to touch its wrist now.

The creature was pond-water cold and the point of contact sent out a ripple, making the Agony yelp.

'Sorry,' Ayingbi mumbled.

The Agony, however, after rubbing its wrist, appeared soothed. It returned its hand to a touchable distance, and when Ayingbi touched it again, it did not yelp, but stared down at her, breathing heavily, its belly pulsing up and down.

This time, Ayingbi could enjoy its texture—it felt like a sensory bag—a sort of learning tool they used to calm hyperactive children down. The Agony's eyes were still leaking.

'Woh-hoh-hah, woh-hoh-hah,' it cried, kneading its eyes with the back of its ape-like hands. This time, the crying was softer, dutiful more than anything.

Like a baby brought outside its nursery for the first time, it began to gaze upon its surroundings, then at the city lights unfolding in two or three horizons, until finally, its watery gaze settled on its own tummy. Placated, it stopped crying and scooted sideways into Ayingbi, as if for warmth.

Its stomach gave a little rumble, and something oozed out sideways, plopping to the roof with a wet splat.

The Teeterling looked nothing like what Ayingbi had imagined, nothing at all like the Welsh demon.

It looked like a bullet hole through a mirror, a warped thing, twenty feet across, crystallized and immobile. Matter seemed to repel it, as if the physical world could recognize it as a foreigner, and the shards that comprised it seemed to swell or shrink depending on how long Ayingbi stared at them.

The creature that had tormented her all summer, here it was now.

Ayingbi checked her phone. 'Hello?'

The Agony shook its head.

Ayingbi realized she was staring at the Teeterling's corpse. It had been defeated at last.

But how?

'Is it . . . dead?'

As soon as she said it, there was a horrible sucking noise, as the corpse of the Teeterling began to tremble and twist. The crystals began to shatter and explode. Somewhere, Ayingbi could hear a distant screech, an echo of the same shriek she had heard inside the Agony, as the last of the Teeterling vanished.

In disbelief, Ayingbi looked up at the Agony.

The Agony looked abashed, as if destroying an inter-dimensional demon was much the same as failing to suppress a belch in polite company.

'You did it?'

The Agony raised a hand and scratched the top of its massive head. It itself didn't know how.

Toothpaste. The Agony had the look and consistency of blue gel toothpaste. Was it actually cute? Ayingbi had been trying to mentally steer clear of the word as a descriptor.

In a rush, Ayingbi poked the Agony in the belly—her arm vanished up to the elbow without breaking the surface tension. The Agony seemed to enjoy it. It let out a croon; booming ripples spread across its form. Ayingbi realized it was finding it ticklish, and she began to tickle it with relish, rolling up her sleeves and getting to work with both hands.

'You did a good thing,' she said, as the Agony continued to bounce and giggle, stubby legs patting the ground up and down. 'Saved me a world of pain.'

The Agony looked much happier now, with the malignancy of the Teeterling outside of it, and without the pressure of having to comfort it, Ayingbi was free to ponder its nature. She would not have had the explanation, had she not thrown herself inside the Agony and seen for herself what was going on.

In retrospect, it was obvious that the Teeterling's plan could never have worked. It had hoped to weaponize the rage and pain of suicidal people in the form of the Agony, overlooking one incredibly basic detail.

That rage and pain had only been self-directed.

If anything, the Agony was a pressure cooker, in no actual mood to hurt others.

That was its true nature.

It was true, the Teeterling had put up a fight. The thing Ayingbi had faced off against in the initial minutes was probably the Agony as it was intended to be. But the violence the Teeterling had hoped ran deep was easily doused. It was merely a film—an oil slick of anger; beneath it all, there was an ocean of pain the Teeterling had not foreseen.

But then again, how could it have?

Regardless, as Ayingbi saw it, this was the Teeterling's great and fatal mistake.

'So . . . the pain of all those people . . . killed the Teeterling?' she whispered aloud.

It was oddly fitting.

Ayingbi looked at the Agony. 'So, I guess, it must be uncomfortable to stick around, huh?'

The Agony did not seem to be listening. It was batting at its belly, seemingly mystified by the petal-faces inside.

'I still don't know what Sir was hiding,' Ayingbi mumbled. It had been weighing her down. For some strange reason, she felt like she could confide to the creature. 'I think he's got a dungeon full of dead people or something. And I think he was like a cannibal, trying to go clean. There's no chance Suggi could tell us, right? She's in there.' When the Agony did not respond, but continued to gaze peacefully at her, she muttered, 'Or maybe not. They

couldn't find anything in a search of the house.' She sighed.
'You don't have to stick around, by the way. I hope you're
not only being polite.'

The Agony seemed stunned by the fact.

'You don't have to be here,' pressed Ayingbi gently.
'You can go.' Together they looked at the kids, who were
still huddled together. 'Er, before that, I don't suppose you
could drop them home, could you? Otherwise I'd be Uber-
ing all night.'

The Agony gently picked the sleeping children up, one
by one, and placed them on its shoulder, where they sank
all the way up to their necks, looking like human-head
mushrooms. Finally, the Agony scooped up Ayingbi. She
did not sink all the way in but only up to her waist.

'You know where they live, right? Seeing as you got
them here?' whispered Ayingbi, cupping her hands at the
Agony's great head, where she hoped there might be an
ear.

The Agony looked sideways at her, stretched its arms
out fully and jerked a big, gelatinous thumb at itself.

'Okay. Woe betide you if send them to the wrong
houses!'

And they were off. It was a wild ride. Ayingbi's insides
felt like they were floating about a void, like she was inside
an elevator shooting up and down its shaft . . . She could
see the city passing as a blur on either side—dark sky
alternating with flashes of trees, cars, parks, shops, houses
as the Agony leapt, bounded and cartwheeled silently
through, apparently unseen and unheard.

What Ayingbi thought would take hours wound up taking minutes. Every so often, the Agony would stop, pluck a kid off its shoulder, crank up a window inside some house and tuck them inside. And finally, with all children safely returned, the Agony brought Ayingbi back to Hamelin Towers, plucking her off its shoulder and gently lowering her to the road outside the under-construction tower.

'Ayingbi? Is that you?'

Rastogi's voice was coming from somewhere inside the building. He must've arrived when they were off returning the kids.

'Go on,' said Ayingbi gently, looking in that direction. 'Get out of here.' She threw her arms around the Agony— it was like hugging the side of a bouncy castle. 'Go on, quickly.'

The Agony looked at her uncertainly.

'Seriously, go!' said Ayingbi. 'It'll be super weird to have to explain this with you around.'

The Agony blinked stupidly.

'Fly! Be free!' cried Ayingbi, wiggling her wrists like a bird.

Finally, the Agony seemed to get the hint. It enveloped her in its arms one last time; Ayingbi could not get enough of how cosy its embrace now felt; the little petal-faces inside it appeared to be smiling slightly.

The Agony released her, closed its eyes and tilted back its head. It began to disintegrate. The head was the first to dissolve into vaporous flowers and then its shoulders, its body—its dissolution appeared to have released the petal-faces trapped within, and they rose like helium balloons, now grinning from ear to ear, vanishing into the night.

The Agony's feet were the last to go, still wiggling slightly even as they turned to mist.

There was a pulse.

And then, from where the Agony had vanished, there erupted outward, for just a moment, a golden bloom—an upwelling of such rapturous ecstasy, that even in its brevity, it felt everlasting. Ayingbi closed her eyes and let it wash over her, heal her wounds, both inside and out, feeling its radiance sweep across all of creation, blossoming out of every door and window, a promise of eternal spring, and peace and bliss . . .

But then the moment was gone, and Ayingbi opened her eyes to find the road deserted once again, and only a weird, bluish mist remaining from where the Agony had vanished.

'Ayingbi? Ayingbi?!' Chatty and Hardy's voices were right around the corner.

Ayingbi wiped her eyes. She picked up the sword and began to walk in that direction, the mist occluding her vision slightly. Once it had finally cleared, she found Dr Rastogi, Chatty and Hardy standing in a panicked triangle, facing outward, trembling swords brandished.

'Ayingbi!' cried Hardy. 'The Teeterling's raised the Agony! It's here somewhere, right now!'

'The Doc got a call about an hour ago!' yelled Chatty. 'We got here as fast as we could!'

They faltered when they saw Ayingbi standing there, with a small, secret smile.

'I know,' she said.

She strolled towards a wonder-struck Rastogi and held the sword out.

'I didn't need it.'

FOURTEEN

THE PURPLE PART OF THE RAINBOW

Ayingbi told them what had happened.

There was no debriefing, no cross-questioning, just a quick enquiry from Rastogi regarding the ultimate fate of the Teeterling. Ayingbi was grateful that they did not want to sit down and exchange notes right now—she was exhausted and, more than anything, she wanted to go home and sleep. Afterwards they parted ways quietly, agreeing to regroup the next afternoon.

Nothing unusual on the events in Hamelin Towers was reported the following morning. There was some property damage reported on the roads, but it was ascribed to a dust storm that had blown in later that night.

The dust storm hadn't managed to wake Ayingbi up.

A hurricane wouldn't have.

'Do you know,' said Ayingbi, the following afternoon, in Rastogi's office, 'what happened just after the Agony vanished? This was right before you found me.'

'Yes,' said Rastogi. 'I felt it too.'

'I felt happiness like I've never felt before,' said Ayingbi. 'You know the happiest you've ever felt and you think that's the upper limit? It made that happiness feel like a false ceiling.'

'I've been thinking about it,' said Rastogi. 'It makes sense. After all, the Agony was a . . . compacted clay of human misery. I like to imagine the implosion sucked all that negativity out of existence. It was . . . a strangely scientific occurrence, going by the laws the Teeterling operated by. It's nice to imagine it was the universe celebrating our victory, but I think it was . . . more of a . . . self-correction.'

'It sure felt like a celebration,' said Ayingbi. 'It showed me what a truly happy world can look like. And then it made me sad, because we'll never get there. No matter how hard we try.' She shrugged. 'I feel a bit wrung out, to be honest. I don't know if I'll ever feel normal again. Maybe I've met too many Debbie Downers. It's like I've been at the beach too long, and now my hair and toes are always full of sand. I don't know if it'll wash out.' She looked around, as if the curios adorning Rastogi's office strengthened the point she was trying to make.

'It's like we keep saying around here, you can't spend so much time on the edge of glass without being cut yourself,' said Rastogi, absently fiddling with the Newton's cradle. 'Never believed it, though.'

'You're made of sterner stuff than I am, then. I don't know how you've been doing this for twenty-five years.'

'Just practice and experience, Ayingbi,' said Rastogi. 'I started off with tube and floaters. You, on the other hand, were thrown into the deep end without the slightest idea of what to expect. I don't think I can quite put into words the admiration I have for you. Well.'

He tapped a knuckle on his tabletop, looking embarrassed. He set the Newton's cradle going again to break the silence.

'It feels like a design flaw,' said Ayingbi. 'Being suicidal. Like . . . we know very little about what our great cosmic purpose is, right? Except to survive. All creatures have that instinct—even bugs and plants, life that can barely think. So, in circumstances of fierce and unnatural pain, we can walk against these grand design wheels. I don't know if this says more about the universe or more about us. Either the universe is fundamentally broken, or we are. And I don't know which is worse.'

'I don't have an answer for you, Ayingbi,' said Rastogi. 'Or words of comfort. I have nothing to say. These are questions bigger than any of us.'

'But we have insight, Dr Rastogi,' said Ayingbi, raising a hand. 'Insight counts. There are horrors we can barely comprehend. There are such terrible things happening to so many people, and their pain, their suffering—it doesn't even have a voice at times . . . but we can feel it . . .'

'You felt it?' said Rastogi. 'Within the Agony?'

Shaking, Ayingbi nodded. 'Like a sickness. It was so much worse than I'd imagined. I could actually feel what they'd gone through. What they had run away from. Too awful for words, Dr Rastogi . . . too awful . . .' Her face screwed up. Rastogi pushed a napkin box towards her.

Ayingbi seized a fistful of tissues and trumpeted her nose into them. 'I think this is the whole problem. We keep talking them off the edge. But the circumstances that drove them there remain. Being call operators truly is lip service after all, even with our little jaunts. It's the . . . iceberg of formal conversation . . . we ever negotiate with—their real, authentic selves are buried far within. The real battles are fought alone. Who's going to make them feel genuinely loved and wanted? Who's going to give them their place in history? Who's going to get inside their brains and fix everything? Not you, Dr Rastogi. Not I. All your precious Phantom Router's done is gamified the whole thing—who can be saved, who can't, yada yada.'

'But we knew this before as well,' said Rastogi softly. 'We never pretended to be therapists. This cannot possibly be revelatory.'

'Knowing it was one thing,' sniffed Ayingbi. 'Experiencing it was another. My first thought was: how is this kind of suffering possible? How does the order of things permit this? It was overwhelming. I can no longer make a persuasive argument against it. I can't assure them that things will get better, if they keep on trucking. A magic wand doesn't come along and wave their problems away, Dr Rastogi, once someone has suffered enough. It's not like everyone has a quota of happiness and sadness. Some people just wither away. Help never comes. They suffer and they suffer and they suffer some more, and then they die. That's how it is.'

Rastogi was quiet.

'And that,' went on Ayingbi, 'was why the Agony failed. The Teeterling itself had no idea about what it was trying to control. It was too unique, too awful, too traumatizing . . . too much, even for the Teeterling . . . It was bound to collapse under its own weight, like a . . . neutron star of pain,' Round two of tears commenced. 'All that soul-searching, all those talks, they have all amounted to nothing. And nothing you say can convince me otherwise, because this time, there's a difference between you and me. You didn't feel what I felt. You *think* you know their pain, through inference, observation and reading. But you don't *know* their pain, and the two are worlds apart.'

Rastogi, however, merely shrugged. 'Okay.'

Ayingbi blinked. 'Okay? That's it?'

Rastogi gave a solemn nod. 'You're right, of course. About everything.'

Ayingbi stood upright. 'You're not going to convince me I'm wrong?'

'No,' said Rastogi. 'But either way, it doesn't matter. Because whatever happens, I'm going to be sitting right . . . here . . .' He jabbed a finger at his chair. 'And these phones . . . are going to be right in front of me . . .' He indicated the two phones. Then he looked up at her. 'I'm ready to fail ten thousand times over. I'm ready to send them back to a life of misery ten thousand times over. If you still find yourself torn or conflicted, well . . . that is justified. I am ever grateful for all that you have done, of course, and always available as a friend. However, if you can find it in yourself to believe that the microscopic chance things *do* get better for them . . . is worth a fight to the death from our end—' Rastogi extended a hand for her to shake. '—I hope to see you again next summer.'

Ayingbi uncertainly shook his hand. Rastogi's expression was even, he did not even appear to want to defend his position. Ayingbi let it slide. It felt strange to have argued with him right after their great victory, but this time, there was only warmth and trust behind it.

*

Outside, Chatty was taking the day shift. Hardy had come in to say goodbye, in spite of Ayingbi's protests.

'So, dinner at my place next?' said Chatty.

'Done,' said Ayingbi.

'Will we see you again at the office next summer, Ayingbi?' said Hardy.

'I dunno.'

'It'll be better next year for sure,' said Chatty earnestly. 'Rastogi's getting air-conditioning, finally. As well as Caribbean rum.'

'And the Teeterling won't be there, either, so that's a plus,' said Hardy, making Ayingbi and Chatty laugh.

'Look, I'll think about it,' said Ayingbi. 'I'm open to it.'

'It's been a lot of fun working with you, Ayingbi,' said Hardy. 'You made the summer interesting.'

'So, what'll you guys be doing?'

'Oh, we're both rich, so we don't really need to work,' said Chatty. 'Nah, I'm kidding. Only Hardy's rich. I have some solid investments that put food on the table. So, yeah, this is a full-time gig for us.'

'I think Mandy would be proud of you,' said Ayingbi, to Hardy.

'Proud of *us*,' corrected Hardy.

Chatty's eyes moistened. 'Alright, guys, bring it in.'

The three of them hugged, and Ayingbi was surprised to find her own eyes damp as they parted. 'Keep an eye on those telephone demons for me, will you?'

'You know it,' grinned Hardy.

'Take care, Ayingbi,' said Chatty. 'Have a nice school session.'

Ayingbi was quiet and contemplative on the cab ride home. Still no closure, pleasant as the partings had been. How could you pour your soul into something over a month, then expect to shrug it all aside?

Her landlady was standing outside the apartment building, where a delivery boy was standing with a big cardboard box.

The delivery boy squinted at a pink card taped to the top of the box. 'Aa . . . aa . . . yee . . . unguh . . .'

'Ayingbi Mayengbam?' said Ayingbi.

'No. Aa . . . aa . . . yee . . .'

'Ayingbi Mayengbam?'

The delivery boy squinted some more, running his finger on every letter. 'Yes. Sign here, please.'

The box had come from the Rastogis. Ayingbi hurried up to her room to open it—thinking it would be a totem, something inspirational, a symbolic continuation of the pep talk Rastogi had refused to give, but it only turned out to be a dark, creamy chocolate cake.

*

'So, a suicide hotline, huh,' said Nimmi in the café, on the last Sunday of the summer break. 'That's what you were doing all this while?'

Ayingbi was looking through the glass wall, at the traffic outside. 'Yeah.'

'Shit, no wonder you always sounded like you've been through the wringer.'

Ayingbi sipped her granita, which had sat too long from her absent staring and gotten diluted. 'Yeah, sometimes it was a bit tough.'

'You don't need to tell me,' said Nimmi. 'It's written all over your face.'

Ayingbi, in truth, was still having difficulty sleeping. Presuming it was garden-variety PTSD from Sir's attack, it was its own beast, something that came with a lifespan autonomous from the inciting incident. She still hadn't gotten her appetite back, and she found herself only lightly picking at the onion rings she'd promised to help Nimmi with.

'Therapy can help,' said Nimmi, sipping her green tea, the purpose of which she'd defeated with four spoons of sugar.

'I guess,' said Ayingbi. 'But in a way, I was the therapist myself.'

'A lot of therapists have therapists,' said Nimmi. 'You think if we make a daisy chain of all the therapists and their therapists, it'll eventually loop back in on itself?'

'I think there's bound to be some great master therapist at the end of that trail,' said Ayingbi.

'Kanishka Varshney, probably.'

'Who?'

'Kanishka Varshney.'

'Never heard of him.'

'Wait. Seriously?' Nimmi's eyes widened.

'Yeah . . . who is he?'

'Come on! Krazy-K? You've never seen the ads? He has this skit routine with a sad clown mask on!' Nimmi's thumbs were already patting away on her phone. 'No wonder you're bummed out. He's the best. Look!' Nimmi showed Ayingbi. 'He uploads mental health vlogs on Wednesdays and Fridays. Lectured at Yale and everything!'

Ayingbi looked at the video titles. *'Is Your Psoriasis because of Sleep Deprivation?'* And *'Think Twice Before Starting a Workplace Romance!'*

Probably something Ribs and Sonal could use. There was a chubby, bespectacled man in all the thumbnails. He looked familiar.

Too familiar.

'His videos are chewable aspirin for the urban spirit,' said Nimmi. *'Time* magazine's words, not mine.'

Ayingbi was still frowning at the thumbnails. 'May I take a closer look, please?' She clicked on the most recent video (*Top Ten Worst Depictions of OCD in Film and Television*), and immediately, she recognized the man speaking. The voice was distinctive. She recognized the receded hairline, small indent between the eyebrows; the leopard print spectacle frames . . . it was him.

She'd met him.

She'd more than simply met him.

Kanishka Varshney, the man with the mental health channel, had, no more than a month ago, tried to kill himself.

And Ayingbi had been there.

This was for the simple reason that Kanishka Varshney was no other than Mister 309 from Hotel Spotlight.

'You should read the testies,' said Nimmi.

Ayingbi blinked. 'Huh?'

'The testimonials. Soooo many people write to him every day. Thank him for bringing them out of a tough spot in life. See!'

She indicated the most recent video (*Unboxing your Gifts #37. Thank you!*)

And just like that, everything fell into place.

Why Ayingbi's pursuit and rescue of Mister 309 had put her in the Teeterling's crosshairs. Why Rastogi had not wanted her to get involved in the matter of Kanishka Varshney, and assume all repercussions for him not killing himself. Maybe he was one of those people the Teeterling had really wanted to claim, and had tried to bargain with Rastogi for.

From the Teeterling's point of view, Mister 309 committing suicide would've been a major win—a most vocal emissary of mental health doing the deed—it would've been perfect. It would've been a pleasure to harvest. Mister 309 was undoubtedly an invaluable part of the Teeterling's plan in raising the Agony. That's why it had been so angry when Ayingbi had intervened. That's why it had sent her to Sir's house.

'Was Mister . . . ah . . . Kanishka Varshney depressed himself?' said Ayingbi.

'Funny you should say that.'

'Why?'

'For the longest time, he always came across as the sunniest ray of sunshine,' said Nimmi. 'But as it turns out, he'd been going through a lot of shit. He's addressed it in a recent video, I think this one . . .'

She pointed at another video, from a couple of weeks ago (*My Confession . . .*). Ayingbi did the math; it was only a few days after her intervention. Mister 309 seemed to be doing better since then; he had uploaded frequently. One of the more recent videos (*My Confession—UPDATE*) had him grinning ear to ear.

'I guess the people who appear the happiest have the most to hide,' said Nimmi philosophically. 'But it was very brave of him to come clean. He himself seems the happier for it.'

Ayingbi stared at the thumbnail; even without Nimmi's contextualization, it did look like Mister 309 had a bit of a twinkle in his eye.

Ayingbi smiled to herself as a wave of deep satisfaction washed over her.

The final piece of the puzzle.

'I'm still feeling peckish,' said Nimmi, perusing the menu. 'Do you want to split a medium pizza or something with me?'

'Large,' said Ayingbi, suddenly famished. 'With the works.'

*

The next morning, schools reopened.

Ayingbi was, in fact, a little scared and apprehensive about facing her kindergarteners. She wondered if the ones who were there would remember the Hamelin incident.

The parents had come to see them off. They regaled Ayingbi with tales of what the kids had been up to. Many of them had grown quite a bit over the summer. Others appeared to have sprouted new teeth.

It was magical. It was the happiest Ayingbi had felt since the Agony had vanished.

Perhaps, including it as well.

They gave her a rockstar's welcome when she appeared, and Ayingbi hugged them all longer than she usually did, especially the ones from that night. They told her about the places they'd been to, the things they'd done, and Ayingbi allowed herself a happy day, just listening, absorbing. Today, she was the learner.

As the end of the day approached, it was revealed that they had all made drawings of Bing-Bee ma'am. Some of them had drawn her holding a hand fan, like a geisha. Others had her in a rice hat. Ayingbi scrutinized the drawings drawn by the kidnapped children in particular, looking for subliminal imagery. There was none—it was all simple and earnest.

'So, all in all, did you all have a good summer?' she asked.

'Yes, Bing-Bee ma'am!' they chorused.

'Were you all good little boys and girls?'

'Yes, Bing-Bee ma'am!'

Ayingbi stared at all of them, the collected drawings scooped in her arms, her chest heaving. She was in two minds of doing what she was about to do, but then she decided to do it anyway.

'Um, do you mind if I say something real quick?' She hurried and shut the classroom door. Her voice was normally a little high-pitched when talking to kids. It wasn't deliberate nor was it something she could help very much. But her tone, when she had spoken just now, was much the same as speaking to an adult.

The class looked interested. They were perceptive; they had picked up on the change.

'So . . . something happened over the summer . . .' said Ayingbi. 'And some of you were a part of it . . . now, I don't think you remember . . . do you remember?'

The children looked puzzled.

'Something . . . a few nights ago? Any of you?'

Heads shook.

'Well, you were there and I was there too.'

'We would have remembered that, Bing-Bee ma'am!' one little girl yelled, and everyone laughed.

'Maybe some things are for the best,' mused Ayingbi. 'Heck . . . I don't even know why I'm talking about this. It's weird. It's like a dream we all shared together.'

Ayingbi stared at their faces, so innocent, unable to link this with what she had witnessed on the roof. It was overwhelming, and before she knew it, her eyes were leaking.

'I . . . ah . . .' Ayingbi's voice was trembling.

The kids' amused, curious faces changed to alarm as one. Immediately Ayingbi was swarmed, and she felt warm, comforting little hands all over her.

'Oh, I'm sorry, I'm so sorry, children,' she wept, keeled over the teacher's desk. 'Please, I'm all right . . . take your seats . . . I'm not done . . .'

Ayingbi exhaled, dabbing her eyes with her handkerchief, and she stood up straight, gulping air through the mouth.

'So . . . I wanted to talk to you about . . . certain things . . . if that's okay.'

The class had gone deathly quiet. They had never seen Ayingbi crying. Dutifully they returned to their seats, clasping their hands over their desks.

'Life . . . is not easy, kids,' said Ayingbi. 'And I hope it takes you as long as possible to learn that . . . things will be tough . . . in ways you cannot understand just now . . . someone you love may get sick . . . you may lose something precious . . . you may fail over and over again at something you try . . . but whatever it is, I want you to promise me you'll hang on.'

The kids looked scared to see Ayingbi like this.

'I guess, that's what growing up really boils down to . . . this one thing . . . hanging on.'

They wouldn't get it. But she needed to tell them. For herself.

'Promise me you'll hang on! Promise me!'

'We promise, ma'am . . . ' mumbled the kids, even though they weren't sure of what they were promising. The usual promises they made to Bing-Bee ma'am had to do with putting pencil shavings in the bin or saying the three magic words.

'And . . . and . . . I don't know if you will remember this, either . . . but one day, you will be all grown up, and you won't remember me . . . when that time comes, know that Bing-Bee ma'am loves you . . . and . . . she always has you in her heart . . . whatever battle you're fighting, reach out to me . . . I'll be there . . . and if you cannot hang on . . . I will try to hang on for you . . .'

Ayingbi was fighting tears again.

*

After school, Ayingbi went to the local lake gardens. She liked walking there, passively enjoying the community spirit the other frequenters brought.

Some people had arrived early for a yoga class. Meditators hogged the benches beneath the oldest trees. College kids—in identical shirts, rubber boots, masks and gloves—impaled litter with sticks and hauled the lot into big black bags.

It had rained a bit during the day but the sun was already back out, gently shrinking the shine of the wet pavements.

After the ordeal of the summer, Ayingbi badly wanted to re-belong. And so, she began to wander.

She spotted a young couple, hand in hand, slinking in the shadows of a mango tree. The boy was rather direct in his engagement, the girl kept looking furtively over her shoulder. Ayingbi thought of Honour Boy and Honour Girl, and she hoped they would be alright, wherever they were. Custard-Mustard and her boyfriend might be here, too—she just had to look hard enough. Or maybe Hash-Brown or Instox.

She sent them as much as love as she could. She squeezed every prayer she could muster out of her system towards them. She believed in prayer. She would never stop believing in it.

A group of kids was crowding around the ice-cream stall. Ayingbi bought herself a grape bar.

She found, on a square of benches beneath a weeping fig tree, three old men whom she had a passing familiarity with.

They hailed Ayingbi. They said it had been a long time.

Ayingbi, smiling, agreed.

They asked Ayingbi if she'd had a good summer.

Ayingbi said she had.

One of them eagerly showed Ayingbi a slightly tattered newspaper—he'd won the daily caption contest. Ayingbi discreetly checked the date—the newspaper was from last week. It amused her to think the man had been proudly carrying the paper around ever since.

The second old man fretted about a hip surgery his ninety-four-year-old mother had coming up, and Ayingbi assured him it would be all right.

The third old man declared he'd managed to teach one of the stray dogs to high-five. The dog wasn't around at the time, but he would show Ayingbi once it did show up. Ayingbi said she couldn't wait to see it.

She chit-chatted with them without concern of time. After a while, the voices of the men seemed to fade and blend into the background of leaves rustling in the wind and water lapping against the stones, and Ayingbi's mind began to drift once more.

Her ears sought laughter, any laughter, and did not have to wait long to hear it. She sought the birds and heard them too.

Ayingbi took her leave and resumed wandering.

It had rained just enough for a very thin rainbow. Just a squirt of colour, a caress of a paintbrush in the sky. Ayingbi counted each colour out from top to bottom.

'Red,' she mumbled, for she could see it the clearest— the longest arc, a curving curtain rod.

She couldn't see the orange, but she could make out the yellow, and she imagined it must be sandwiched within. She could see the green, but she had always been unsure about where blue stopped and indigo began.

Richard Of York Gave Battle In Vain.

Vibgyor.

Ayingbi preferred Vibgyor. It got the point across more quickly and without the pessimism.

Without the pessimism.

It registered as a life-affirming little victory—preferring Vibgyor as an acronym for the colours of the rainbow.

Ayingbi felt a prick of gratitude for being able to see this rainbow. She latched fiercely onto the gratitude prick, protecting it like dying embers in a wind, encouraging it to live and swell, and devour more of her in its glow. So parched was Ayingbi's spirit of any nourishment, the trick worked without effort. Ayingbi revelled in her own upwelling of gratitude in absolute amazement.

Gratitude for the little knob of grape ice still clinging to the stick. Gratitude for the people around her, fighting quietly for their joys, hopes and dreams. Gratitude for the fact that she was still alive, having made it through the gauntlet of the summer. Gratitude for the fact that gratitude had come when she had given up on it.

Ayingbi licked the last of the ice lolly and wedged the stick into an overflowing bin. She walked with a smile, and found smiles returned. It was true—what she had said to Rastogi—there was no way of truly knowing if things would get any better.

But you didn't know that they wouldn't.

Perhaps that little scrap of not knowing was enough. At least, in that moment, for Ayingbi, it was enough. And if it wasn't enough, she would make it enough. Richard of York may have given battle in vain, but she, Ayingbi, would not.

'I'll keep fighting, and I'll win,' she whispered quietly. 'I hope you will too.'

She put her hands in her pockets, maintaining a hint of a smile even when there was nobody to return it, and did not feel so terrible anymore.

Scan QR code to access the
Penguin Random House India website